The Former Things

Steadham's *The Former Things* is an excellent redemption story. The writing has authenticity to it that is often missing in Christian fiction about non-religious characters' paths to redemption, and that was a refreshing element to the story. Steadham well portrays a troubled atheist with a bad experience with Christians and his aversion to God and scornful disbelief. It rings true to reality, which is not often something I have been able to say about most Christian realistic fiction.

I am happy to say I would highly recommend the book to those looking for a brief story that really explores the difficult questions in life, such as why a good God has so many followers who don't look like Him or whether forgiveness is possible after making some of the worst mistakes possible in life. Exploring these questions through the eyes of a disbelieving atheist who encounters those answers at every turn makes the story a relatable one and frees the reader to ask the same questions in the privacy of their own minds, even if they might otherwise feel they cannot voice them.

The book would be of special comfort and encouragement to struggling Christians seeking a story that acts as a reminder that though life is difficult, God works in wonderful and mysterious ways, even in seemingly horrible situations. It speaks to all believers and those searching for answers by meeting each of us in the place of difficult questions and heartache that we have been at, may be now, or will be in the future.

Ariel Paiement

Author of *The Legends of Alcardia* series

The Former Things by Allen Steadham relates a story of love and redemption told from the point of view of the main character, Sean Winter. A troubled man, Sean stumbles his way through life with few friends and no real purpose. He considers himself an atheist, and Christians repulse him. Then he meets Keith and an old friend he once loved, Jennie Lou. Through Sean's journey, we learn about finding love in the wrong way, about forgiveness, and about redemption. If we're honest, parts of Sean, Keith, Jennie Lou, and Kalea live in all of us. This story brings joy as well as some tears but, most of all, brings hope and knowledge of Jesus' love for us all.

Deb Haggerty
Author of *These Are the Days of My Life*
Coauthor of *Experiencing God's Love in a Broken World*
Publisher and editor in chief of Elk Lake Publishing, Inc.

Allen Steadham's *The Former Things* is a stirring, thoughtful exploration of life's unexpected twists, personal growth, and what it means when we submit to Christ and His will. An inspirational read that will stay with you long after you've read the end.

Parker J. Cole
Author and CEO of PJC Media Worldwide Network

ALLEN STEADHAM

The Former

Things

AMBASSADOR INTERNATIONAL
GREENVILLE, SOUTH CAROLINA & BELFAST, NORTHERN IRELAND

www.ambassador-international.com

The Former Things

ISBN: 978-1-64960-301-2
eISBN: 978-1-64960-323-4
Library of Congress Control Number: 2022936343

This is a work of fiction. Names, characters, and incidents are all products of the author's imagination or are used for fictional purposes. Any resemblance to actual events or persons, living or dead, is entirely coincidental. Any mentioned brand names, places, and trademarks remain the property of their respective owners, bear no association with the author or the publisher, and are used for fictional purposes only.

Editing by Daphne Self
Cover design by Hannah Linder Designs
Interior typesetting by Dentelle Design

Scripture taken from the King James Version. Public Domain.

AMBASSADOR INTERNATIONAL
Emerald House
411 University Ridge, Suite B14
Greenville, SC 29601
United States
www.ambassador-international.com

AMBASSADOR BOOKS
The Mount
2 Woodstock Link
Belfast, BT6 8DD
Northern Ireland, United Kingdom
www.ambassadormedia.co.uk

The colophon is a trademark of Ambassador, a Christian publishing company.

"And God shall wipe away all tears from their eyes; and there shall be no more death, neither sorrow, nor crying, neither shall there be any more pain: for the former things are passed away."

–Revelation 21:4

I

THE STORM

It would have to be raining on my first day of work, wouldn't it? THOOM! The window glass rattles at thunder that could wake the dead. My mouth is dry like a desert; my tongue feels as rough as sand; and there's a dull throbbing in my head. I figure I probably snored again. Water bursts against my bedroom window. It must be really coming down in waves outside. I sit up and check the weather app on my phone. Like I figured, the county is under a severe thunderstorm warning.

"Well, that's encouraging," I gripe. Even so, I'm grateful it's not worse, like a tornado warning.

I force myself to stand up, only to stumble into the bathroom. I wait for the water to get truly cold before I dip my hands into it and splash it on my face. That shocks me awake even more. I follow it up with a quick, hot shower that invigorates me to full consciousness. Revitalized, I then eradicate the presence of overnight grime buildup on my teeth. As a final touch for my cleaning regimen, I swish around a shot of sharp-tasting mouthwash for half a minute.

Still barefoot, I cross the soft bedroom carpet, enter my closet, and flick on the light switch. It only takes a minute to get dressed in the clothes I set out last night. I like the crisp feel of my dress shirt over my undershirt, the reassuring touch of its collar around my neck. A glance in the mirror convinces me that navy blue is a good match with my black slacks and dress shoes. I considered adding a tie, but that wouldn't be "business casual." I make a few combing tweaks to my hair and smile at myself. Now, I look ready to go to work.

Out of habit, I check on Sparky before I leave. He's my imaginary Cocker Spaniel. I know he's not real, but I can't afford the pet fees or the effort to take care of an actual animal. Pretending I have a fun and scruffy little buddy helps ease a bit of my loneliness. I glance at the metal food and water bowls in the kitchen next to the pantry. Each night, I take comfort from the idea of this happy, golden-furred guy sleeping at the foot of my bed.

I lean over and act like I'm scratching Sparky behind his ears for a few seconds. I imagine his brown eyes brightening with joy as he leans into it.

"That's my boy, Sparky!" I tell him. "Keep the place safe while I'm gone, okay?" I envision him barking in response and smile at the thought.

I just wish I didn't have to walk through this monsoon to get to work, even though Prosaic Industries is only a block and a half away. I secure my black trench coat and grab the umbrella on the way out of my apartment.

As soon as I'm outside, the frigid wind and rain slam into me. I wipe away some of the water that blew into my eyes. I realize my poor umbrella won't last two seconds in this mess. I keep it closed and make it around the corner to find warm and dry refuge inside Greenbacks Coffee. As I stand in line, I verify the time on my phone. Cool, I'm running a half-hour early.

"What can I get you?" the short, blonde barista asks, shining a smile that contrasts sharply with this weather. She looks younger than me.

"A smoked bacon and egg sandwich, please."

"Anything to drink with that?" she adds.

"Yes," I reply. "A medium caramel macchiato with an extra shot of espresso. No sense in being hungry or sleepy this morning, right?"

"Absolutely!" she beams. *How much coffee has she already had?* I wonder.

. . .

At a quarter 'til eight, I practically swim up to the local office of Prosaic Industries. This powerhouse storm isn't showing any signs of weakening. The lightning is near-constant, making me wince occasionally. As I enter the building, I see a handful of people in the brightly lit lobby near the front windows. They're probably talking about how bad the weather is. They sound muffled, huddled together as they are. They're also all as drenched as me. The drumbeat of raindrops against the windows taps away against the glass.

My phone's weather app demands my attention with a shrill beep. Great, we're in a tornado watch now, I think. Just my luck. Shrugging off my concern, I focus on my job instead. I see the elevator mere feet away, but I can't risk using it. What if the power goes out? I'd be stuck in there. Then again, if we lose power, how will we do our jobs? I sigh. *You're thinking too much, Sean. Focus. Let the coffee kick in.* Just then, I spot the stairs.

I grip the wooden rail tightly as I ascend the slippery steps toward my work area on the second floor. Opening the wooden door to the Call Center, I'm relieved to see carpeted floor and several dozen people already working. There are a few coat racks near the entrance, and I'm happy to hang mine up to dry on one of them.

"Good morning, Mr. Winter!" A bright and cheery female voice pierces through a busy chorus of my fellow employees. "Are you ready to start helping our needy customers?"

I recognize my supervisor, Jessica McCormick, as she walks toward me. I think she's in her thirties. Her lips are smiling, but her amber-eyed gaze is no-nonsense. She projects kindness and confidence, along with an air of warning. Combined with her imposing stature, it makes me hope I never disappoint her. She's wearing a wine-colored pantsuit with a white blouse. It compliments her hazelnut skin and dark, braided hair.

"Yes, ma'am," I say, returning her smile.

"How about you call me Jessica, and I'll call you Sean?"

"Sure, Jessica."

Satisfied, she leads me over to the cubicle area. I think the whole Greenbacks Coffee building would fit into this room. It's a full call center, immersed in more bright lighting and filled with dozens of desk areas separated by half-partitions. Each wall has a number of widescreen monitors. Most of them display call queue information. A few show varied pictures of perfect-looking Prosaic Industries "employees" at their desks and overlay them with encouraging company slogans like, "Our customers are like family to us" and "All problems have solutions. Do your best to provide them." I'm inspired to see that my decidedly average-looking coworkers sound pleasant as they talk to customers while operating their computers. They look like they're taking their jobs seriously.

I'm pleased with how dry my shirt is. I put my hands in my coat pockets and pull my arms closer to combat the chill in here. That doesn't do anything for my drenched hair and lower half. I hope I don't get sick.

Jessica stops next to a husky man with short, curly, blond hair. He looks a few years older than I. The nameplate on his cubicle reads "Keith Farris." Jessica waits for him to complete the call he's on. Then he maneuvers his mouse and clicks something on screen.

"There, I'm out of the queue now," he says, rolling his office chair to fully face me and Jessica. He seems a bit stressed but forces a smile. "What's up, boss?"

"Keith, this is Sean Winter," Jessica answers. "He just started, and I'd like him to train with you today."

He nods, standing up before he offers me his hand. "Welcome aboard, Sean."

Accepting with a firm shake, I reply, "Thanks," and then let go.

Jessica puts one hand on my shoulder. She motions toward Keith with the other as he sits back down.

"Keith's been here a few years, and he's my best trainer," she says. "I'll check in on you later, okay?"

"Thanks, Jessica."

With that, she leaves, and Keith turns his attention to me.

"We use Gzelle desktops running the latest Pane operating system," Keith tells me. "But Prosaic makes its own ticketing software. Have you worked with ticketing systems before?"

"No," I reply honestly. "But I'm pretty comfortable with computers, and I learn quickly."

"Okay," he says, relieved. "You should do fine then. Let me take you through the basics."

After Keith demonstrates how to edit an existing ticket, he lets me listen in on a few calls so I can watch him make tickets from scratch. His voice is warm but raspy, and his demeanor is very professional.

"I'm sorry to hear your services are out, sir," Keith says to a customer. "Let me take a look at your account. Can you please confirm your phone number and address? Thank you. Well, it looks like your payment was due yesterday. Yes, sir."

Keith is surprisingly quiet as the customer begins to curse him out, slightly grimacing only for a moment.

"Now, sir, we can turn your services back on," Keith assures him. "If you can make that payment now, I'll take care of everything. That's right. I can restore service in less than a minute, once we receive payment."

The customer ends up complying, and he restores his service. I'm impressed that Keith never lost control of the conversation.

Thirty minutes later, a tremendous boom overhead makes a lot of us look skyward. A second later, the lights flicker and then fail altogether. The computer screens blink out next. I hear several people gasp in response while others begin to murmur and complain. I have no clue what to say, and apparently, neither does Keith.

This shouldn't be scary to me. I've been in power outages before. But there's something different about this time. I have a sinking feeling in my stomach, like something bad is about to happen. I clench my fists at my sides: was the building struck by lightning? Are we safe? Could things get worse? A sense of dread builds in my chest, constricting me slowly.

"It's all right," I hear Jessica's voice resound above the commotion. "The generator should kick in soon!"

I follow the voice to where she is on the other side of the room, her face illuminated by the flashlight she's holding. I hear a whirring sound and a few clicks, but it stops. The power isn't coming back, at least not right away. Jessica mutters a curse. Then she sighs and takes in a breath.

"Everyone, stay calm," she continues. "I'll see what I can do about the power. Just stay put. This is the safest place any of us could be right now."

She's right. There are no windows in the call center area. We're literally in the middle of the building. It would take something worse than rain and lightning to threaten us.

Nervous, I stand up and peer around. I can see small lights from people's phone screens. The thunder continues to threaten overhead. My coworkers mostly look like silhouettes, and their unease is palpable, like another presence in the room.

I startle as a strong hand grips my shoulder.

"Sorry about that," Keith says. "I just wanted to see if you're all right."

Am I okay? My whole body is rigid like a statue. When I touch my arm, it's ice cold. I decide to sit back down. Keith does, too.

"I guess I'm more spooked than I thought." My voice is surprisingly shaky.

"Probably not the best experience to have on your first day," Keith sympathizes. "Don't worry. This happened last year, too."

"Really?"

"Yeah. The engineers jury-rigged the generator until the power came back on, but the higher-ups didn't want to buy a new one." He shrugs. "So, this was bound to happen again."

"Wow," I respond.

Keith pats me on the back reassuringly. "Trust me. Either the generator or the power will be back up in an hour or so."

I appreciate the confidence in his tone. I want to believe him.

"Sure, Keith."

I turn on my phone's light and set it between us on the desk. The thunder outside is colossal now, almost deafening. Keith and I exchange a glance acknowledging the storm before I change the subject.

"So, uh, how long have you worked here?"

"Four years. How long ago did you graduate college?"

I sigh. "That obvious, huh? In December."

He smiles. "Don't feel bad. It's common knowledge that Prosaic likes hiring college grads."

There's a moment of awkward silence between us. I don't know anything about him, and I'm not sure what to ask. Even in this barely lit room, I see a small, framed picture beside Keith's phone. It appears to be a blonde-haired little girl.

"Keith, can I ask you a personal question?"

"Sure."

"Who's that a picture of?"

"My daughter, Karen. It's from a few years ago. She's seven now."

"That's cool. She looks sweet."

"Thanks. She is."

I'm glad for him. He's clearly proud of her. But as I continue to glance at the photo, an old sadness claws at me from within, a sense of loss I thought I'd left behind.

Turning away from the photo, I squint, even though I don't mean to. I know I'm trying to block the bad memories, but it isn't working.

"Is something the matter, Sean?"

I'm terrible at hiding my feelings. The chill of the past creeps up within me, and my anxiety builds. I resist it, but it's hard. The darkness from the power being out is pressure enough, but the storm outside is screaming like a monster. The awful combination pummels me from every side, emotionally overwhelming me. I feel clammy. I need something—anything—to distract me from it. Normally, this wouldn't be my first choice, but maybe talking to Keith will help.

"I envy your daughter. She looks happy, like she had a good childhood. I . . . didn't," I admit, still not sure if this is a good idea. I grip the right armrest of my chair. "My mother died when I was pretty young. I was raised by my grandparents."

"I'm so sorry for your loss," he replies with a sincere voice.

"I was about the age your daughter is now, so I barely remember my mother," I add. A wave of bitterness washes over me.

In the low phone light, I see him contemplate my words. When he looks at me, he seems like he's trying to understand me. I guess he's a compassionate person.

"Actually, I do want to know, Sean. You can feel free to talk with me."

There's a new roaring noise outside. It's incredibly loud, like metal being torn apart and glass shattering, a nightmarish freight train barreling through the city. People start screaming and hiding under their desks. I already know it's a tornado.

I'm locked in combat with my anxiety now, and I'm losing! I'm afraid that this building will start shaking. And if it does, I know that's the beginning of the end. I imagine the ceiling or walls suddenly ripping away, and that's it—we'll all get sucked up and killed by the twister.

I shake off that painful thought and look at Keith. He appears concerned, but he's calmer than me. He's closed his eyes, and his mouth is moving. Is . . . is he praying? I can't tell. I listen closer, and a moment later, I can understand his final words: "In Jesus' name. Amen."

My mouth hangs open, and anger seethes in my heart. I can't help but feel betrayed. I thought he was a good person. But I was wrong. He's a Christian!

Keith looks up and sees me. He seems genuinely perplexed.

"What is it, Sean? What's wrong?"

It takes all of my will to keep my voice low. The tumult outside has started to move away, but my nerves are strained to their limit. I can feel my heart pounding in my chest. I want to hit something, but I can't move.

"You," I almost growl. "I thought you were normal. I was . . . really starting to respect you. But you're one of them." I see his brow furrow in confusion, and I spit the words at him: "a Christian."

Keith's only visible reaction is to blink in stunned silence. He puts his hands in his lap, lowers his head, and takes a deep breath. It's a few seconds before he looks up and says anything.

"Yes, I am a Christian," Keith replies slowly. "What about it? Why does that bother you so much?"

I release the armrest of my chair and clench my fist in my lap.

"It bothers me because it's a placebo! There is no God, and religion doesn't solve anything."

Keith waits to respond again. In a way, I'm grateful. It gives me a chance to calm down a little. The tornado sounds are gone now. All I can hear is the rain lashing against the sides of the building and occasional thunder. Most of our coworkers are out of sight, probably still under their desks. I can hear some of them whispering now and then. I don't see or hear Jessica. She must be out of the call center, probably trying to see who can get the power back on.

Just then, Keith slowly leans forward in his chair. He's actually pretty calm.

"You're an atheist then?" he finally says.

"Yes."

"If you don't believe in God, that's your choice," Keith continues. "And I respect that."

That's surprising to hear.

"But let me ask you something, Sean. Why does it matter to you if someone else does believe in God?"

What? Did he really just ask that? Is he stupid? This is making me madder.

"It matters to me if I see someone is choosing to be a mean, selfish hypocrite, yeah."

"So, all Christians are mean, selfish hypocrites to you?"

I stare at him, my irritation simmering. I take a deep breath.

"There is no evidence of any Supreme Being ever existing," I tell Keith. "But there is plenty of evidence to support rational and scientific explanations for what used to be attributed to superstition, gods, and other silly belief systems."

"Science has helped us understand a lot of things," Keith acknowledges. He's serious, at first. Then he smiles, amused. "We know the Earth isn't flat, for example."

I sigh. "We know a lot more than that."

"Do we know everything about everything?" he asks.

If the power ever comes back on, I'm asking Jessica to sit me with someone else.

"No, of course not," I reply. "But we're learning more all the time."

"Granted. Will that be enough?"

What is he talking about? "Enough for what?"

"Enough to satisfy human knowledge and curiosity. Will we ever know it all?"

He's carried this debate further than I thought he would. Maybe this isn't such a bad way to pass the time.

"No, I doubt we'll ever know it all," I suggest. "Humans will always have questions and seek knowledge."

"I agree," Keith adds. "But is intellectual knowledge enough to satisfy us humans? Can we live off of knowledge alone? Or do we need more?"

That's an interesting question, I have to admit.

"I suppose we need emotional satisfaction also," I answer.

"How do we attain that?" Keith inquires.

I give that some thought.

"By accomplishing goals we set for ourselves."

"Like what—school, work, marriage, and family? Things like that?"

"I guess. I mean, not everyone wants to get married or have kids. But there are all kinds of goals people can set for themselves."

He looks as intrigued by this discussion as me. It's also relieving to hear the rain finally dying down outside.

"And what if a person fails to achieve their goals?" he asks me. "Are they a failure and doomed to be miserable for the rest of their life?"

"Obviously not," I counter. "If one goal doesn't work out, a person can always make up new dreams to follow."

"New dreams," Keith repeats, nodding. "What's your dream, Sean?"

I don't mind the question. It makes sense. So, I oblige him.

"The only dream I've had so far is to live on my own," I tell him truthfully. "And I've achieved that."

"Good for you," he replies with a smile. "It sounds like that was no small feat."

"No, it wasn't."

The lights flicker back on, and the computers begin to boot up again. Several employees begin clapping at the achievement.

Jessica walks to the front of the room and gathers everyone's attention. She's joined by a male security guard.

"As you can see, we do have power now. But a tornado damaged two buildings next to ours. Our security personnel have first aid training and can assist with minor cuts and bruises. If anyone has more significant injuries, emergency responders are on the way," Jessica says in a commanding tone. "In addition, the city has sent engineers to inspect the building and make sure it's structurally sound. They will need several hours. I have been in communication with our corporate headquarters, and they are ordering a mandatory evacuation of the building until at least tomorrow. Check your company email and wait for the okay to return to work."

I find myself just wanting to go home. I feel tired, and even though my anxiety has lessened, it's not all the way gone. My vision is hazy around the edges, and my legs are sluggish. It takes all my focus to get out of the building. I don't talk to anyone as we all gather our personal items. I just leave.

Once outside, I look up—it's overcast; the rain is now a light mist; and the only lightning is in the distance. Leaves are scattered everywhere, along with numerous broken branches torn from trees and bushes. The temperature has dropped, and there's a northern breeze. A few people have emerged from the shelter of their buildings like me.

I have to stop myself suddenly. I barely avoided walking into an overturned Jeep that was deposited onto the sidewalk. Its hood is smashed into the ground. The wheels are twisted in different directions; the windshield is shattered; and the driver's side door is missing. I crouch down, squinting into the half-crushed cab. I look inside for occupants. Thankfully, no one's in there. I hope that means they're safe somewhere else.

The parking garage across the street is in similar shape to the smashed vehicle. Parts of the top two floors are demolished or missing entirely. There's smoke rising from the second and third floors. The back half of a Ford F-150 truck is hanging perilously over one side of the building. At street level, a city bus is turned on its side. People are trying to help survivors escape through its emergency exit at the back. I hear piercing emergency sirens closing in.

"You okay?" I hear Keith say behind me. Is he asking me?

I turn around and see him talking on his mobile phone, facing away from me. He nods his head, looking relieved.

"I guess the worst of it was centered on downtown," he says. "I'm fine. Yes, I'm fine. Please, tell her I'm all right. Thanks. I'll call you later, Julia. Bye."

I walk toward him. All of this still feels surreal.

"Your wife and daughter are okay, then?" I ask.

"Ex-wife," he clarifies. "But yes, they're in another part of town. They're fine."

I didn't expect that. Still, I find myself glad they're unharmed. If I had family I cared about, I'd want to know they were okay, too.

Keith looks behind me and gasps.

"Oh man, this . . . this isn't good," he says with a mournful sigh. He scratches the back of his head quizzically.

"What's the matter?" I wonder aloud.

He slowly lifts his hand to point behind me.

"That's my Jeep," he says.

2

PAINFUL RECOLLECTIONS

As I walk back to my apartment, I'm still in a daze. Emergency vehicle sirens seem to be everywhere, the telltale red and white lights flashing as they zoom by. The rain is gone, but the humidity is thick, almost stifling. I have to walk around one downed tree and its broken and scattered branches. I hear the crunch when I step on the smaller debris like concrete "rocks" and broken glass. When I look at people, most are frantically using their mobile phones, appearing as stunned as I feel. I finally get to my front door and enter. It should make me feel safe. It usually does, but not this time. I feel unsettled, restless, like I've forgotten something. It's unnerving. Even as I hang up my trench coat in the living room closet, something nags at me. A part of me is saying, "You still have something left to do out there. Don't do that. Stay ready." But that doesn't make sense to me, so I try to ignore it. It seems like Sparky's sleeping, so I leave him alone. I smooth my hair with my comb, but even that is unsatisfying.

Go.

Go where? This weird feeling is so frustrating.

I start heating some water for chamomile tea on the stove. A few minutes later, the whistle of the kettle alerts me that it's ready. While I wait for the tea to steep, I flip on the TV and remain standing. It seems our tornado made the national news.

"According to the National Weather Service, the Oklahoma City tornado that hit this morning was a strong F3 on the Fujita Scale. Local storm chasers have claimed it was more like an F4," the female news anchor says. "Whichever the case, we have verified reports of serious damage throughout the city, at least eighty-four people were injured, and six are confirmed dead."

Given how violent the storm was, it's incredible that it wasn't far worse. I sit down on the couch and look at the screen. I see the news anchors talking with a reporter on the scene, but I don't hear their words. I'm lost in thought. I think I'm starting to see how close I came to dying today. It could have been our building that the tornado ravaged. It was right outside, across the street. My fears about us all being sucked up into oblivion almost became reality. The people in that bus and the parking garage weren't so fortunate.

I keep thinking about Keith and his vehicle. They weren't lucky, either. I mean, he's fortunate to be alive. Vehicles can be replaced. But I do feel bad for him. He'll have to file a police report and wait for the vehicle to be towed. Then he'll have to get a ride home and find other means of transportation.

If I had a car, I would have given him a lift. Why should it matter to me? I have no obligations to him, none at all. Except that, for some reason, I care.

I take a sip of my tea and nearly burn my tongue. I try to shake off the sting from the heat before I lean forward, grab the remote, and immediately change the channel. Maybe some sci-fi will take my mind off things. At first, I'm excited—one of my favorite shows, *Battlecruiser Amsterdam,* is on.

It starts with a visual recap with voiceover by lead actress, Chance Powers, who plays Commander Sylvia Michaels. "Previously on *Battlecruiser Amsterdam*, the crew encountered an ion storm, which severely damaged the ship. Will the crew be able to survive long enough to repair the ship and make it out of the storm?"

Frowning, I turn off the TV.

The tea is so weak, it tastes like someone put grass in water. But it's the right temperature now, so I gulp it down. I hope it can steady my nerves. I lean back against the couch and try to unburden my mind. Think good thoughts, right? But I keep seeing the destruction outside the Prosaic building and reliving the tornado sounds. I close my eyes and slowly tilt my head from side to side for a few seconds, feeling the crick-crack noises of my joints popping and relieving their tension. I breathe deeply a few times, but my right foot keeps tapping erratically, betraying how frayed my nerves still are.

Now, I think about Keith. Even though I may not agree with Keith's belief system, I know he was trying to help me through the whole experience. His actions helped quell my anxiety attack. He didn't overreact when I was freaking out. That got me through two storms—the one outside and the one inside. And I walked away from the disaster without a scratch. But he lost his vehicle. He's the one who needs help now. Is that what I'm really wrestling with? How am I supposed to do anything?

My finger starts tapping on the armrest. I can't help it.

Keith couldn't do anything about the weather. He just did what he could for me. He acted like a friend. He stayed with me, listened to me. Why should it matter to me if someone else believes in a god?

People believe in all kinds of crazy things. Besides, it's not like he forced me to pray with him.

. . .

IN THE PAST

Twelve-year-old me was sitting at the dinner table with Grandma and Grandpa for supper. I stared down at the blackened crust atop Grandpa's overcooked meatloaf. As he sawed through its center to distribute slices to me and Grandma, I knew it would taste just like last time—saltier than instant ramen. The green beans and corn side dishes were equally brined. And while I didn't like Grandma, I wished she had made supper. At least she could cook.

"Sean," Grandma barked suddenly in her smoky voice. "Say the prayer for us, boy."

"Yes, ma'am," I complied, resigned to the inevitable. Still, I knew how to say the prayer the way she liked—short, sweet, and respectful. I closed my eyes and clasped my fingers together in front of me. "Lord, we thank you for this food. Please bless it. Amen."

When I opened my eyes and looked at her, she briefly smiled at me, verifying her acceptance. Then she took a bite of the meatloaf and almost spit it out. Aggravated, she cursed and focused her ire on Grandpa. Her deep blue eyes were like lasers.

"Jeremy Winter, what is this supposed to be?"

"Meatloaf," he replied apathetically.

She cursed again, picked up her slice from the plate, and threw it at him. He barely deflected it with his right arm. The tomato sauce covering the meatloaf splashed across the top of his long-sleeved, white shirt. He sighed. I could see he was mentally bracing for what came next.

"I've had juicier cereal—before adding milk!" she yelled. "You're gonna get on the phone right now. Order us some pizza. And you better not mess that up!"

"All right," Grandpa said without looking up as he wiped off his hands and shirt with his napkin. Then he took out his mobile phone from his pocket.

"Honestly, do you expect me and your grandson to go without?" she muttered.

Grandma crossed her arms over her chest in a huff and looked away. She was shorter than Grandpa, and her wide and angular shoulders made her drab, gray blouse spread out like a tent, especially the way she always hunched forward. Her bitterness had aged her beyond her fifty-eight years. Frown lines tugged the sides of her mouth, and she had developed a permanently furrowed brow above the thick, square-framed bifocal glasses she'd be blind without. She dyed her shoulder-length hair black, but her natural silver roots were starting to shine through.

I'd seen pictures of her and Grandpa from when they were much younger. Grandpa appeared to be a stylish charmer, based on his confident poses next to Grandma, who was very beautiful back then. She had a bright complexion and long, wavy hair. She seemed easygoing and had a wide, infectious smile that complemented Grandpa's boyish face, crisp mustache, and goatee. He'd lost the goatee, but he still had the mustache and a full head of white hair.

I liked Grandpa, especially talking with him one-on-one. He showed the most positive interest in me since I came to live with them. He was closer to my mother, too, based on our conversations. She'd told him when she was pregnant with me, and he'd broken the news to Grandma.

Grandpa still refused to look up from the phone. "I'm calling right now, Debra."

He sounded miserable already. I felt sorry for him.

I'd learned to stay quiet when Grandma was this angry. She grabbed a cigarette from her purse on the table and lit up right there. The odor of the burning tobacco immediately saturated the air. Then, without another word, she walked to the dining room door, opened it, and walked directly onto the back porch. It was what she did when she wanted to calm down. Grandpa finished making the pizza order and grabbed a beer from the refrigerator.

. . .

IN THE PRESENT

Fifteen minutes have passed. I see Keith, who is still in front of the Prosaic Industries building as I walk up. He's on his phone, facing away from me, and a wrecker is driving off with the remains of his Jeep. He hangs up and lets his hand drop to his side, breathing in as he looks skyward. It seems as though things haven't been going well.

"Excuse me, Keith?" I say carefully, trying not to startle him.

He turns around, at first surprised. Then his frown reverses into a smile. "Sean? I thought you'd gone home."

"I did, but I came back," I reply, shrugging slightly. "May I ask how things have been going?"

I'm not sure what I'm hoping to accomplish by this. It's not like I can help him get another car or even give him a ride home. But I feel like I need to do something.

"I'd just paid the Jeep off three months ago, so at least there's that," Keith answers. "I don't look forward to a new car payment, but I can handle it. I'm kind of sad, though. I really liked my little Jeep. Julia—my ex-wife—she picked it out when we were still together."

"You have a lot of memories with it," I suggest. He nods.

His eyes are misty, but he shakes it off and smiles.

"Maybe it's time to move on, leave the past behind," Keith says gruffly. Then he lifts his head and straightens his posture.

"Maybe so," I agree with a single nod. "I don't have a car yet, either. But if you're hungry, I can spring for pizza at Loggie's."

"Are they even open after this storm?" he asks.

"I can call and find out," I reply. "If they're not, we can get delivery to my place. I live within walking distance."

Keith looks extremely relieved and grins widely. "Deal, my friend! I'll take you up on that."

Are we friends? I'm not sure I'm there yet. I nod at him and make the call to Loggie's.

"Loggie's Pizza. Always cheap, all the time," a man answers. He has a husky voice with a Bronx accent. "I'm sorry, but this location is closed. We're assessin' damage from the storm."

"Oh, I totally understand," I reply. "Are your other locations open?"

"Yes, sir! The Robinson location is just a couple of blocks over, and they're helping us out today."

I thank him and end the call, turning to Keith.

"The closest location is closed, but another one nearby is open," I tell him. "We can head back to my apartment, and I'll order delivery from their app. Is that okay?"

"Sure, Sean. If that's easier, let's do that."

We start walking around the corner toward my apartment complex. The city crews have moved the downed tree and started sweeping up the debris already. A few minutes later, I let Keith inside my apartment.

"I'm going to open a few windows," I tell Keith. "I didn't realize how stuffy it's gotten in here."

"It's all right," he assures me.

I still take a moment to open the kitchen window over the sink and crack open my balcony door. It takes less than a minute to download the Loggie's Pizza app.

"Feel free to sit down," I suggest as I point to the couch. "I'm getting us two medium pizzas and some bottled drinks. Just tell me what you want."

"Thanks, Sean. That's very generous of you."

I shake my head kind of shyly and say, "It's no trouble." But my eyes end up staying on him as we sit.

"Is something wrong?" Keith asks, his shoulders stiffening.

I must have stared at him too long. Feeling awkward, I look down, embarrassed.

"No," I answer. "Nothing's wrong."

"Okay," he says. "Pepperoni is fine for me."

I nod and start to make our delivery order. The app indicates everything should arrive in half an hour.

My feelings about Christianity haven't changed. Keith's a good guy, but he is a Christian.

So what? He doesn't deserve kindness? He lost a vehicle to the twister and I'm buying us pizza. There's nothing wrong with that. I won't be breaking some "personal ethic" by just making small talk with him.

I briefly shake my head, trying to snap out of my distraction.

"I guess I'm still a little out of it," I manage to blurt out. "You know, with everything that happened."

His shoulders relax again, and he nods. "That's understandable."

"Would you like a bottled water while we're waiting?" I ask.

As peace offerings go, I guess this, and the pizza order, will have to do.

"Yeah, thanks."

After handing him a bottle I grab from the fridge, he asks me, "Can we continue our discussion from before?"

I can't help but tense up a little at that.

"I wanted to keep this civil," I respond. "So, that might not be a good idea."

He nods. "That's fine. I don't want to make you uncomfortable."

I sigh. "That's not it. It wouldn't make me uncomfortable. I just don't want to get into an argument again."

Flashing a smile, he says, "I can promise I won't yell at you or anything."

I need a second to figure out a good response to that. I head over to the fridge and get a bottled water for myself. On the way back to the couch, I find the right words.

"I'm not sure I can make the same promise, Keith."

"Why?"

"It's a subject I feel very strongly about."

"That subject—is it belief in God or Christians themselves?"

Again, I consider my answer for a moment.

"It's both," I acknowledge.

"Then I suggest we keep this simple. Can I ask you about yourself, your life before today?" he ask. "And whatever you don't want to share is fine. It's up to you."

I shrug. "Sure. What do you want to know?"

He takes a drink from his water.

"Are you from around here?" Keith asks.

"No. I grew up near Phoenix, Arizona," I reveal, relaxing back into the couch. I take a sip of my water. "A small town called Sully."

"With your grandparents."

Just the word *grandparents* gives my stomach a sinking feeling.

"Yes," I reply numbly.

"You're a long way from Arizona now," Keith adds.

I smile, but it feels bittersweet. And ironic.

"That was on purpose," I answer. "I moved to Oklahoma City when I got into OU. I applied to Prosaic Industries before I graduated college, and they offered me a job here."

"Did your grandparents help you move?"

I shake my head at that. "No. I worked while I was in school and saved up money. I rented a truck and moved everything myself."

"Oh. Sorry," he says, leaning forward a bit. His eyes are apologetic. "I shouldn't have assumed that."

"It's . . . okay."

Suddenly, I have an idea and sit up straighter. "How about we make this mutual? Where are you from, Keith?"

"Concord City."

That's still in Oklahoma, but pretty far from here.

"Why did you move here?" I wonder aloud.

"Julia has family here. After our daughter was born, we thought it was a good idea to relocate."

"Did that not work out like you thought?"

"No," he replies sadly. "No, it didn't."

"I'm sorry to hear that."

There's an awkwardness in the air for a moment. I take another sip of water.

"What caught your attention about Prosaic Industries?" Keith wonders.

"Well, I looked for service industry companies that were doing well financially and whose employees enjoyed working there," I answer. "Prosaic was my second choice. Valdivian doesn't have any offices in-state."

Keith nods, his eyes warm with intrigue. "Impressive choices."

His approval helps me relax some, and I rest my hands in my lap.

"Thanks," I reply. "From what I've seen, I'm glad I got in at Prosaic."

"Yeah? Even though you were in danger on your very first day?"

I laugh a little, nervously. I lift my hand and start slowly massaging the right side of my neck.

"Yeah. I mean, if Valdivian had an office here, I would have been just as threatened."

"Hm, I guess you're right," Keith replies.

Just then, there's a birdlike "cheap cheap" notification from the Loggie's app. I take a quick look.

"The driver is on the way with our pizza," I tell Keith. "It'll only be about ten more minutes."

"Cool."

"Can you tell me more about yourself?" I ask.

"All right," Keith answers. "What would you like to know?"

"I'm sorry if this is a sensitive topic, but . . . I'd like to know about your marriage if that's okay?"

I can see the sadness in his eyes more than anything else. Regret immediately tugs at me for asking him. I start to say, "Never mind," but he shakes his head.

"It's okay," Keith says with a slightly forced smile. "I need to get used to talking about that part of my life."

Did I just step on a landmine? I feel really bad about this.

"I'm sorry, Keith. I should have known that was a poor choice of subject. I don't know what I was thinking."

He shakes his head again and takes another drink of water. This time when he looks up, his smile looks voluntary.

"I don't want you to feel bad for asking, Sean. What happened in my marriage was my fault."

How do I change subjects from this?

"I wasn't a Christian yet," Keith continues. Just hearing the word *Christian* makes me bristle inwardly. I wrestle back any facial reactions. "Julia and I met at a party. We had instant chemistry and started going out. We got married within a year, and our daughter was born a year after that."

"That's impressive," I confess.

He beams with the memories, but that look quickly fades. He looks to the side a moment, as if collecting his thoughts, and then he sighs somberly.

"I was impressed, too. Maybe that was part of the problem," Keith adds. "Julia and I started out all passion and excitement. I had a good customer service job, and Julia's a paralegal. We'd saved some money and were planning to buy a house, maybe have more kids."

"I don't understand. What went wrong?" I ask.

He looks down, seemingly lost for words. Then he looks up at me again.

"I went wrong. I had an affair with a woman from work," Keith admits. "She approached me about a relationship, and . . . I didn't resist."

I thought he might be heading in this direction, but it's still shocking to hear. He doesn't seem like someone who would cheat on his wife. Then again, I remind myself that I hardly know him.

"Things had gotten kind of routine at home. And this other woman, Linda, was seductive and exciting," Keith shares. "But that brief spark came with a terribly high cost. It didn't take long for Julia to figure it out. Late nights at work, pathetic excuses . . . and then she checked the text messages and call logs on my phone. I wasn't exactly what you might call stealthy."

I remain silent. He exudes regret like a volcano overflowing with lava. He becomes emotional, gripping his arms as his head remains lowered in shame.

"I—I'll never forget the look on her face when she confronted me," he says pensively. "She'd given her love, trust, and life to me . . . and I'd destroyed that. She was devastated."

"She may forgive you someday," I tell him, trying to offer what little hope I can. "Maybe you two could—"

He shakes his head. "She says she's forgiven me. We share custody of our daughter and see each other pretty often. But when she looks at me, even when she tries not to show it, the hurt is still there."

I don't know what to say. I'm completely out of my depth here. I'm the last person to offer some kind of relationship advice.

"After my divorce, I was pretty broken and had a lot of soul-searching to do," Keith says. "I had ended my relationship with Linda, even though it came too late. It was hard to live with all my regrets. Drinking didn't help, and I didn't want to pursue any new relationships. Work was all I had. About three years ago, a couple of my coworkers saw how heartsick I was and invited me to their church. I was so low at that point, I was willing to try anything. That's all I'll say."

It's enough. I am grateful he didn't go further.

"Thanks for answering my question," I say.

A minute later, there's a knock on the door. Our order has arrived. Opening one of the boxes, I'm pleased to see the pizza is steaming hot, and the aroma alone is delicious. I close the lid and go grab a couple of plates and ice-filled cups for us from the kitchen. Before he begins to eat, Keith closes his eyes, and I already know he's saying grace for his food. But at least he's being silent about it. I find myself waiting till he's done to get my first slice of pizza.

I lift the gorgeous, greasy food to my mouth and take a generous bite. The infusion of mozzarella cheese, bacon, and mushrooms melts into my mouth; and I close my eyes as I savor it. I take three more bites before I remember I have a two-liter soda. I pour some of it into my cup and take a gulp. The sting of strong carbonation is followed by a lovely syrupy sweetness.

I look at Keith, and he smiles, still chewing his food as he lifts his cup in a toasting gesture to me. I smile back.

"I've had Loggie's before, but I don't think it's ever been this good!" Keith says a moment later.

"Maybe we've got reason to enjoy it more today," I suggest.

Keith nods. "True. This is one of those days to stop and . . . smell the pizza?"

We both laugh at that.

Ten minutes and some small talk later, Keith closes up his pizza box and puts the cap on his soda.

"Thanks again, Sean, for everything."

"You're welcome, Keith."

My apartment feels a little emptier when he leaves.

. . .

That night as I'm about to go to sleep, I get an email from Jessica McCormick. The small text pierces through the room's dimmed lighting: "The Prosaic building has passed its safety inspection. All employees are to report to work for their shifts as usual tomorrow. Thank you, and please stay safe."

I'm relieved by this information. I was concerned we might be shut down a while, and I need all the hours I can get to pay my bills on time.

Now there's only one question I have: do I want to keep training with Keith, or should I ask Jessica to pair me with someone else? He hasn't done anything wrong, and he is very good at the job. I could learn a lot from his expertise. But I'm not sure it's a good idea anymore.

. . .

IN THE PAST

"What is it you really want to do, Sean?" Grandpa had asked.

"I want to get a bachelor's degree and get a good job," I answered, looking at him.

"That's a given, son. But what else?"

He's turned toward me, sitting at his drafting desk. He was an engineering consultant, even after he retired from the state. He had a way of seeing right into me, and I think he already knew my answer.

He just wanted me to admit it. I felt like he'd accept what I had to say, no matter what it was.

"I want to live on campus, Grandpa. It's time for me to get out of here."

He smiled. "You're right. You're ready to stand on your own. So do it."

"What about Grandma? She doesn't approve."

"Is she going to take the classes for you?" he asked. I shook my head. "It's your decision. She'll get over it."

. . .

IN THE PRESENT

I realize that's still true. There's really only one answer. If Keith is the most experienced trainer, then I should learn from him. All things considered, as long as the building isn't threatening to come crashing down around us, I think I can maintain a professional demeanor.

I sigh in relief. That wasn't so hard.

I'll sleep easy tonight.

3

SPECTERS

I know it's a dream. It has to be. Last I checked, elevators weren't twenty feet wide. And they usually don't have aquariums built into all of the walls made of white clouds that softly reflect the blues, greens, and ambers from the rock formations and various fish in each tank. If I saw this in real life, I'd question my sanity. But it's a dream, so I just accept it. I feel the hum and the gradual ascension of the elevator. The destination floor numbers appear as wisps of air on the wall in front of me. We just passed number fourteen. There are no doors. Somehow, I already know passengers are supposed to go through the clouds to enter or exit the elevator.

I'm not alone in the elevator. Right now, there are two men, a woman, and her child in here. Like I said, there's plenty of room. Even so, we don't speak to each other. Everyone seems closed off, distant. I'd like to think maybe they're focused on where they're going, but that's not the vibe I'm getting from them.

A brown-hued man in a silky, dark blue suit exits the lift. He's followed by the other man, who is bald and in green overalls. When I look over at the woman and her child, I recognize the plump, little girl as Keith's daughter, Karen. I suppose the woman next to her must be her mother. If that is Julia, she's about my height. She has an inverted triangle figure. Studying her, I note she has short, wavy, brown hair, a small nose, and a beauty mark on her left cheek. The child has her eyes and lips. Julia is wearing a plain blue dress and shows no expression. Neither does Karen.

"Excuse me, is your name Julia?" I ask, since we've never actually met.

She turns her head and makes eye contact with me.

"Yes," she replies flatly.

"My name is Sean. I work with Keith Farris."

"Do you?" she asks suspiciously, looking over the thin-framed, oval-shaped glasses that just appeared on her face. "That's interesting."

She looks at the floor number, which just reached nineteen, then at her daughter.

"We're here, Lemon Drop," she tells the girl, sounding impatient. "Let's go."

Karen looks up, now grinning. "Okay, Mommy!" She has Keith's smile.

They walk through the front of the elevator without saying anything else to me, disappearing into the mist. This doesn't feel right. I want to know more about them, so I go after them.

Then I find myself sitting in a lecture hall at Oklahoma University. I don't question that I'm the only student in a room that can seat over a hundred. Front and center is my favorite teacher, Dr. Leonard Stringfellow. He always wears a white dress shirt and black slacks with maroon suspenders and a bow tie. His trademark black fedora hat is resting on his desk. He always likes to pace in a circle and gesture with his hands during his lectures.

I only had him for two semesters while attending the university, but he made a tremendous impression on me. A very smart man, he specialized in teaching humanities courses, such as Interpretive Methodologies, Philosophy, and World Religion.

"Mr. Winter, do I have your attention?" Dr. Stringfellow comes to a stop near his lectern at the center of the floor.

I sit up straight, suddenly very alert as I feel the need to answer him. "Yes, Dr. Stringfellow!"

Why can I easily picture this trim man walking or jogging daily down some long, circular path around a park, lake, or even the campus? He'd probably talk to himself during those strolls, just so he could continue to make his compelling gestures. Suddenly, I hear him clear his throat to redirect my focus again.

"Then can you please explain to me how you came to the conclusion that bunny rabbits have feelings?" Dr. Stringfellow asks.

Wait, what? Did he just say "bunny rabbits?" Oh yeah, I'm dreaming.

Suddenly, I'm inspired to answer.

"Certainly, Dr. Stringfellow. Bunny rabbits have social habits, including mating, raising, and protecting their young. For that kind of complex behavior to occur, they would need to have feelings."

The bearded African American man wags his finger at me, closes his eyes, and makes a "tut tut" sound. When he looks at me again, I already know I must have given the wrong answer.

"You were so close, Mr. Winter," he replies. "While what you said about their socialization is an approximation, you are neglecting the fact that these are animals. They have instincts that comprise their habits. But there is not enough evidence to conclude that bunny rabbits actually have feelings."

"Dogs are animals, and they demonstrate feelings," I interject.

"Ah, but we were not discussing dogs," Dr. Stringfellow rebuts. "We were discussing bunny rabbits. Please stay on topic."

After another fifteen minutes, my one-on-one lecture lets out. I thank Dr. Stringfellow; then I leave the room and begin to walk across campus.

There's a shift in the air, and then I find myself with the Campus Revival group I joined during my freshman year. That means it's three years ago.

Jennie Lou Harris and I are manning a table along a walkway that runs through the central region of the university. I'm reliving a memory. I know that, and I don't care. I'm just happy because it's her. I haven't seen her since that day.

. . .

I wake up from the dream, the image of Jennie Lou fresh in my mind. Jennie Lou was a sophomore. She grew up in Texas, somewhere near Dallas. We're the same height, though she was heavier than me. She had bright blue eyes; long, strawberry blonde hair; and a kind smile. I thought I was in love with her. She led Campus Revival for two years and had recruited me to the cause a few months earlier.

For such an attractive woman, she had a surprisingly rough voice. It reminded me of Peppermint Patty from the Peanuts gang, if she grew up and went to college. She could be kind of bossy like her, too, but I didn't mind. I was completely devoted to her, which was probably the worst reason to join a college club.

"At least he looked at it, Sean," she told me after we saw one young man throw away one of our group's pamphlets. "You never know how the Lord may work with him later."

Jennie Lou always rebuilt the club's—or rather, *my*—confidence when people rejected our efforts. Despite her encouragement, I hadn't been convinced this time. I felt like we were wasting our time. But I didn't want to openly disagree with her. I didn't want to disappoint her.

"I suppose you're right, Jennie," I said, still sounding dejected.

She took me by the shoulders and practically held me up with her own strength. In that moment, all my attention was on her gorgeous, heart-shaped face. Just seeing it and being so close to her lifted my spirits in ways nothing else could. I saw that her faith was unshakable. And I would follow wherever she led . . . like a grinning idiot.

"Sean, listen to me," she said, letting go and turning around to face the greater campus. She was wearing one of the purple Campus Revival t-shirts she'd designed. The logo was a white cross rising over the yellow blocky letters "Campus Revival OU." It was the same on the front and back. I thought it complemented her figure, along with the blue jeans and white sneakers. Still looking away, she stretched out her right arm and opened her palm toward the students walking down the sidewalk. "We're like front line soldiers for Jesus. We've been given a responsibility—us—and this is something we're uniquely qualified to do."

Then she swung around and faced me, looking determined. "All we have to do is reach out to the students. It's up to them whether they accept us or not. But if we don't try, then the work doesn't get done at all. Do you understand?"

I didn't understand at all. Every time we went out in public, we were mocked, even laughed at. Only club members came to our events—and not all of them at that. I didn't feel like we reached anybody. But this was Jennie Lou. I would have climbed a mountain for her. Or endured a thousand insults to protect her honor and beliefs.

But what about my beliefs? I felt like a liar inside. I had attended church services ever since I came to live with my grandparents. I had even learned some Scriptures. I could behave just like a Christian, but it was all just an act. Smile, say the right words, keep out of trouble, and say the blessing. I could do those things. But I had no deep devotion.

And then came Derek Simmons walking up the sidewalk toward us. He was the head of Campus Freedom, an atheist group. He was tall, athletic, handsome, and smart. Worse still, he was confident and proud.

"Afternoon," he smirked with a shark-like glint to his gaze. "I'd like to know more about your group."

I've played these moments a hundred times in my head since that day. It never ends well.

"Certainly," I said pleasantly. "We're glad you stopped by, um . . . ?"

"Derek." He continued his kind façade, smiling with perfectly white teeth. "Derek Simmons."

"What do you want to know?" I asked.

Jennie Lou gently tapped my arm and stepped in front of me.

"Doesn't this get old, even for you, Derek?" she complained, her voice rougher than normal as she pointed a finger at Derek. Her gaze was like steel.

"Oh no, never!" he boasted, slowly shaking his head. It made his gel-styled auburn hair wobble some. "You guys are the gift that keeps on giving."

"You know this is harassment," she insisted, now crossing her arms.

Derek leaned close. "Prove it." Then he pulled back and laughed. "Oh, that's right—your group isn't so good at that, is it?"

I'd had enough, stepping forward. He was messing with Jennie Lou. That was reason enough for me to intervene.

"Why can't you just run your group and let us run ours, Derek?" I asked him.

"I'm not stopping you. In fact, I'm going to help your little group.. I'm going to test your Bible knowledge."

My heart sank.

"What does John 3:16 say?" Derek asked.

At least he started easy, I thought. I knew that verse.

"'For God so loved the world that he gave his only begotten Son,'" I quoted. "'That whosoever believeth in him should not perish, but have everlasting life.'"

Derek clapped slowly. "Good for you. You even memorized the King James Version. I'm impressed; that's not easy. Now . . . what is that verse supposed to mean?"

"Excuse me?" I wondered aloud.

"Well, I'm one of the 'heathen,' right? So, I'm not supposed to know what the Scriptures are about," he mocked. "And I want you to enlighten me. What is John 3:16 talking about?"

Jennie Lou stepped forward. "It—"

Derek turned to Jennie Lou and held up his index finger. "Not you, Club Leader," he warned sharply, cutting her off. "I want *him* to tell me."

I tensed up, realizing I'd walked right into the trap he'd been setting. But I couldn't back down.

"It's talking about the reason Jesus came to earth," I answered.

"And that reason *was…?*" Derek's tone was dripping in condescension.

"To save the world—to save us—from our sins," I completed my thought.

"Well, which was it—the world or us? And by 'us,' who do you mean?" Derek piled on.

I twisted my mouth and clenched my jaw. I did not want to get angry. But he was so disrespectful to both me and Jennie Lou. I took a deep breath and shoved down my indignation.

"Jesus' death on the cross, burial, and resurrection was for everyone in the world, back then and now," I said proudly from memory. I'd learned this from a sermon once. "Jesus made it possible for anyone to receive His salvation."

Derek nodded slowly. "You have a good memory. I'll give you that."

"Thanks," I replied.

"So, Who said this Scripture?" Derek asked.

In that moment, I was stumped. Was it John the Baptist? One of the disciples? To my shame, Derek was clearly reading me like a book. He snickered but stopped himself. I could tell he was trying to give me one more chance to figure it out. And I blew it. I couldn't answer.

He howled in laughter. "You don't know! You honestly don't know Who said those words! That's hilarious!"

I looked to Jennie Lou for help. Her cheeks were flush with embarrassment as she frowned. Her arms were still crossed, visibly pressing into her abdomen.

"It was Jesus Who said those words," she said quietly.

"Yes!" Derek said, slapping his hands together in satisfaction. "I knew that *she* knew it!"

He stepped over to Jennie Lou but kept a respectful distance this time. His grin was truly aggravating.

"Y'know, I just did you a favor, Club Leader," Derek taunted. "Now you know who's working for you."

"What is *that* supposed to mean?" she replied icily.

He stared at me, finding my name tag before returning his gaze to Jennie Lou. "'Sean isn't here to tell the world about Jesus. His heart's not in it. I can tell."

She raised an eyebrow, maintaining a defiant stare.

"Is that so?" she retorted. "Then how about you tell me why he's in this club?"

"No, that's not my place. It's too rich," he said, his manner serpentine. "I'll let him do that. My work here is done."

And with that, Derek walked away with his head held high, casually clasping his hands behind his neck. He began to caustically whistle "When The Roll Is Called Up Yonder." It continued to taunt us in the wind, even once he was out of sight.

"He can be so infuriating," Jennie Lou said at a low volume, clearly upset. She finally unclasped her arms and let them fall to her sides. They were red where she had been gripping them.

I was speechless. I hadn't just let her down. I'd let myself down. I felt like my lie was on full display.

"You didn't have to take his bait, you know," she added, gazing at me with hurt in her eyes. "He would have left after a few minutes."

I sighed. She was probably right.

"Sean, *is* there some other reason you joined this club?" she asked. "I mean, the other members and I—we don't know the whole Bible, either. But I'd like to think we all have one thing in common—that we all love Jesus and want to do His will."

I took in a deep breath. "I have . . . always been taught those things. I've tried to do His will. But . . . that's not the reason I joined the club."

As soon as the words left my mouth, I was ashamed of how shallow they sounded. Jennie Lou's eyes widened a little in comprehension. I could tell she'd deduced the truth.

She slowly shook her head in denial. Her voice was hushed, only for me to hear.

"You didn't join just for me . . . did you?"

"I . . . did."

A few seconds passed in silence.

"Why?" she asked with a wounded and confused expression.

It had all fallen apart in a minute's time. I had nothing left to lose in telling the truth.

"I love you, Jennie."

She didn't look angry as she comprehended my words. Actually, she briefly smiled. But I had sensed something else from her. Was that disappointment? Pity? I really couldn't tell.

"I appreciate you finally being honest about your feelings for me," Jennie Lou said, looking at me. "But surely, you can see how this will cause problems in the club . . . and between us?"

I nodded.

"I think you're a good person," she told me.

"You don't have to say the rest," I interrupted.

"Yes, I do. Sean. I can't be in any relationships right now," she said. Then she looked down. "I want to finish my bachelor's degree, maybe get a master's. Then I can focus on marriage—"

At that, she suddenly lifted her head and looked at me again. In that moment, she blushed bright pink. "I mean . . . I just need to focus on school right now," she added. I think she was trying to be serious, but all I could focus on was how cute she looked. "You know?"

I did. And that gave me hope. She hadn't ended things.

"I can wait for you, Jennie Lou."

Her expression immediately soured. It smacked me like a door closing in my face.

"Sean, when I do pursue a relationship, I want it to be with someone who shares my values. And you've just made it very apparent that you don't. I'm sorry."

"Jennie Lou, I'm sorry. I didn't—"

"I think you should leave now," she interrupted abruptly, turning her face away.

In that instant, all my romantic aspirations crumbled to dust. Any faith I had was gone. I felt empty.

And I followed her final instruction. I walked away numbly.

. . .

Lost in my memories of Jennie Lou, I soon fall back asleep.

I'm planted on a wooden bench next to a full-grown elm. The giant tree casts a calming shadow that stretches thirty feet.

"It's all right, son," Grandpa answers, now sitting alongside me on the bench.

He's got a six-pack of beer with him. He pulls one out of its plastic ring and offers it to me.

"You're old enough now," Grandpa says. "Want one?"

"No, thanks, Grandpa. I don't drink, remember?"

"That's a shame. Why is that, anyway?"

A chill goes down my spine. "Because I don't want to be like you and Grandma."

He chuckles. "That's a harsh thing to say . . . even if it makes sense."

I can tell this isn't his first beer. He's very relaxed.

"Now your Grandma, she can drink!" he adds.

I sigh and roll my eyes. "That's because you always buy her whiskey."

"I do that for our protection, Sean," he says with a mellow nod and knowing grin. "Yours and mine." He's been using Grandma's cigarettes, too. I'd know that sweet-yet-burned tobacco smell anywhere.

Before I can blink again, the college campus is gone, and I'm sitting alone at Grandpa's work bench in his home office. The floor in the room is cherrywood. The wooden chairs and bookshelves match the tan and brown color scheme of the one-story house.

He and Grandma half-stumble into the room, drunk and laughing arm-in-arm, and bump against some of the furniture. Grandma's eyes are only half-open, and she's holding a bottle of Irish whiskey in her free hand. Grandpa's devoted gaze at Grandma shows me that he still loves her. I can see his relief at her joy, but also an underlying sadness that it takes this to achieve it. I feel even more sorry for him. The only thing I can do is stay quiet and out of the way for as long as I can. They barely know I'm here, anyway.

"Wow, I can see why you have a problem with them," someone says next to me.

It's Keith! How did he get into my dream? It makes me mad and embarrassed at the same time. The intensity I felt toward him during the storm returns.

"There!" I shout, pointing at my inebriated family members. "You see why I don't trust you? One day, you're gonna turn out to be just like them. They're Christians, too!"

Keith looks at me with concern and what could be pity. He takes in a breath and releases it slowly.

"They began the race, but they did not finish," Keith tells me.

"What? What does that mean?"

"They didn't keep the faith," Keith says sadly. "They denied Christ through their actions. They do not represent Him."

. . .

I open my eyes and see I'm in my bedroom with the lights out. The reds and pinks of dawn's light hug the horizon's edge. I check my phone, verifying I woke up twenty minutes early. I shut off my alarm.

Stumbling out of bed, my eyes burn. My limbs scream for more sleep, but my mind's fully awake. As I stand to my full height, I rub my eyes in frustration. It's gonna be a long day.

I need coffee.

4

NOT A WALK IN THE PARK

I gulp down my "Catapultcino" from Greenbacks Coffee in record time and wipe the corner of my mouth with my sleeve. The barista stares at me in amazement.

"Uh, you know there's five shots of espresso in that, right?" she asks. "You want some food to even that out?"

"Thanks, but I don't have time," I reply. "I'll manage."

As I exit the coffee shop, I can already feel a tingling at the base of my neck. It spreads throughout my head and chases away my grogginess within a couple of minutes. Now, I'm walking with a little extra zing, and it feels good.

As I near the Prosaic Industries building, I can't help but notice that the parking garage across the street has been completely blocked off to the public. The tornado stripped parts of the walls bare and tore off sections of the top two floors. My walk slows and then stops. Near the top of the garage, uneven metal beams are twisted upward in different directions. The concrete walls are pitted with holes or splintered by cracks.

How did our office come out of this unscathed when the tornado was so close? Death was literally a hundred feet away. That sends a chill down my spine.

A few minutes later when I enter the Prosaic lobby, Jessica rushes up to meet me. She looks excited and worried at the same time.

"Sean! I'm so glad you made it," she tells me. "I've been personally welcoming everyone back."

There's no warning behind her gaze today, only relief. The oval-shaped woman pulls me into a bear hug. I didn't know she was this strong or sentimental. When she releases me, her eyes are misty.

"You're the last of my employees to arrive, Sean, and you're *early*," Jessica says proudly. "Everybody knows we dodged a bullet yesterday. I don't know what I'd do if something happened to any of you."

"It's okay, Jessica," I reply. "We're all here, right?"

"Yes, except for Keith."

That's surprising.

"What happened to Keith?"

"Oh, he needed to take time off to replace his Jeep," she answers thoughtfully. "It got demolished by the twister. He told me he may be in later today."

I nod. It makes sense.

"That's cool. Who will I be training with then?" I ask her.

She smiles and gently leads me toward the call center. "I'll have you sit with Miranda Guerra. She'll have you taking your own calls by the end of the day."

Miranda Guerra is a short and slender woman in her mid-forties. She has her chair turned away from the aisle, gripping its handle tightly. Finally, she gives me and Jessica a "why are you trespassing in my domain?" glare as she faces us. Great.

"Miranda, this is Sean Winter." Jessica beams.

Miranda looks at me like I'm a used car salesman.

"Do I have to?" she deadpans to Jessica.

Jessica leans forward and smiles at Miranda with menace.

"You do if you *ever* want another raise," Jessica tells her through her smile. Some of the color drains from Miranda's face.

"Fine," Miranda replies. Then she looks at me. "Nice to meet you."

I deliberately raise an eyebrow and give a barely noticeable sneer. "Charmed . . . I'm sure."

Miranda nods slowly, and a hint of a smile appears then vanishes. Did I just earn some level of respect from Miranda? Go, sarcasm!

"See?" Jessica adds. "You two will get along great." With a wave of her hand, she says, "Later!" and walks off.

By lunch break, I've taken four calls and logged as many tickets under Miranda's training. Part of me feels like she's letting me do her work for her, but I'm glad for the experience.

Now, I'm famished, and my caffeine buzz is pretty much gone. My body drags, feet heavy with each step I take toward the ground floor. Hunger propels me outside, but I'm not sure where to go. I don't feel like pizza again. Should I go to Burger Empire or Damar's Fried Chicken?

Before I can decide, a dark blue SUV pulls up in front of the Prosaic Industries building and parks along the curb. The passenger-side door opens, and Keith gets out. He jogs around to the driver's side door. Its window slides down with electric precision, and I can better see the driver. Then I freeze. It's the woman from my dream—the one who I imagined was his ex-wife, Julia! How is this possible? She looks *exactly* the same, only friendlier. I think she may even be wearing the same dress.

"Thanks for the ride, Julia," Keith tells her. "I'll take a cab home."

"No, you won't," she replies with a lopsided grin. "Your daughter has already *informed* me that I'm picking you up after work so you can have dinner with us tonight."

Keith lowers his shoulders. "Do you . . . think that's a good idea? I don't want to make you uncomfortable."

There's a moment of uneasy silence.

"This isn't about our comfort, Keith. This is for our daughter," Julia answers, reflecting Keith's humble manner. "She's feeling extra-protective of her daddy, given what . . . almost happened yesterday. Even she knows you're lucky to still be alive. And . . . she loves you. She doesn't want to lose you."

"Yeah," he concedes. "You're right."

I do my best to play ignorant and turn my head away. I look down the block toward the restaurants I should be frequenting right now.

"Julia, I—" Keith starts to say.

"I'll be back at five sharp, Keith," she interrupts. "Be ready."

"Uh, sure. No problem."

He stands there with his shoulders still slumped and his hands in his pockets. He watches the SUV drive away.

I'm mystified. How could I have a dream with *her* in it?

Just then, I spot the B. Torres Tacos food truck and decide to make a dash for it. I get three spicy chicken fajita tacos and a bottled water. I chow down next to the food truck. Small, but oh, so scrumptious. Tender grilled chicken, onions, and jalapeños with shredded cheese inside freshly made flour tortillas. As I head back to the office, I wish I'd bought two more. But this should get me through the rest of my shift.

. . .

By five o'clock, Miranda is bragging about me to Jessica.

"Oh yeah, he's totally got this," Miranda tells her. "I mean, if he still has questions, he can chat them to me, but he's good."

Jessica tentatively looks at me for confirmation.

"Yeah, I'm good, Jessica," I agree. "And I'm not shy about asking questions."

"No, he's not," Miranda adds.

She says it sweetly, but I think she's just doing that for Jessica's sake. Miranda just wants to get rid of me. And that's okay. The feeling's mutual.

Jessica narrows her eyes, closely scrutinizing me and Miranda. Then she shrugs.

"Whatever," Jessica says. "If you feel okay to be solo tomorrow, Sean, go for it."

As I walk off, I hear her tell Miranda in a low voice, "If I get complaints about him tomorrow, I will not be happy. And then *you* will not be happy. Got it?"

"Yeah, boss," Miranda answers.

. . .

I don't feel like heading straight home. Between everything that's happened so far today, I'm agitated and restless. I need to clear my head. I'm not far from a park, maybe a few blocks. I hope it wasn't too damaged by the storm.

It takes me about ten minutes to get there. I see a large, white tent set up on one side of the grounds next to some large dogwood trees with vibrant white flowers. I see some people going in and out of the tent, but I can't tell what they're doing. Curious, I walk closer for a better view.

Of course, I think bitterly as I come to a halt. *It's a Christian group.* The Hopes and Prayers Relief Organization. It figures. One crisis arises, and they swoop in like vultures under the guise of "helping." I start to feel a little queasy at the thought. But as I turn around, I almost bump into someone.

"Sean?"

Our eyes meet, and there's instant recognition. Of all people, it's *her.*

"Jennie, is that you?" I ask, not believing my eyes.

She's with a young woman I don't know. But Jennie Lou Harris looks as stunned as I feel. After a few seconds, she remembers how to smile.

"Yes. Yes, it's me," she replies. "This is . . . quite a surprise. How are you?"

Her companion, a short Asian woman in a white t-shirt and khaki skirt, wisely stays silent. She's probably waiting for Jennie Lou to introduce us.

Part of me hoped I'd never see Jennie Lou again. And another part is thrilled that she's here. She hasn't changed much, except cutting her hair to shoulder-length. She and her friend are wearing Hopes and Prayers t-shirts, which sport ocean blue lettering on a white background. Jennie Lou is wearing blue jeans with hers. She always liked blue jeans.

I almost wish she wasn't as beautiful as I remembered. I nearly don't comprehend what she says; I'm so absorbed in her appearance.

"Did you not hear me, Sean? I asked how you're doing."

My verbal recovery is less than stellar.

"Uh, I . . . um, I'm fine, thanks," I manage to say. "You're here with them?" I point at her t-shirt.

She smiles uneasily. "Yes. We're here to help the community recover from the tornado."

I start tensing up. *Don't say anything. It won't make any difference. And it will mess up any chance of—*

"How?"

The word is out of my mouth before I can contain it. And it's filled with contempt.

Both of them stiffen and go quiet. Jennie Lou's friend frowns, and Jennie Lou's brow furrows. I need to fix my blunder.

I clear my throat. "I mean, what service is the organization providing?"

That seems to diffuse some of their alarm, especially Jennie Lou. She considers my question.

"Hopes and Prayers has a mobile hospital," Jennie Lou replied. "Since yesterday, the city's hospitals have been pushed to capacity. This organization has medical professionals who volunteer their time and services. They can help treat those who can't afford medical treatment."

Jennie Lou's friend steps forward and offers her hand. "Hi, I'm Lynn Wilson. I'm a volunteer like Jennie."

I accept her handshake and give her a polite smile.

"We also have a musical group that will be giving a free concert," Lynn continues. "Some of our volunteers are licensed counselors. And we're providing free food for those who need it."

That all sounds good. Those are all valuable services. Except they're leaving one out.

"And spiritual counseling?" I ask, looking directly at Jennie Lou. I consciously remove as much negativity from my voice as I can.

Jennie Lou keeps a straight face, but I can see the confidence in her eyes. It's just short of defiance.

"Of course, for those who are seeking it," she replies.

"Of course," I repeat, holding my own emotions in check.

More awkward silence.

"I suppose Lynn and I should get back," she suggests. "It was good to see you, Sean. You're looking well."

I nod and start to walk away. I hear their steps on the grass as they head in the opposite direction. Then I stop.

"I'm *not* well!"

I couldn't help it. Those words erupted from me loud and clear. My feet dig into the ground and won't let me proceed.

"I was there!" I continue. "I was in the building across the street from the twister. I heard it roar and scream and destroy while we cowered in the dark next to our desks! We . . . thought we were going to die."

Having said all that, I turn to face them again. Lynn is further away than Jennie Lou. I can't read her expression from here, but she's frozen in a half-turn. Jennie Lou is maybe ten feet from me with eyes wide and mouth open. She heard everything I said.

My cheeks feel wet. I started crying?

Jennie Lou looks more than sympathetic. She jogs toward me, and I can't move. She hugs me with her strong arms. And in that moment, despite how I feel and what I think I want, I feel safe. Loved. It's not romantic love, but a peaceful one. I don't know that I've ever felt this way with anyone before, except maybe hazy memories with my mother.

Part of me wants to fight it. This isn't how I imagined a reunion with Jennie Lou going. My pride rebels. It tells me, "Don't let her see you like this. Don't be weak." Then I hear Jennie Lou's voice, almost a whisper. And it's filled with her own tears.

"I'm sorry you went through that," she says. "That's awful. Everyone must have been terrified."

I nod. "We were."

Inwardly, I tell myself, *Don't think of her as a Christian. She's just an old friend.* My anxiety and frustration lessen. I get a handle on my feelings again. Then I ease back from her hug. She stays close, looking at me with tenderness and concern.

"Thanks," I tell her. "I didn't expect any of that, but thanks."

"I'm glad I could help," she replies, looking slightly embarrassed. She looks to her friend and back at me. "I'm sorry if that was out of bounds."

"It's . . . okay," I respond.

Lynn walks closer, providing her with silent support. Jennie Lou looks mildly frustrated about something for a second. Then she manages a smile.

"Come to our event here tonight, Sean," Jennie Lou offers softly. "It starts in a couple of hours. We're having a spaghetti dinner. The band is really great, too—and it's all free of charge."

I smile. "That's a sweet offer, Jennie Lou, but it's not really my thing anymore."

"What do you mean?" she asks, perplexed.

"I don't believe in your God anymore," I answer honestly and without hostility.

Lynn looks put off by my comment but says nothing. Jennie Lou studies me with her gaze. I expected her to be shocked, but she's not. She looks sad for me.

"May I ask how your grandparents are doing?" Jennie Lou asks out of nowhere.

"They're both dead now," I reply without hesitation.

"Oh! I'm . . . sorry for your loss."

I don't want her pity.

"I'm not," I say angrily. "The world is better without them."

She starts to gasp but stops herself. Quietly, she takes something out of her purse and hands it to me.

"Sean, whether you come tonight or not, please take this," she urges, looking worried for me. "It's my card. I want you to call me if you need to talk. I promise, I will never judge you. I'll just listen. Call me any time of day or night."

I look at the white business card with her name and contact info in dark blue lettering. It fills me with trepidation.

"I'm not sure, Jennie."

Her face softens, and she smiles reassuringly. I know that look; I remember it well. She's serious now, practically on a mission. And helping me is that mission. All things considered, I'm not sure how to feel about this.

"Will you at least take the card?" she asks. "I know you might not call. But if you decide to, you'll have it."

I nod and take the card, putting it in my wallet. I know it would be better to just hand it back to her and say, "No thanks." But I can't. If it were anyone else, especially Lynn, I could do that easily. But it's

Jennie Lou Harris. And even after three years, I still have feelings for her. This reeks!

My pride makes one last attempt to rescue me. *C'mon, you can do this, Sean. Take out the card, tear it in half, and drop it on the ground. Then walk away. It's no big deal. She rejected you, and you got over her. This is just bad memories trying to make a fool of you. Again. Don't let it. You're in control here, so prove it.*

No. There's a stronger voice within me, and it tells me not to listen to the first voice. *You will regret it for the rest of your life if you throw that card away.* I don't have to go to her event, but I have to keep the card. I'll need it someday.

So, I quiet both voices and keep the card where it is.

"Goodbye, Sean," Jennie Lou says, giving me one more quick hug.

Could you stay there for an hour, Jennie? That would be nice. Ah, well, it was a fun thought.

"Goodbye, Jennie."

"It was nice to meet you, Sean," Lynn says as she waves at me.

She and Jennie Lou head back to the white tent. And I start to walk home.

This has got to be the weirdest week of my life.

5

WHEN REASONING ISN'T ENOUGH

Why haven't I seriously decorated my apartment? Maybe a better question is why haven't I cared about it till now? When I moved in, I put a few nails in the wall to hang some framed concert posters. But even those were of techno bands I liked a few years ago. They don't reflect who I am now.

Would it have killed me to go out and get some new music posters and frames? I listen to Pure Indigo and Why Shark Why now, both European indie rock bands. Or I could have picked up or ordered posters or pictures of something else—gaming stuff, science fiction shows or movies. Anything at all. I guess I just didn't feel like trying. It still feels like another lie.

Give yourself a break. It's not like you were expecting visitors.

I shake off my introspective mood. Then I sigh. I spent five minutes with my former crush, and now I'm questioning my own identity? Great.

Jennie Lou has always had this effect on me. I've always cared what she thinks about me. But why should I do that now? It's been three years, and aside from her volunteer work, I don't know anything about her. Did she get her bachelor's degree? Did she . . . get married?

This kind of thinking isn't going to go anywhere, Sean.

If I really want answers to these questions, Jennie Lou will have to give them to me. And she is going to be at that event until it's over tonight.

I turn to look at my laptop lying on one end of the couch. Should I pass a few hours watching stuff on NetAddixion? Or I could play *Star Wars: Droid Wars* or *Knights of Kashyyyk*. For that matter, there's a gazillion internet dating sites.

I shake my head. Who am I kidding? I have to pretend I have a dog. I have no life.

As I lock the apartment door and wonder what in the world I'm up to, I remind myself that I never really had anything better to do in the first place. I'm heading back to the park.

. . .

IN THE PAST

The cool night air makes me glad I wore a jacket. I can hear music from a block away. It sounds like they're playing CDs. I can see a spotlight focused over the area where I know the park is. Hopes and Prayers has a budget, it seems.

There's a few other people walking in the same direction as me, looking curious or excited. One or two of them are holding flyers. I keep my hands in my pockets and continue my slow pace toward the event. The bright white lights near the tent also illuminate the nearby trees. The silhouetted timberline further back is a stark contrast to the twilight sky transitioning to night.

My nose detects the tantalizing scent of garlic. Either that's some zesty spaghetti, or Hopes and Prayers is serving garlic bread with dinner.

"—want to thank all of you for joining us tonight," I hear a man say over the public address system. It makes him sound tinny and adds a slight reverb to his tenor voice.

I recognize the voice, too. And when I get closer, I confirm it. It's Stephen Manor, a well-known evangelist. There's a large screen above the stage projecting the image of him standing on a stage they've erected next to the white tent. He's wearing a dark blue jacket over one of the organization's t-shirts. I guess it makes sense that he's associated with Hopes and Prayers in some way.

. . .

Seeing the evangelist triggers a long-buried memory—ten years ago, my grandparents dragged me to an event similar to this one in Phoenix. It was inside a big church, but the atmosphere was similar. People gathered to hear a different famous preacher who brought in singers and a music director, making it a big production. Grandma and Grandpa thought I'd be impressed. They certainly were. But it all felt fake to me, like seeing a model demonstrate makeup or clothes you know they'll never personally wear.

On the surface, it was very polished-looking. The choir sang beautifully in their glittering robes. The preacher waved his arms about and called on the people to repent and get right with Jesus before it's too late. Many of the people cried out their sorrow and regret. Dozens came forward at the end to rededicate their lives to the Lord. It seemed like a lot of good had been accomplished, but something felt off to me about the whole thing.

Six months later, that same pastor made national news when he was arrested for charges of tax evasion and grand larceny.

Ever since then, I haven't trusted pastors.

· · ·

IN THE PRESENT

"I grew up in rural Kansas," Manor continues. "I've seen my share of tornadoes. And I know Oklahoma has, too. Hopes and Prayers is committed to serving your needs. Tonight, we also want to offer you hope. You are already in our prayers."

Nice speech. But can you deliver on that?

He looks out over the crowd of about two hundred people. There's a grimness in his expression. It reminds me of the way Jennie Lou looked at me—sympathetically.

"Our volunteers have been working hard to provide you with good meals tonight," he continues. "And I've met with the band Psalms of Asaph. They're excited to perform some songs for you. Between all that, I'm going to share some passages from the Word of God that I hope will comfort and encourage you tonight."

Many in the crowd start clapping, while others look tired or preoccupied. I think some people showed up only for the free food.

"But now, we want to share our hospitality and the delicious food our volunteers have prepared for you," Manor said, gesturing toward the serving tables. "Please form a line, and we ask that you be patient. There's plenty for everyone."

He surprises me by leaving the stage and donning an apron. He's going to be serving food, too? Most of the preachers I've seen and known wouldn't do that. They'd consider it beneath their position.

Why am I analyzing things this way? Why am I even here? This was a mistake. Even if the food and music are good, I don't want to hear the preaching. I've closed that door, and I don't want to risk opening it again.

And then I see her again: Jennie Lou. She's serving food, too, along with her friend Lynn. There's a few other volunteers I don't know.

My belly gurgles in hunger. *Et tu, stomach?* This is getting ridiculous. I should walk right out of here and pick up a burger on the way home.

But just then, Jennie Lou sees me and waves happily. I'm unsure what to do. She motions for me to come get some food, and my legs start moving toward her on their own. My whole body is rebelling against me! Why couldn't I have had a snack or something before I left?

I go to the back of the line that's formed. There's about twenty people ahead of me, but we move fairly quickly. I approach the chain of white cloth-covered tables where they're serving the meal.

"Hello," a woman says into the stage microphone. "The live music will start in about twenty minutes. We hope you enjoy it. Thank you."

I'll give Hopes and Prayers credit for being well-organized. Garage Band Fest could learn a few things from them.

I've gotten my plate of food and a bottled water and take a seat at one of the tables.

"Excuse me," a Hispanic man about Keith's age says from the stage. "My name is Hector Espinosa, and I'm an evangelist who has been working with Hopes and Prayers for about five years. I'd like to take a moment to bless this food, so please close your eyes and stop your conversations."

My eyes stay open, and I keep eating my bread as he says the blessing. I know it's rude and kind of pointless, but there's an odd satisfaction in my resistance.

The spaghetti sauce smells good but is a little bland for my tastes. I add pepper to it, trying to enliven it some. But that just makes it taste like bland spaghetti sauce with pepper in it. And the pasta is overcooked. What did I expect? It's free. I should just be grateful I didn't have to cook tonight. And at least the garlic bread is delicious.

I don't notice Jennie Lou until she sits next to me. Her eyes look sunken from exhaustion, but somehow, she still displays a great mood.

"Sean, I'm so happy you made it!" she tells me. "Is the food okay?"

"It's okay," I say truthfully. "Good garlic bread."

"I know, right?"

She looks momentarily hesitant to continue, as though she's struggling with something.

"I wasn't a good friend to you in college, Sean. You were going through things, and I should have seen it."

"What are you talking about?" I wonder aloud.

She looks toward the serving area, then back to me, a little flustered.

"I only have a moment," she says. "I want to apologize for the way I treated you back then. I feel just awful about it. I want to discuss it, but now's not a good time."

She had me at "I want to apologize."

"I hope you'll stay and enjoy the rest of the evening," she adds. "I'm glad you made it!"

With that, she rushes back to the serving area. I feel warm inside, almost goofy. I blink a few times, dumbfounded at what had just happened.

. . .

I made it through the first three songs by Psalms of Asaph before they started grating on my nerves. They have a solid music section, but the two vocalists, a male and female, are pretty obnoxious. How many times can people say the word "hallelujah" instead of their song's lyrics? I don't think I'm the only one getting annoyed by that.

It gives me the excuse I need to leave.

Then Stephen Manor steps up to the microphone again.

"Isn't this band great?" Manor says. He smiles and makes eye contact with the group before turning back to the audience. Many clap and holler their praise. He waits for them to quiet down before continuing. "I really appreciate their faithfulness to the Lord in supporting this ministry. Hopes and Prayers will be in Oklahoma City as long as the people have need. In the coming weeks, we will be assisting with the rebuilding efforts, offering medical help, and counseling or praying with victims' families and survivors."

Good. That's what they should be doing—giving to the community and not taking.

"All right, that's enough from me," Manor adds. "Let's get back to praising the Lord. It's His love that makes this all possible. Give another round of applause to Psalms of Asaph!"

That's my cue to go, and I start walking away.

"Excuse me, sir," a male volunteer says. He seems a little younger than me. "Is everything okay?"

"Thanks for your concern," I reply with a smile. "Nothing's wrong. I just need to head home."

"Oh, okay. Would you like to take a bottled water or some food with you?"

I shake my head. "No, thank you. That's very kind, though."

I wave at him as I head toward the tree line.

Rational thought tells me that the Hopes and Prayers volunteers are just well-intentioned people trying to help others. And that part is fine to me. But their worship! It's superstitious nonsense grounded in trying to cope with the random nature of the universe. The Bible is a book written by men to create a moral code for people to live by. But in the end, everyone dies. There is no afterlife. There is no God. Life and death and everything that happens in between are all part of a biological cycle. If there is a destiny of some kind, we make our own.

I walk in silence, even in my thoughts, for several minutes.

If everything I just thought is true, why does it make me feel so sad now? These concepts have been my foundation for a few years now. They brought me solace when I thought I'd lost everything. But are they not enough anymore? If there is no God but there's also no solace in pure reasoning, does that only leave emotion? Isn't there supposed to be a proper balance between intellect and emotion? If nothing lasts, what is the point of making anything? Why not just jump right to the end and get it over with?

No! A sensation from deep within me refuses to accept that kind of hopeless thinking.

I'm only twenty-four; I've barely lived at all. There's a lot I still want to do, even if I'm not sure what it is yet.

And I've got something else to focus on. I've decided to call Jennie Lou. That's enough to keep me going. I make my way home and find my bed. I'm too exhausted to play with my invisible dog. I just collapse and embrace sleep.

. . .

I wake up groggily sometime later. What do I smell? Must be the garlic. I hear the deep hum of the air conditioner and wonder why I'm still in my clothes. I guess I was too tired to change.

Wait! What time is it? Did I sleep through the night? It's still dark in my room and outside, so I guess not. I try to find my phone and see it facing downward on the floor. I grab it, and the motion lights up the screen, which I pull close to my face. It's 11:42 p.m. That's not too bad. I sit on the side of my bed and gather my thoughts. My throat is burning. I must have snored pretty hard. I push myself up from the bed and stagger forward to grab a bottled water from the refrigerator. The water goes down, refreshing like an icy spring. It soothes my tender esophagus. I consider making some coffee, but the water is actually waking me up.

Feeling a little better, I turn on a lamp and plant myself on the couch. I lean forward, grab the folded business card from my pocket, and type the numbers into my phone. It starts ringing. One time, two times, then three. Did I wait too long? Is she already asleep?

"Hello?" Jennie Lou answers. Her voice sounds tired.

"This is Sean," I make myself say. "Sean Winter. Did I wake you? I'm—"

"Sean! I'm so glad you called," she replies, perking up. "Thank you."

"I would have called sooner, but I fell asleep when I got home."

"That's okay," she assures me. "I only got back about fifteen minutes ago myself. We had a lot of cleanup to do."

First one there, last one to leave. That's the Jennie Lou I remember.

"You wanted to tell me something earlier but didn't have time," I recall. "What was it?"

"Right," she says. "I . . . made some serious mistakes during our time in Campus Revival. It took me a long time to admit it to myself, but I was very unfair to you."

I didn't expect her to say something like that. I actually thought, under the circumstances, she was right to do what she did. I never questioned it.

"Why do you think that?" I wonder aloud.

She pauses several seconds. Did the call disconnect? Suddenly, I hear her clear her throat.

"On that day, I was really angry at Derek Simmons for what he did," Jennie Lou continues. "But I took that out on you. I judged you, and I shouldn't have. You opened up to me . . . and I turned you away."

"Look, Jennie Lou, you had every right to be angry that day," I reply.

She sighs. "I may have had the right, but that didn't help anyone. It only caused more problems."

"More problems?" I repeated. This is news to me.

"I couldn't run the group after I, um, expelled you. I didn't trust the members anymore," she says. "Maybe I didn't trust my leadership anymore. I don't know. I had my own crisis of faith."

I didn't even know that was *possible* for her. I have no idea how to respond. I hear her sigh heavily and then take a deep breath before continuing.

"That day, I accused you of not sharing my Christian values," she begins in a soft and regretful voice. "But I was the one not living those values. I was blind to what I had become—a self-righteous hypocrite."

I don't have the heart to tell her what I'm feeling—that's usually the way it works with Christians.

"You were the brave one, Sean. You challenged Derek, even knowing you might not be up to it. You defended the club."

"I was defending you more than the club, Jennie Lou."

"I know," she replies, pausing briefly. "But that took courage, and I should have recognized that. Then you showed even more bravery. You told me your feelings. And I rejected you outright."

I appreciate what she's saying, but I don't understand where she's going with this. Is this just an extended apology? A way of becoming friends again?

"Jennie, that's all in the past. What's—?"

"I loved you, too!" she blurts.

What?

There's complete silence for thirty seconds. Her breathing is a little ragged. She must be really tired. Focus, Sean. She just told you she loved you.

"You did?" I ask, shaking myself out of my confusion.

"I couldn't tell you. I was carrying a lot of people's expectations," she admits. "My parents, my grandparents, my little sister, the group, my friends, and my church. It's like I told you back then; my plan was to get my degree, maybe a master's, and start a career."

And then marriage, my dream had reminded me. When she mentioned marriage plans, had she meant . . . with me?

"But all of that was for my own security," Jennie Lou continues. "It was to make myself look like a 'good Christian girl' to the people I looked up to. It was what I thought I was supposed to do. But that's why it failed."

"Why? I've seen people make plans like that my whole life," I add. "And isn't failing part of the journey sometimes?"

She laughs, and her cheer lifts my mood.

"You're right, Sean," she replies. "People put those kinds of weights on themselves every day. But it's wrong. I found that out the hard way."

"How? What do you mean?"

"I was so concerned about what others thought of me that I lost sight of what Jesus might think of me. Was I doing His will? Was I being like Him toward others?" she laments. "And I wasn't. I was worried about my offended pride. So, I hurt you . . . and also myself."

I still don't really understand, but I keep listening. I shift positions on the couch.

"I wasn't honest with myself about you," she answers. "I truly enjoyed the time we spent together, both in the group and outside the group. Deep down, I loved you. I just didn't feel comfortable sharing that. I was worried people might misunderstand. Or I might lead you, on and things might go too far. I kept all of that inside, and it was tearing at me."

This is mind-blowing. We felt the same about one another! And we both kept it inside to protect each other.

"And even worse, you—"

She stops herself, but I know what she was going to say.

"I became an atheist. Look, Jennie Lou, you didn't cause that. It was a long time coming."

Her silence tells me she's not convinced.

"Can I ask what happened?" she asks a few seconds later. "Did it have anything to do with your grandparents?"

I grit my teeth at that. "It had *everything* to do with them."

Another brief silence. I can't tell her everything now. It would take all night, and neither of us is ready for that.

"We'll . . . have to talk about them another time," I tell her. "It's not a quick discussion topic."

"I see," she responds. "But you will tell me sometime?"

"Yes."

Why did I just do that? Now, I'm committed to her again.

"Thank you," she adds. "Is there anything you would like to talk about tonight?"

"Yes," I reply. "Would you tell me about your life the last few years?"

I hear a small gasp on the other end of the phone.

"Oh! Well, that's a little complicated, too," she replies. "Er, I did get my bachelor's degree in social work . . . but I decided against pursuing a master's."

"Really? You were so set on it," I remember.

"A little *too* set on it," she acknowledges. "I needed to step back and reassess . . . no . . . no, that's not it. I'm sorry. That . . . I . . . "

She's quiet again. All I can hear is her timid breathing. Why is she so tense?

"I had a nervous breakdown," she finally admits.

"What?"

"It's true."

"What . . . what happened?"

She exhales slowly. "I put myself under too much stress," she explains. "I was all balled up inside with anxiety. It got worse and worse over a period of months. Then I couldn't take it anymore. I had a complete meltdown in front of my family."

That's another way she was like me! Jennie Lou Harris suffered from anxiety and stress. Wow, I would never have known.

"So, you got help?" I ask. "You're okay now?"

"It took . . . a while, but yes, I'm better than I was. I have to take things day to day. I'm working really hard at being open and honest with myself and others."

"You weren't being honest before?"

"No," she replies. "That was such a hard thing to own up to. But with counseling and the Lord's help, I was able to see myself and start to change. Working with Hopes and Prayers assisted with that. I like being a part of an organization that helps others, but I don't have to be the one in charge. I can just do my part."

She sounds so much more vulnerable than I remember.

"I'm glad you found something you enjoy." That sounds weird coming from me.

"Thanks. What about you, Sean? What have you been doing?"

"I got my bachelor's, too. I just started working full-time in a customer service position. I also got my own apartment here in town."

"That's great," she says. But there's something off in her tone. Does she not mean what she's saying? I can't tell. "That's great, really."

"What's wrong, Jennie?"

Another hesitation.

"Will you call me tomorrow after work? Or can I call you at this number? Oh! That sounded weird, didn't it? I'm so tired. I'm sorry."

"It's fine, really. You can call anytime."

"I wish I'd been honest with you then," she says softly, repeating herself. "And I don't know why it's so hard to share this now."

I understand that all too well.

"Relax, Jennie Lou. It's me, Sean. You can tell me anything, and I won't think less of you."

"Even today at the park, you were brave. I'm not brave," she tells me.

"It's not like I planned that. It just happened."

"But you did it. And I need to do the same. I need to do the same."

What could be so hard for her to tell me? It's only been three years.

She takes a quick breath. "I still love you."

Jaw, meet floor.

"I know it's been a long time, and it's selfish of me to admit this now," she adds, speaking quickly in her natural, gruff tones. "I rejected and hurt you. I was an awful person. Maybe I still am. So, you can hang up on me or tell me off . . . but I needed to tell you this."

My mouth is still hanging open. I shake myself out of my mental haze.

"I'm . . . uh . . . "

"It's okay. You don't have to say anything," she interrupts. "Just . . . um . . . thanks for listening."

This feels like the beginning of something pivotal. And I want to keep it going.

"Call me tomorrow after six p.m.," I tell her before confirming my mobile number.

6

THE BEST OF INTENTIONS

"Hey! Sean, isn't it?"

Just outside the breakroom, I startle and turn to see a tall, bald man in a red, short-sleeved dress shirt and khakis standing right behind me. My co-worker is trim but athletic. He has wire-frame glasses hanging from a thin strap around his neck.

"Um, yeah. That's me," I say, trying to recover some composure.

"I'm Ben Deconde. Jessica said we had some new team members, so I wanted to get to know ya!"

"Oh, so you already met the other newbies?"

He grins widely. "Yeah, I met Connie and Jamie yesterday when I got back."

"Back?"

"I went to Cali for a week to visit family," he says brightly. "It was nice to get a change of scenery, too."

"Sounds nice," I reply, perhaps a little too impatiently. I only have a few more minutes on my break.

Ben extends a hand for me. "Yeah, thanks. It was."

I shake firmly and let go. I don't see any reason to be rude to a teammate.

"I'm having a little after-work party at my place tonight," Ben tells me. "I wanted to invite you."

"Really?"

"I've invited most of the team, but I suspect it will only be five or ten of us," he answers. "Jim, Kalea, maybe Connie and a few others. I'll grill some burgers; we'll have some drinks and just socialize. It'll be fun."

"I don't drink, but the rest sounds good."

The idea of getting to know my coworkers is appealing. Actually, having *anything* to do after work sounds good.

"So, are you in?" Ben asks enthusiastically.

"I'm in," I reply with a grin. "What time are you getting things started?"

He looks off a moment, as though considering something.

"I'll need to get a few things from the store on the way home. How does seven o'clock sound?"

That's perfect. I give Ben my phone number.

"Text me your address," I suggest. "I'll get a ride there."

"Sure thing, man. This is gonna rock!"

. . .

I tried calling Jennie Lou three times. But I couldn't reach her before the PayMeRide app indicated my driver was only two blocks away. I have to leave a voicemail for her instead.

"Hi, Jennie, it's Sean. Sorry I missed you. I'm going out for a while, but I'll call you when I get back. Bye!"

That'll have to do. I hurry out the door, excited at having somewhere to go.

It takes only fifteen minutes to get to Ben's place. It's a big, one-story, red brick house with a large backyard surrounded by a chain link fence. I can smell the burgers grilling as soon as I exit the car. I hear joking and laughter, too. I walk up the driveway and to the left of the garage. The fence gate is open, so I enter.

"Hey! Sean!" Ben shouts, even though he's only ten feet away. I see the beer bottle in his hand and figure he's had a couple already. There are three other people with him. They're all wearing t-shirts or blouses and shorts.

The one closest to me is a short, diamond-shaped young woman with frilly, long, brown hair. She's either Asian or mixed race. Our eyes meet, and she gives me a sweet smile. She's remarkably beautiful! It takes effort, but a second later, I tear my eyes from her visage.

Connie Evans is next to her, a slender woman in her mid-fifties with short, dark red hair. Connie started work the same day as me. She's no-nonsense in the office but seems more mellow here. She's drinking from a beer bottle but tilts her head up at me and gives me a thumbs up.

Opposite Connie is a stocky African American man I haven't met before. He looks maybe Keith's age and pleasant.

"This is our co-worker, Sean Winter!" Ben tells them. "Man, I'm so glad you could make it! Of course, you already know Connie."

"Hey, Sean," Connie finally says with a smile.

"Hey," I say back to her.

Ben effortlessly swings me around to face the woman who entranced me. "Let me introduce Kalea Nadeaux."

She smiles and lifts her beer bottle in my direction. "Nice to meet you."

Something clicks, and I speak without thinking again. "You're Hawaiian?"

Her eyes warm at my observation, and she smiles. "Half-Hawaiian. My dad is French."

"Very cool," I add.

"I think so." She smirks.

The African American man walks up to me, and we shake hands. He has an intimidating grip. I try not to squint, but it kind of hurts.

"I'm Jim Geribo, but you can call me Jimbo for short," he says. "I do the network support for the office. Ben and I go way back."

"Thanks, Jimbo. Nice to meet you."

"Same, Sean."

Connie gives me a curious look. "Did you come straight from the office, Sean? You're still wearing your work clothes."

Great. I was so focused on calling Jennie Lou that I forgot to change clothes.

"Something like that," I say nervously. "I had an errand to do, and it ended up taking too much time. So, I just headed on over."

"That's okay, man," Ben interjects, pointing to his right. "But you'll need something less formal if you want to take a dip in the pool."

I gaze where he's pointing and see a rectangular twelve-by-twenty-foot swimming pool. It looks clean and very inviting. But of course, I'm not at all dressed for it.

"You didn't mention a pool earlier," I deadpan, slightly annoyed.

"I didn't?" he asks, genuinely surprised. "I'm sorry. Don't worry, though. You and I are close in size, and I've got some extra trunks you can borrow."

Nope. That's not happening.

"I, uh, I appreciate that, Ben, but I can't ask that of you."

"It's no big deal, man," he replies. "Anyway, I hope you're hungry. The burgers are almost done!"

Upon his mention, the smell of grilled food captures my focus. On the table next to the two grills, there's a variety of potato chip bags, sodas, and plenty of beer.

When Ben places the first plateful of burger patties on the table, I get to work making a cheeseburger loaded with vegetables. I slather the top bun with mustard and ketchup and scrunch it together. Then I grab a bag of plain chips and a cola and sit down at one of the white plastic chairs by the pool. I'm caught off-guard when Kalea joins me.

"Relax, Sean. Last time Ben had a get-together like this, I was the fresh face. So, I know what it's like," she says, leaning over slightly. Honestly, I wouldn't mind if she got a little closer. "Ben, Jimbo, and their friends had to help me loosen up. I'm just paying it forward."

"Thanks?" I say awkwardly. "I'm not great at being social."

She sits in the chair next to mine while I take a drink from my soda.

She smiles. "You made the effort to be here. We're coworkers, and this is a friendly get-together. It's all good."

My cheeks are warm. I smile, knowing I'm blushing. But I'm not sure what to say next.

Kalea scoots her chair closer and gently puts a hand on my shoulder. "Loosen up. Why don't you tell us a little about yourself?"

I blink a couple of times.

Can we not? The party doesn't need to be brought down like that.

"There's not a lot to tell," I say instead. "I went to OU, graduated with my bachelor's, and came to work at Prosaic."

"Are you from around here?" Jimbo asks from the pool.

"No, I'm from Phoenix. But I moved here as soon as I could."

"You like it here then?" Connie wonders. She's in the pool, too.

"Oh, yes! I love it here."

The momentum fizzles as I let that answer hang in the air without adding anything to it. Don't everyone speak up at once.

I feel a woman's fingers touch the top of my shoulders from behind me. They tighten briefly into a grip, then release.

"Whoa, Sean! You are so tense," Kalea says. "You *are* among friends, okay?"

I sigh. "Believe me, I know. It's just . . . it can be tough for me to relax sometimes."

"I can tell," she agrees.

Ben shoves a beer bottle in front of my face. He's standing over me with his near-permanent smile.

"It helps, Sean. We've all been there," he says.

"I told you, I don't drink."

"Are you allergic to alcohol or something?"

"No. Personal preference."

He nods. "I can respect that. But one beer will just take some of the edge off, you know?"

I do. I used to sneak some of Grandpa's beer every once in a while. But that was years ago. I've avoided it since I started college.

But do I want to have a war with my principles at a social event? I mean, I could politely decline and then leave. But then, why did I come here tonight? I already know the answer: to meet these people and get to know them better.

Ten seconds feels like ten minutes, but I make up my mind. I hold out my hand to receive the drink from Ben.

"There you go, man!" he cheers.

I gulp some down. It's cold and watered down but not horrible. Over the next few minutes, I can feel my tension easing. I resume enjoying my burger and chips.

Soon, I finish my first beer, and Kalea opens another before she gives it to me.

"Do you like sci-fi stuff?" she asks while leaning against one of her chair's armrests.

"Yeah," I answer. "*Star Wars* or *Star Trek?*"

She looks up at me slyly. "*Total Trek* girl here." She appraises me a moment. "You're a *Star Wars* guy, aren't you?"

I nod. "But most sci-fi interests me."

"I prefer retro sci-fi the most," she says before taking a swig from her own beer. "The stuff from the seventies and eighties was the best!"

"What about the sixties?" I ask out of curiosity.

She suddenly raises her bottle high. "Original Series *Trek*! The first, the best!"

I laugh, but not to make fun. Her enthusiasm is as disarming as it is amusing. She starts cracking up, too.

"F-favorite Star Wars movie?" she asks a minute later, still giggling some.

"Too easy," I say confidently. "*Empire Strikes Back.*"

"The prequels?"

I shrug.

After finishing my second beer, I lose all fear of consuming more. What I care about is spending time with Kalea. I get lost a few times in her lovely nut-brown eyes, rounded nose, and cute smile. The sun sets, and I can't keep track of time anymore.

"Who wants margaritas?" Jimbo booms. "Regular or strawberry!"

Kalea stands up too quickly and almost loses her balance. Somehow, I get to her in time to steady her.

"Me!" she shouts happily, even as she can't stand still.

"Are you sure? You're already kinda—"

She puts one arm around me and leans her head close to mine. She stares into my eyes and smiles.

"Yes. I'm sure," she tells me. "Wanna join me? Jimbo makes killer 'ritas, 'specially the strawwwberry ones."

"Okay?"

The night becomes a haze of silly jokes, more food, margaritas, and increasingly loud music. Ben's playlist is booming through waterproof Bluetooth speakers.

The others are either eating and drinking or swimming and splashing around in the pool, but Kalea stays with me the whole time.

"Didn't you want to get in the pool, too?" I ask her.

"I did," she admits. "I'm wearing my swimsuit under my clothes, but I'm having more fun being with you."

"Being with me is 'fun'? That's new."

She just smiles in a goofy way and giggles, swaying back and forth a little bit. That's when I finally realize how very drunk we both are.

"I feel like I can be myself around you," Kalea says, grinning and blushing. "And I feel like we're the same . . . in a lot of ways."

"Really? Like what?"

She puts her hand to my cheek and looks in my eyes.

"You have lonely eyes," she says, her voice almost purring. "Eyes that say you don't want to be alone."

Before I can react, she steals a kiss.

"I can relate to that," she adds softly.

I start to say something, but she puts her fingertip to her lips and shushes me. As she walks over to get more refreshments, I begin to lose consciousness.

Sometime later, I try to open my eyes; but everything is blurry, and I can't focus.

"He's too wasted, Kalea," I hear Ben say. "I'm gonna take him home."

"You're wasted, too, Ben!" she snaps back in her slurring/purring voice. "We all are!"

"I'll be fine ta take him," Ben insists.

"Yeah? What's two plus two?" she retorts.

"Nine! See? I'm not drunk!"

I hear her gasp. "Dude, you will *kill* someone if you try ta drive! It's PayMeRides or cabs tonight! And that'z that!"

"Okay, okay! You win!"

I'm glad she talked him out of that. I don't want to end up a drunk driving statistic.

Then everything fades to black again.

. . .

Whoa! Where . . . where am I? This *isn't* my apartment! I don't know this place!

So dizzy! C'mon, room, stop moving! This isn't fair.

Mmmm. Cool breeze. I like that smell. Is that cinnamon? Focus on that. Good. *Shake it off, Sean. Figure out where you are . . . what's goin' on.*

I'm lying on carpet. Very soft carpet. And this place is *really* blue! The walls are white, but when I turn my head, I see the carpet is deep blue. There's a dark blue couch over there. Even the room's light has a blue tint to it. What's with all the blue?

Then I put my hands on my chest. Where's my shirt?

I still have on pants and shoes. Really, where'd my shirt go? What happened?

It's hard to sit up. I'm still drunk, and my balance is lousy. I have to close my eyes until the room stops moving again, which takes a few seconds. When I look again, I think this place is—what do they call these? Townhomes? Yeah, I think so. There's a big HDTV on the wall to my right with a soundbar under it. Nice.

Wait! I have no shirt on! Did I take it off? Did someone else take it off? This is bad. Very bad.

I make myself get to my feet. I have to grip the wall to keep from falling back down. Note to self: *all* of this is why you don't drink! I use my hands to follow the wall past the couch. I try not to bump into the little table next to the couch. It has a blue-purple lamp on it. More blue, great. This must be the living room. Lots of posters on the wall, but I can't see them clearly from here. There's a kitchen area in front of me. The breeze is coming from an open window over the sink. The cool air is helping clear my head some.

I push off from the wall to haphazardly cross over to the stairway. The cinnamon smell is coming from upstairs.

"Hello?" I call out, looking up the stairway from the bottom.

"Oh! You're up!" Kalea's voice replies from just out of view. "Hold on, I'll be right there!"

I must be at her place. Wait! Why *am* I at her place . . . with no shirt on?

She steps into view, a curvy silhouette at the top of the stairs. As she walks down toward me, I see she's wearing a navy blue nightshirt.

She's happy and relaxed, smiling as she looks at me. I'm doing my best to remain calm.

When she reaches me, she pulls me into a hug and releases me. Then she tilts her head, confused, and breaks into laughter.

"You should see your expression, Sean!" She sounds less inebriated than before. "A deer's got nothing on you right now."

"Kalea, what's . . . what happened?" I ask. At least I sound more sober than I feel.

"Oh . . . well, that's kinda funny, too," she answers sweetly, standing a little too close to me. "We all kinda drank too much at Ben's party."

I nod. "You told him not to drive me home," I recall.

"That's right!" she says happily, tapping her index finger against my chest. Her eyes are only half-open, and I smell strawberry on her breath from the margaritas. Yep, she's still hammered. "So, my *intention* was to get a cab and take you home first."

"Your . . . intention?"

Still facing me, she crosses her arms and looks down, embarrassed.

"Right. Y'see, the cab arrived before I got your address . . . because you were too wasted to tell me," she begins slowly. "And I couldn't unlock your phone. Plus, I was a little drunk myself." Then she brightens up. "But I remembered my own address! So, I gave that to the cab driver!"

Go with what you know, huh? Okay.

I nod. "That explains how I got here. So, what happened to my shirt?"

"That was my bad. I spilled some of my drink on your shirt while I was getting you into the cab," she admits with a giggle. She tries to walk up a couple of stairs but loses her balance and has to grab the railing. Without thinking, I rush up to help steady her. "Thanks! Anyway, don't worry; it's washing upstairs right now."

"Oh."

I'm surprised she's able to stand, much less do laundry and hold a conversation. I help her down the stairs. When we reach the floor, she turns to face me and looks into my eyes with fondness and a smile. She's a tempting sight, but my walls are up now. I've got to figure this out. Too much doesn't make sense.

"It's all right, Sean. You're safe with me."

I don't know how to respond to that. What does it mean?

"I've got a pretty good idea who you are now," she tells me in her purring voice. "Your secret is safe with me. I won't tell anyone."

I stiffen at that. *Now* I feel like a deer in headlights.

"I don't understand," I say cautiously.

"I've seen what they did to you," she tells me, making eye contact again. "And you talk in your sleep."

This is worse than bad. This is a nightmare! A chill runs through me, and I feel a lot more sober all of a sudden. I want to get out of here and run home. But that wouldn't do any good. I have to deal with this, here and now.

"What do you want?" I ask her coldly.

I can hear her sigh in disappointment. "I don't want to *blackmail* you, Sean. I want you to trust me."

I can't do that. I don't know her. I just met her. And I don't trust anyone! Every time I have, I've gotten hurt.

Wait a second! I'm not wearing a shirt, and she has only a nightshirt on. Do I want to ask her about that? Do I really want to know?

I don't think I do.

The moment lingers. I feel drawn to her eyes. Her full lips are luscious. We did have a good kiss. I feel like I kissed her again. Did I?

Focus on right now, Sean!

She breaks eye contact and looks at something behind me.

"Um, are you hungry?" she asks, breaking the silence. "I don't have a lot of food, but there's some leftover pizza in the fridge. And I can get you some ice water."

"I'd like that," I answer, giving myself some space.

She nods and goes to get that for me from the kitchen. I wish I didn't feel so conflicted. Did I lead her on? Did I say or do something stupid earlier and can't remember it? She's a beautiful woman; I can't deny that. I did enjoy her kiss. And she kept me safe when I passed out. But something feels wrong about this.

We sit down on her couch.

"Nice place," I tell her.

"Thanks," she replies.

"A lot of blue."

She laughs. "Yeah. It's my favorite color."

Awkward silence.

"How long did you say it'd take for the shirt to be ready?" I ask.

She thinks about it. "Maybe, I dunno, ten minutes to wash. Another ten or fifteen to dry?"

I nod. "Okay."

For all our small talk, we're avoiding the biggest question: what are we going to do now? She doesn't have to tell me she likes me; it's obvious in her gaze and how close she sits to me.

I turn my head to break eye contact again. I know I need time to think, away from these circumstances. I need to be at home in my own bed. Even without knowing all the details, I can tell I've made a colossal mistake. And I don't know what to do.

"I can see you torturing yourself over there, Sean," Kalea says. She stands up and goes into the kitchen to rinse off her plate in the sink. "You really don't have to."

How can she say that? A moment later, she returns and sits down next to me again, taking my hands in hers. It makes me uncomfortable, so I gently pull them free. She closes her eyes and lightly chuckles.

"I told you, you talk in your sleep," she continues. Then she opens her eyes again and looks at me. "I know there's a girl you love. Her name is Jennie Lou."

Thank you for reminding me of my other blazing failure today. How am I going to explain this fiasco to Jennie Lou?

I'm a mess inside, and Kalea looks amazingly content. What am I missing here?

"We can just be friends, if you like," she assures me. "At least, I hope we can still be friends. Like you, I didn't expect for us to connect like we did at the party. And I wasn't planning for you to end up here."

I nod slowly. "Friends."

At this point, she stands up and goes to check on the laundry upstairs. She grips the railing tightly and maintains her balance this time.

Twenty minutes later, I'm fastening the buttons on my cleaned shirt, looking at myself in the downstairs bathroom mirror. When I finish, I try to make some sense of my ruffled hair.

I look at my phone and see that it's 1:30 in the morning. And I have four voicemails from Jennie Lou. I'm not ready to listen to them yet. It's not like I can call her back right now anyway.

When I head back into the living room, Kalea is watching television. She turns her head and looks at me. She doesn't seem as content as before.

"Thanks for taking care of me," I tell her.

"Anytime."

We sit in silence in her living room until my driver arrives. She stands by the door and watches as I get in the vehicle and it pulls away.

7

DEGREES OF FRIENDSHIP

I drag myself into my apartment feeling miserable, with each step dragging more than the last. The door booms shut, and the clicking of the lock slaps my ears. Now my head is starting to pound. I supposed I shouldn't be surprised I'm getting a hangover.

This is why you don't drink, Sean.

I gently tap my phone, and even its soft light hurts my eyes. I have to bear with it, so I can make sure I set my alarm and thirty minutes early, too. That might let me compensate for how terrible I'm gonna feel with the three hours' sleep I *hope* to get.

The phone opens directly into my photo app. And there are new pictures in it. Lots of new pictures. Of Kalea. She may not have been able to unlock the phone, but she certainly figured out how to access the camera.

I blink in amazement and disbelief. There are quite a few vanity selfies. Some are pretty cute. Others make it clear she was trying to impress me. She also made two videos. The first one is me laying on the floor snoring softly with her giggling behind the camera. The second video only lasts about thirty seconds. It's a close up of her face as she blows kisses toward the camera.

"These kissuz are jussst for you, Sean! Only you!" she purrs. She grins, her eyes barely open, and falls to her knees. She's not hurt; it just surprises her. She laughs at herself, then me, and blows another kiss. "They're just for you! Only you, Sean!"

Then the video abruptly stops.

I can't even think about this anymore. I set my alarm and force my wobbly legs forward toward the bedroom. I collapse onto the bed and let the phone drop to the floor.

. . .

When my alarm goes off, I feel like I only closed my eyes a second earlier. My head feels like it's in a vise, but at least there's no more pounding. I lean my head toward the edge of the bed and spot my phone on the floor. The motion alone makes me feel like I'm underwater. I must still be a little bit drunk. With effort, I grab the mobile device and verify the time; it's really 5:30.

I have got to get ready for work, no matter how I feel. I plant my feet on the floor and will my legs to stand up. I manage to stagger into the bathroom, turn on the light, and start the shower. I make it super-hot to combat my muscle fatigue and restore a basic sense of coherence and consciousness. The near-scalding embrace of the water has the intended effect. A few minutes later, I find my way out of the steam-drenched bathroom and back to the bedroom to get dressed.

A quick glance at the phone assures me I'm still running ahead of schedule. I start a pot of strong coffee, knowing I'll need at least two cups to graduate from coherence to near-human status. Breakfast will have to be cinnamon toast and a bottled water to drink while I'm waiting for the coffee to brew.

A couple of minutes later, I plop down on the couch with a plate of toast and my water and look toward the wall.

"Sparky, you are not gonna believe what happened to me last night," I tell my imaginary canine. "I met this really beautiful girl at a party; we got really drunk; and I ended up at her place."

It sounds even weirder when I say it out loud. It makes it real. As real as that kiss. Plus, the selfies and videos.

I get a sudden sinking feeling as I recall something important— Jennie Lou's voicemails from last night.

"Hi, Sean! It's Jennie Lou. I'm so sorry I missed your calls," her voicemail begins. "We had a mandatory Hopes and Prayers meeting after I left work. There are so many people in need after the tornado; the organization is bringing in volunteers from other cities and states to help. Our group will be training them, so we had a lot to go over and pray about. I'll try back in a while. Bye!"

There's another voicemail from an hour later. "Hi, it's Jennie again. I guess you're still out. I'll try later."

The last one came ninety minutes after that. "Hey, Sean . . . um, it's getting kinda late. Are you all right? Would you mind giving me a call when you get in? It can be whenever . . . a quick call just to say you're okay. Thanks."

I hate that I made her so worried. It's too early to call now, but I can try on my break.

Another notification on my screen. Who sent me ten text messages since last night? Of course. Kalea sent the texts. All between two and 2:30 in the morning.

Hey Kalea here!

Put me in ur contacts k?

I hope u dont mind. Ben gave me ur #

Lemme know when u get home

R U OK?

Hope ur ok

G'nite

Dream of me – lol

C U 2moro

Nite-nite

I really want to dismiss it as a drunken text string. I guess it is. But I don't understand why she did it.

Sean, face facts: You hardly know anything about her. She's friends with Ben and Jimbo, who you know even less about.

"I'll grill some burgers; we'll have some drinks and just socialize. It'll be fun."

Thanks, Ben. Thanks a whole lot. I think last night proved to everyone that fun and I don't get along. I manage to mess it up, just about every time.

I look through Kalea's pictures again. Of those, I only retain two of her selfies. But I still have both of her videos. I'm not sure what to do with them. I should delete them, but I can't bring myself to. Not yet.

Do they mean something to me?

My phone rings. At six in the morning? It's Jennie Lou, so I answer.

"Hello, Jennie," I say cautiously. I wish I felt more sober, but at least, my headache has gone down some. The coffee is waking me up.

"Sean, are you all right?"

"More or less. I stayed out later than I meant to. I didn't get much sleep."

"Oh," she says.

I can't find words that work. Do I admit I got drunk? What do I say?

"H-how was the meeting?" I ask.

"Good. We made solid plans," she replied. "And the leaders answered a lot of our questions. We're ready."

"Good."

Did I really just say "good?" I sound like a moron. And an awkward silence builds.

"Sean, are you sure you're okay?"

"I'll . . . talk to you soon, Jennie. Have a great day."

"You, too."

After that, I make sure to drink the rest of my bottled water. I stand up too quickly and feel dizzy. I steady myself against the couch armrest. I am such a mess right now.

Time for that second cup of coffee.

. . .

I arrive at work about twenty minutes early and look for Kalea. Even before eight o'clock, this place is abuzz with activity. When I find her, she's already working at her desk. She catches a side-glance of me, smiles, and waves before refocusing on the call. She looks as exhausted as I do but appears positive. I'm still trying to get past my tired grumpiness. I hope we can talk later.

When I turn around, I'm face-to-face with Smiling Ben. How did I not hear him walk up? And how does he stay so chipper?

"Sean! Hey, I'm so glad you got home okay, man."

"Yeah, it's all good," I mutter. Not wanting to come across angry, I force a semi-smile and speak up. "Thanks."

"Did you enjoy yourself at the party?"

"What I remember of it, yeah."

He slaps me on the back and laughs. "Good deal, man. Good deal," he says. "See you later."

I'm not so sure about that.

"Oh, hey, I forgot to ask," he adds.

"Hm? What's that, Ben?"

"How'd things go with Kalea?"

"What do you mean?"

Maybe he'll shed some light on this situation. I hope. He walks back over to me.

"Well, you two seemed to really dig each other," he says with a more confidential tone. "And she was super protective of you, even after you tripped and spilled your drink all over her."

"I spilled my drink on *her?*" I say, startled. "She said she spilled hers on me."

"That's just Kalea," he tells me, grinning. "Big-hearted and very protective."

That matches what I've seen.

"She does seem to be all that," I reply. "But why would she be interested in me?"

"She relates to you," he responds. "When you loosened up, you told us you had kind of a rough childhood with your grandparents. Kalea lost both her parents and was brought up by her aunt and uncle."

Maybe that's what she meant when she told me, "I have a pretty good idea who you are now."

I see Keith enter the call center, and I feel relieved. He seems pretty alert and ready for his shift. I could use some of that positivity I see in his confident stride toward his desk. I'd like to talk with him. He's my only real friend right now.

. . .

"Sean!"

"Hi, Kalea."

I guess now's as good a time as any. I just logged out of my computer for the day and locked my desk. I stand up and turn to face her with a tired but sincere smile.

She has dark circles under her eyes but a radiant expression.

"Can I see you for a minute?" she asks.

"Sure. In the breakroom?"

She fidgets at that. "I think it should be more private. I don't want people to talk."

That makes sense. "We could go for a walk."

Her eyes soften in response, and she nods. "Yes. Great idea. Let's go for a walk."

After we exit the building together, I decide to head away from the park. Instead, we go about two blocks east of Prosaic and sit together on a public bench. People are strolling by, but it's no one we know.

She turns her head to face me, looking more serious. "I guess you saw your phone by now, huh?" she says.

"Um, yeah."

"Sorry if that made you uncomfortable."

I sigh. "It did."

"I keep my feelings bottled up most of the time," she admits. "So, they kind of come out when I get drunk."

"I can relate to the first part."

"I know you do," she tells me, looking into my eyes. "I do want to be a good friend to you, Sean. But I'll be honest, I don't know if I can *just* be friends with you."

She takes my hand in hers and laces her fingers with mine. I look down at our clasped hands and then at her. Her hand feels warm and tender like her gaze.

"Can you explain why you . . . feel so strongly about me? We've only known each other a day."

"I told you last night. I feel like I know you already," she explains. "I learned so much about you. I feel bad that I haven't shared as much with you in return."

"You can tell me now, if you want."

She considers that for a moment.

"All right. I'm an orphan," she says. "I was raised by relatives, like you."

"I'm sorry for your loss, Kalea."

"You don't have to . . . well, thanks."

She's quiet and reflective for several more seconds, seeming almost apologetic.

"My aunt and uncle weren't bad people really, just too strict," she tells me. "There was no room for me to be me."

"What does that mean?"

"They had a plan for my life. I was going to graduate high school as salutatorian or valedictorian and go to Stanford. I was supposed to become a lawyer to establish myself and help support them."

"I'm guessing you didn't do either of those things," I suggest.

She offers me a bittersweet smile, releasing my hand.

"That's right. I dropped out of high school, and they kicked me out. I was old enough to get a job, so I moved in with some of my friends who had already graduated," she replies, putting both hands in her lap. "Then I went back later, got my GED, and learned customer service skills from the state work commission. It took a few years, but I landed this job, and I'm doing all right for myself."

"Yeah, that's a pretty nice house you have."

"It's a rental, but at least I can afford it."

I can tell there's more to her story, but I'll wait for her to fill in the details.

"Anyway, I respect you for surviving your own situation with your grandparents," she continues.

"How much did I tell you?" I ask.

"You dreamed about the last time you saw them alive. And like I said before, you talk in your sleep."

"So . . . you do know," I confirm. She nods sadly.

Kalea leans her head against my shoulder. Her long hair caresses my cheek briefly. I feel a tinge of wariness, but it doesn't last. I kind of like that she wants to be this close.

"I can support you, Sean," she says lovingly. "I'm offering to be here for you, however you need me to be. A listening ear, a shoulder . . . or more."

I'm still confused. As good as this feels, I don't want to move away from her or seem uncaring. But I don't understand it.

"Why does it matter to you so much what happens to me?" I query.

She waits a moment to answer me, still leaning against me.

"I've met a lot of people in my life but very few whose circumstances are so close to mine," she reveals. "No one was there to protect either of us. But I can protect myself now. And I'll protect you."

I wonder what she means by "I can protect myself now"? I'm not sure what to think about any of this. I believe she won't share my private details. But I'm getting even more uncomfortable with how forward she's being. And as long as I'm sober, I think I can protect myself just fine.

And really, who does she think she is? I open my mouth to offer some protest, but she speaks first, cutting me off.

"Let me ask you this, Sean," she purrs before showing a mischievous grin. "Are you really content for us to just be friends?"

She obviously isn't.

"I get that we have similar backgrounds, and you feel protective of me because of that," I begin, determined to sound respectful. I know this could go south very quickly. "Some people might develop a sisterly affection out of that, but not a romantic one. What makes this distinction you have toward me?"

She laughs at that, long and loud. What on earth?

"You are trying so hard to analyze this logically and protect my feelings at the same time. I can see that. It's kind of sweet," she says, turning toward me. Her gaze makes me think she's frustrated for me, not at me. She relaxes some. "Can you take a moment to think less and feel more? You may find that the answers you're looking for are closer than you realize."

So there *are* answers, Kalea? I knew she wasn't telling me something before. She is right about one thing—I have been clamping down my emotions, even more than usual. Why?

Then it becomes glaringly obvious. I've been afraid to. Why?

I take in a deep breath and release it.

A memory flashes through my mind and sends a shiver down my spine.

Kissing Kalea. Not the quick kiss at the party—this was later. At her place. We kissed . . . much more passionately. I was the one who took my shirt off. She was so beautiful, alluring. And we crossed that line together, willingly.

I'd never been with anyone before. We were unprotected. I didn't consider her sexual history. How could I do something so stupid? I didn't want to face this, but now I have to.

I look at Kalea with new understanding. Her attachment to me makes so much more sense.

"We . . . were together last night," I say quietly.

Her eyes take on a contented look. "Oh, yes."

Kalea leans back against the bench, crosses her arms over her chest, and closes her eyes. Her face beams with satisfaction.

"We never could have been 'just friends,' Sean."

. . .

The walk home is surreal. What kind of relationship do I want with Kalea? I mean, I could treat last night like a mistake. I could walk away from her. Move on, like they do in TV shows and movies. But I'm not that cold. She's a stunningly attractive woman who likes me. And I'm starting to have feelings for her, too.

But what about Jennie Lou? She loves me. And I thought I loved her, too. Don't I?

I stop, suddenly feeling cold all over. I can't keep this from Jennie Lou. The idea is terrifying, but I have to tell her.

8

THE FOURTH WHEEL

Saturdays are always weird for me. I don't mind the break from work, but I never know what to do. I enjoy the structure that a schedule brings, which I have on weekdays.

But this Saturday morning, fatigue gnaws at me like a hungry animal. I spent too much time last night worrying about explaining myself to Jennie Lou and stayed up too late. Worse, the sleep I did get wasn't refreshing. I've been laying in my bed slipping in and out of consciousness. It's really bugging me. I don't want to spend my whole day like this.

Is it too late to volunteer for an extra work shift? *Bad idea, Sean.*

I sit up, and inspiration dawns on me. Should I look into getting a car? I mean, I don't know how to drive, but I could take a night class and learn in a few weeks. I spend a lot of money on rides. In that regard, a vehicle would be a worthwhile investment. And it's not like I'd be getting anything fancy.

I grab my phone and go straight to the SearchYoo app. I type in "car dealerships near me" and get a few results. Hm, I don't think I'll be getting a Jaguar in my lifetime. Maybe I should change it to "used car dealerships near me." Ah, there's one: Jellico's Re-Auto Emporium. After a shower and change of clothes, it takes me about fifteen minutes to walk there. I'm surprised at how many people are outside

105

in the lot looking at various vehicles. It's perfect weather for it—not too warm, only a few clouds in the sky.

Then I see the sign: "Some hail damage for us means deep discounts for you! Must Sell!" That's right, there was hail in the storm. I picked a good time to come here.

"Sean?" I hear the deep male voice from behind me. I turn around and see Jimbo.

"Hey, man," I reply when I recognize him. We shake hands, and I ask how he's doing. He looks energized, almost rushed.

"I'm good, but my girlfriend's car got smashed by the tornado. I stopped by to see what kind of deals I could find."

I nod; that makes sense to me. "Anything look good?"

He looks across the showroom and back before shaking his head.

"Olivia is not gonna want a car that reminds her of the storm," he tells me. "She's got a rental for now. In a couple of weeks, this place will get new stock. I'll probably come back then."

"I think that's a good plan, Jimbo. Good luck on that."

Jimbo gives me a thumbs up and starts to walk away but stops.

"Hey, Sean," he says. "I won some tickets to the Crushin' It Monster Truck Rally tonight at the Arena. Wanna join me and Olivia?"

"It seems like a fun idea, but are you sure you wanna invite me? I don't want to get in the way of a date with your girlfriend."

"Olivia's cool. And we're bringing her son. He's thirteen."

Shall I check my blank schedule? Nah, I'm good.

"What time?" I ask, my mood now improving.

"Well, it starts at eight o'clock, but we'll pick you up around seven, okay?"

. . .

"My favorite is Master of Disaster!" Olivia's son, Kendrick, tells me. We're on the way to Chesapeake Energy Arena. "It's black and red and has a sixteen-hundred-horsepower engine! I've seen it win twelve races in the last three years. And he always crushes the competition!"

Sitting next to me, Kendrick is tall and slender with caramel-colored skin. His short, natural hair is styled into a fade on the sides. He's wearing oval-shaped glasses that draw attention to his deep brown eyes. He's sporting a simple black t-shirt, jeans, and sneakers

"That's pretty impressive," I reply. I love his enthusiasm. It actually makes me curious about these motorized beasts.

"Sean, you're really in for a treat," Jimbo adds, briefly turning to look at me and Kendrick in the back seat of his truck. "Master of Disaster will probably race its toughest rival tonight, Sidewinder. Somehow, that truck makes super-wide turns and recovers instantly. I don't know how the owner tweaked the suspension, but it's amazing to watch!"

I know next to nothing about cars, but it all sounds interesting. "I'm looking forward to it!"

Olivia is sitting in the front passenger seat. She turns to look at me, drawing my attention to her impressive, shoulder-length braids and black cap with yellow letters that read "CRUSH THEM!"

Olivia is African American, close in age and size to Jimbo. She's wearing a black jacket with matching blouse, pants, and boots.

"I'm glad you could make it, Sean," she says. "I love my guys, but it's great to see a fresh face. How long have you been a fan?"

"Um, since this morning . . . ?" I chuckle.

She laughs. "That's okay! You'll have fun, believe me. Kendrick has been passionate about monster trucks since he was nine. He went to his first show at ten, and where he goes, I go!"

"And now that includes me, too," Jimbo interjected, turning to smile at Olivia.

She blows him a kiss in response.

"Mom," Kendrick warns, looking sour.

"Kendrick, what is mom's rule number one?" she asks Kendrick with a stern expression.

He rolls his eyes. "Mom makes all the rules."

He says it insincerely, but Olivia nods in approval.

"And what is mom's rule number two?'" she adds.

"'Always remember Mom's rule number one," he recites as though it's a punishment.

She smiles, but there's menace in it. "I'm glad we *understand* each other."

"Y'know, you could let up on him now and then, Olivia," Jimbo says, not looking over.

Now, it's Olivia's expression that sours as she turns her head toward Jimbo. She stares at him for several seconds.

"James Geribo," she says in a frosty tone, "is this your son? Did you raise him?"

"No."

"Who did?"

"You."

She nods slowly.

"So, maybe I know how to handle my son *just a little better* than anyone else?"

"I'm not questioning how you raised him," Jimbo replies calmly. "I just think, now that he's a teenager—"

She raises a hand to stop him.

"Let's look at this another way, hon," she says. "What was my son doing when I corrected him?"

Jimbo took in a breath to begin his reply when Olivia lifts the "Hand of Silence" again.

"He was expressing disapproval at our display of affection," she continues. "Do you want me to *allow* my son to oppose our relationship?"

"No?" Jimbo replies.

Having never taken her eyes off him, she smiles.

"Good answer. So . . . about my 'letting up' on Kendrick, you were saying?"

Jimbo shakes his head and keeps looking straight ahead. "Did I say something? I forgot."

Olivia turns her head to face Kendrick. "And this is why I'm keeping him."

Kendrick simmers at that but says nothing further. I get the impression he's not really opposed to their relationship. Maybe he's just jealous for his mom's attention.

The whole conversation was pretty amusing. And it makes me feel good that they're comfortable being themselves around me. I could learn from them. I've spent so much of my life protecting myself. But it's okay to have a little disagreement if everyone genuinely cares about each other.

. . .

This is definitely the place to be tonight! As we enter, the welcome screen flashes facts about the arena, including that it can seat between fifteen and eighteen thousand people, depending on the event. I'd say at least ten thousand are here. The crowd spans all ages and ethnicities.

I didn't know these events were particularly family-friendly, but clearly they are. On the way to our seats, I saw a big sandbox area where kids could play with their toy monster trucks, imitating races or just pushing their toys up large sand mounds.

Sitting here now and facing the competition area, surrounded by fans, the energy is contagious. I begin to feel a surge of anticipation as I see the first two trucks, Obnoxious Antagonizer and Raptor Claws, line up to race.

Obnoxious Antagonizer is big, even for a monster truck. Its frame is black with painted green and yellow flames, and the engine roars to everyone's delight. Raptor Claws is more streamlined with a charcoal gray and red color scheme. The driver pulses the engine, sounding like a beast about to strike.

Raptor Claws surges ahead, using a ramp to increase its lead over its competitor. Obnoxious Antagonizer leaps further but can't close the gap between them. It almost rolls over taking an outer turn in the mud while Raptor Claws slips and slides but never slows down. A moment later, Raptor Claws is declared the victor and will advance to the next race.

Jimbo and Kendrick shout in delight, along with thousands of others, at the first win of the night. Olivia looks pleased that they're enjoying themselves. She makes brief eye contact with me as I leap up and shout my satisfaction. This really is fun!

As the night progresses, I decide on a few favorites: Raptor Claws, Amplifier, and Defiant. They all looked like underdogs, but each of them had hidden strengths and capable drivers. And while

I don't know if I'll ever go to another monster truck show, I won't rule it out, either.

Once the event is over, Jimbo stops by a Burger Empire on the way back home.

"Sean, I'm going to go inside to order for all of us," he says. Then he smiles. "Would you go in with me? It may take both of us to haul this load."

"Uh, sure," I reply. "No problem."

He looks to Olivia. "Large combo number one all the way with a lemonade?" She nods. Then he turns to face Kendrick "Large combo number six with no pickles, onion rings instead of fries, and a Dr. Cola?"

"You know it!" Kendrick replies with a thumbs up. Jimbo nods and exits the vehicle.

As we walk into the fast-food restaurant, Jimbo tells me, "Of course, get whatever you want, Sean. I'm treating tonight."

"Thanks, Jimbo. I really appreciate it."

There are several people ahead of us in the line.

"I hope you don't mind, but I was hoping we could talk for a minute," Jimbo says.

"No problem. I really had a great time tonight."

"I'm glad about that, but I wanted to talk about . . . the other night," he adds.

"Oh?"

"I've thought about it a lot. Ben shouldn't have pressured you into drinking, and we shouldn't have gone along with it. *I* shouldn't have. Sorry to do that to you, man."

I didn't know he felt bad about what happened. I didn't think he did anything wrong.

"I'm glad you got home okay," he continues before I can respond.

I can't help but smile. Jimbo is a nice guy.

"Look, I want to tell you this before you hear it from someone else," I tell him. I'm pretty sure we both know I'm talking about Ben. "Some things went on between me and Kalea that night. It's . . . not really a big deal. She and I will figure it out."

Jimbo puts his hand on my upper arm. "I respect that, man. Just know that if you need a friend, you've got one."

"Thanks."

We order the food and bring it out to the SUV. I'd have been content to be dropped off and eat at home, but Jimbo and Olivia insist that we dine together in the vehicle. My burger practically melts in my mouth, and it's delicious. Why doesn't the Burger Empire near my apartment make food this good?

Thirty minutes later, I'm dragging myself into my apartment. I guess my adrenaline finally ran out. I imagine Sparky running up to me and barking a welcome at me. But I'm too tired to do much more than pat him on the head and say a weak, "Good boy."

Man, I must be exhausted. I make my way into the kitchen and grab a water from the fridge. I look at the couch but think better of sitting down. I'd end up falling asleep there, and I don't want that. So, the bedroom becomes my next destination.

I sit on the edge of the bed and stare at the moonlit window. I didn't turn on the light. Why bother?

Smiling, I reflect on the great time I had with Jimbo, Olivia, and Kendrick. I need more friends like that.

I mean, I am friends with Keith. And Kalea. And even Jennie Lou.

Suddenly, I feel like the gravity in my room has doubled. My heart sinks.

Jennie Lou. I still have to talk to Jennie Lou about what happened with Kalea.

I lose my strength and fall back, assuming my head will hit the soft pillow.

It hits the brass bed frame instead.

Hot pain stabs through the left side of my skull, forcing a grunt from my throat as I put my hand to my head. At least, it's not bleeding; it's just a throbbing source of misery.

I finally find the pillow, when its softness isn't going to help me anymore.

That kind of sums up my life right now, doesn't it?

9

TURBULENT WATERS

I almost wish Jennie Lou hadn't come, but I see her briskly walking up the path toward me. This park reunited us a few days ago. Is this where our new relationship ends, too? I hope not.

It's a hot Sunday afternoon, without even a breeze to make this more bearable. At least, there's trees to deflect some of the sunlight. I picked a somewhat remote part of the park, so we'd have a little privacy. It's just us, the insects, and a few ducks in the nearby stream.

Jennie Lou is sweating and breathing hard when she reaches me. She must have hurried all the way here. I'm surprised she didn't put her hair in a ponytail or anything. She looks concerned.

"Your message sounded urgent," she says, appearing winded. "I got here as quick as I could."

"I'm sorry, I didn't mean to worry you," I reply. Then I point to my left. "Why don't we sit down under that tree? You can cool down some, and we can talk."

"All right," she agrees.

The sprawling giant grants us some merciful shade. We sit facing each other, and I wish I'd thought to bring some water.

"Now, what happened?" she asks me. I guess she can still read my moods.

"I made a mistake," I struggle to say. "Several of them. And now, I need to tell you about them."

"What kind of mistakes?" she wonders.

I tell her about Ben's party, the difficult time I was having at first, and my choice to use alcohol to relax. Jennie Lou is tense but says nothing. I knew this would upset her. But I've come too far to turn back now.

"I spent most of my time at the party with a coworker named Kalea," I admit.

"Kalea? A woman?"

"Yes," I nod.

"We started talking and—"

"Was she *pretty*?" Jennie Lou interrupts with a slight edge in her voice.

How do I answer that? Of course, Kalea's pretty! But saying that is pure doom for me. There's no way to get around this, is there?

Jennie Lou's exhale becomes a whistle, and her eyes flash a mixture of surprise and disappointment. "*Very* pretty," she says. Before I can say anything in my defense, she continues. "If she was plain or ugly, you'd have said so. Even if she was kind of pretty, you would've told me she was pretty and left it at that."

She can still read me so easily. I feel like a rat caught in a trap.

Jennie Lou shakes her head and chuckles. "You couldn't even find the words to describe her. She must have been beautiful."

She looks away for a few seconds, saying nothing as I stew in my own guilt. Then she faces me again.

"Go on," she prompts.

"Kalea was kind to me. We talked and found out we had a lot in common. We joked a lot—specially after my coworkers started making margaritas," I answer. "For some reason, Kalea never left my side."

Jennie Lou's eyes narrow.

"'For some reason?'" Jennie Lou repeats, incredulous. "Like maybe she was *attracted* to you?"

I sigh. This is not gonna get any easier.

"By the time the party was winding down, I was barely conscious," I resume. "Ben, the guy whose place we were at, was going to drive me home, but Kalea stopped him. He was just as drunk as the rest of us."

"Good for her!" Jennie Lou interjects. "So how did you get home?"

Here we go down the rabbit hole.

"Kalea got us a cab."

Jennie Lou looks confused. "All of the guests got in the same cab?"

"No, the others got separate cab rides," I explain. "Kalea and I shared a cab."

Jennie Lou considers that a moment, then shrugs.

"Well, it was kind of her to make sure you got home safely."

I wince and scrunch my shoulders. "Yeah, about that . . . "

Jennie Lou's eyebrows raise up. "What? Something *else* happened?"

I sigh. "Kalea didn't know where I lived, and I had passed out. Plus, she was drunk, too."

"What . . . happened?" Jennie Lou says, clearly dreading the answer.

I swallow and brace for what I'm about to say. "She had the cab driver drop us off at her house . . . and she helped me inside until I woke up," I begin. Then the memories fill my thoughts again. "Or that's what I thought at first."

"What? Explain what you mean by that."

I close my eyes and squint, fully feeling my shame. I'm cold all over, and I feel like an awful person.

"Sean?" she says sympathetically.

"At first, I thought nothing had actually happened between us," I tell her. "But that was just fear and wishful thinking. I ended up remembering everything."

She shakes her head very slowly, confused. "What do you mean? What did you remember?" she asked softly.

It's come down to this. I have to tell her the truth. And it's going to hurt her, not me.

"Kalea and I . . . were intimate."

Jennie Lou's eyes convey inner devastation, but she remains silent.

"I feel—I *am*—responsible for all of this," I say. "And I had to tell you. I didn't . . . I didn't want to keep this a secret."

I sit there feeling emotionally numb. In my mind, I imagine bridges on fire. Because everything I said sounded bad. I feel like a man walking toward the gallows. And now, it's time to pay the price.

Jennie Lou looks down, clearly thinking. Her expression is hard to read. Is she holding back a blistering rebuke? Is she disgusted with me now? Does she hate me?

When she finally gazes at me, she's teary-eyed, but I don't see any fury.

"I . . . know you and . . . Kalea just met," Jennie Lou says in a hoarse voice. "But do you already have feelings for her?"

Her question slams into me worse than a punch. It forces me to dig deep within and drag out an answer I don't want to give. But it's the truth. And I can't lie to her.

"I do."

Jennie Lou's jaw clenches, and she inhales harshly through her nostrils.

"Will you . . . be pursuing a relationship with her?"

"I don't know," I answer honestly.

She nods in acknowledgment, still unhappy.

"I believe you," she says, now sounding drained. "It wasn't what I wanted to hear, but thank you for being honest."

I still think she's going to walk away from the park and never speak to me again. It would be justified. For over two years, I lived with the heartache of Jennie Lou's rejection, only to get a second chance. And I ruined it in one night.

My fury at myself suddenly rises within me, and I wonder how I could have been so dumb! Before I can do or say anything more, Jennie Lou speaks.

"You're right. You made a mistake. And it could have a lot of consequences," she adds. "But you're owning up to it. I wouldn't be much of a friend if I rejected you now."

"I don't deserve your friendship after this," I quickly interject.

She looks surprised at that. Then her gaze narrows.

"Listen to me closely, Sean Winter," she says as she stands up unsteadily. She balances against the tree for a couple of seconds while I stand up, too. Then she turns and makes eye contact with me again. "I was your friend before we shared any romantic feelings with each other. And I'm your friend now. Got it?"

Now, it's my turn to be surprised. I close my mouth, which was hanging open, and lower my head. She's right.

"Got it," I answer.

A few more seconds pass.

"I'll be truthful with you, too," she continues. "What you've told me . . . it's heartbreaking. I'm going to need some time, okay?"

I can't believe she's handling this so well. If our positions were reversed, I don't know what I'd do.

"Sure, Jennie. Take what time you need."

I escort her in silence back to her car and watch her get inside. As I'm turning to head back to my place, I see Jennie Lou slump her head against the steering wheel. There's nothing I can do. I have no choice but to go home.

. . .

Later that night, I stand on my balcony and look out at the neighborhood. I don't know anyone here. And I've just messed over one of the only friends I do have. Even though the balcony isn't that big, I can't help pacing around it.

I've made a big mess, and I don't know how to fix it. I need a different perspective.

For a few minutes, I think about calling Keith, but I struggle with the idea. Eventually, though, I know I need to call him. I pull my phone from my pocket and dial his number. After a couple of rings, he answers.

"Hello?"

"Keith, it's Sean. Can you talk right now?"

"Sure," he says. "Is something the matter?"

"You . . . could say that."

I tell him the whole story and ask for his advice.

"When you invited her to the park, were you looking for closure with Jennie Lou?"

That's a good question.

"I knew I couldn't keep it from her," I tell him. "But I didn't want to end our relationship. I probably did, though."

"Sean, admitting to your mistake was the right thing to do. One way or the other, you'll learn from it. But it sounds like the next move is up to Jennie Lou."

I sigh. "You're right."

I'm glad he hasn't been quoting the Bible or offering to pray for me.

"I won't tell you how to live your life," Keith says. "You have some decisions to make, though. No matter what you choose, people's lives are going to be affected. Yours, Kalea's, Jennie's . . . maybe even mine."

"How do I make those kinds of decisions, knowing there will be fallout? I'm not good at that. This mess makes that really clear."

I hear reassurance in Keith's voice. "Your situation is bad, but it's not insurmountable. I'm confident you can handle it. And I want you to know, I'm here for you."

He has no idea how much I appreciate that.

. . .

I head back inside but am unsure what to do with my time now. I plop down on the couch and use the remote to turn on the TV. I feel myself sink deeper into the couch as I channel surf between news, the *Wife Warriors* reality show, and then an episode of the 1970s Western drama *Bandit's Gulch* on the Wayback Channel. The next time I check my phone, over an hour has passed, and I still have no idea what to do. This hasn't helped in the least; it's just made me feel more lethargic.

I'm bored. Lonely and bored. I don't want to be alone, but Jennie Lou's gone. Maybe for good. And I already talked to Keith. I feel like I'm out of options. It's going to keep being a dull night.

That's when I get a text notification from my phone. It's Kalea.

Can I come over?

I pull up one of her selfies from my pictures and study it for a minute. Of all people, do I really want her to come over? Is anybody else standing in line to come see me? Nope. Even so, I have mixed feelings about this.

Then in my thoughts, I see Jennie Lou's face, heartbroken and dejected because of my actions. I see her droop her head against that steering wheel.

It's too soon to see Kalea. I made some poor choices yesterday; I don't need to compound them. I mean, I know there won't be alcohol. I'm not making *that* mistake again. But Kalea and I have chemistry; I can't deny that. If I let her come over, I don't trust myself to hold back. I'll want more.

I take a deep breath. I need to make a decision.

Sorry. Tonight's not good for me.

Need to talk? Can I call instead?

Not up to talking. Got things to figure out.

She waits a minute to respond.

See you tomorrow?

Sure.

Good night, Sean.

Nite, Kalea.

Why is it that the things that seem right also make me feel bad? I didn't want to do that.

But I needed to.

. . .

It takes some effort to get to sleep because I still feel so alone. Not even playing with Sparky for a while—scratching behind his ears the way he likes or playing tug-of-war with some imaginary rope—lifts my spirits.

It's not like this is a new feeling. I've spent almost my entire life feeling alone—ever since Mom died. I've felt that way whether I was living with my grandparents or my college roommates. My thoughts were my only company most of the time. My world and my secrets were my own. I had acquaintances and some friends. But I never let anyone get close. Not even Jennie Lou, even though I loved her.

And then I met Kalea. She found out about my past. She knows who I've become as a result. We're connected—in so many ways—now. Yet I still know so little about her. I want to. At least, I think I do. It's confusing. My people skills aren't great, especially at reading intentions.

With Kalea, that almost doesn't matter. I know her scent, the texture of her hair, the softness of her skin, and the taste of her kiss. I can see her face when I close my eyes. I've never had that kind of rapport with a woman before. Or anyone else, for that matter. But I don't have as much self-control when I'm around her. Control has always been important to me. Yet when I'm with Kalea, I don't have to hold up my walls to protect myself. It's freeing. I can be myself.

So, what about Jennie Lou? Am I giving up on her? I don't want to. That might be a moot point now.

As I toss and turn in my bed, trying to find a relaxing position, I'm suddenly distracted by how warm I feel. The air conditioner is on, and I'm only wearing shorts and a t-shirt, but I'm still uncomfortable. I want the release of drifting off to sleep, but it eludes me.

Left side. Right side. Curled up. Straightened out. On my stomach and then on my back again. Nothing brings relief.

My thoughts drift to a conversation I had with Keith recently. It was a few days ago, after I'd run into Jennie Lou and she'd shared her feelings with me. He'd asked me what I was feeling.

I sighed and looked at him. "Love. For her."

"I thought so," he replied. "You seem like you still have some deep feelings for her."

I shrugged. It was uncomfortable, but I needed to talk about it.

"And it sounds like she has deep feelings for you, too," he added.

"Yeah."

He nodded contemplatively for a few seconds.

"You need a bridge," he suggested.

"A bridge?"

"A bridge," he repeated. "You have some gaps between you two. Gaps in perspective, in belief systems. If you both work at building a bridge, you can overcome them."

That actually made sense.

"How do we build a bridge then?" I wondered.

"Well, consider me and Julia. Even if we transcend the obstacles of rebuilding trust and understanding, I'm a Christian, and she isn't," Keith said. "That kind of bridge takes time and effort to make. I can't just ask her to convert to my faith."

"Good point," I replied, nodding. "No one should expect others to change for them."

"It is a very personal decision," Keith acknowledged.

He's a pretty reasonable guy. I respect that.

"So, for me and Jennie, are you suggesting some kind of counseling, like what you and Julia are doing?" I was only half-serious, but I really had no idea what to do.

"I don't think either of you is there yet," Keith replied. "It took me and Julia years of co-parenting our daughter to get to where we are now in our relationship. Then again, we had a near-impossible gulf between us. Your situation with Jennie is different."

"What do you mean?"

"You didn't actually enter a romantic relationship back then," he clarified. "You seem to be trying to start one now. The bridge—of how you relate to one another—still needs to be created. But it's possible. The distance is achievable."

I appreciated that. It was reasonable.

Now, in the present, that little gap seems like a chasm between me and Jennie Lou.

More time passes with more tossing and turning in bed. Two images continuously swim to the surface in my mind's eye: Jennie Lou and Kalea. I want to reach them, but I can't. Intermittently, I try to make a bridge to Jennie Lou, but I keep failing. I get close to her and run out of building materials. Or the support beams collapse. The wood rapidly rots away. Lastly, I reach her, but she's already gone.

When I focus on Kalea, I can make the bridge easily. But I can't cross it. I get halfway; and the rest of the catwalk disappears, or there's a wall blocking my path.

I realize I'm dreaming, but I can't do anything about it.

I try one more time to get to Jennie Lou. I have a rope ladder and throw it across to her, but it's Kalea who catches it and fastens it to metal stakes in the ground. I'm able to cross the expanse to her. As I stand up, I see that she's calm, with a sweet and welcoming smile.

"You rejected *her* this time," Kalea tells me, pulling me into her embrace. "You chose me instead."

Is that what I did? Still in her arms, I look at her. She's so content, so beautiful.

Then I can't help but wonder, *Where's Jennie Lou?*

Almost as if reading my thoughts, Kalea's smile turns vicious.

"I *protected* you, Sean," she says with an edge of malice. Then she looks down at the chasm below. "She'll never bother us again."

Before I can look over the edge and scream Jennie Lou's name, I awake in a cold sweat. I'm flat on my back in the darkness of my room, staring at the ceiling. I have a sinking feeling in my heart. My breaths are ragged, and I'm stunned at my own imagination. It takes some time before I can free myself from the shock.

When I check the clock on my phone, I see it's three forty-seven in the morning. I feel awful. Not sick. Just so out of sorts that I don't know what to do. Being emotionally worn out before starting the day is not good. It's gonna take a while to get the dream imagery out of my head.

Jennie Lou mentioned being honest with herself. I need to do the same. I don't deserve Jennie Lou's love, really. I'm just going to let her down. Jennie Lou doesn't know much about my life, especially about my grandparents. I never told her. I guess I didn't trust her enough to do that.

If Kalea hadn't learned my circumstances on her own, would I have volunteered that information to her? Would that have changed things between us? When Kalea learned about it, she didn't turn away. She's made it clear she wants to be with me.

She feels . . . safe to me.

This really isn't such a difficult decision, is it?

I put on my black night robe and walk across the living room. I head out onto the balcony again to get some fresh air for a few minutes. Looking at the neighborhood under the night sky, I lean against the metal railing surrounding the terrace. There's actually a couple of people walking below and a few cars driving by. It's calming to observe the nearby businesses and residences by moonlight. The scant clouds above have become dark wisps, and there's barely any breeze.

I need to get Jennie Lou out of my thoughts. I have to let her move on without me.

My instincts tell me it's too soon to make this decision. And my heart is tired of hurting, of being alone, always afraid.

Then my mind intervenes. Make a decision. *Any* decision. And don't turn back! *I shouldn't have tried to be a part of your life again, Jennie Lou. You'll have a better one without me. I can live with that.*

The mind wins. I won't live with the doubt and fear anymore. I've decided.

I don't have to make rocket science out of filling a jug with water. There's not much to this.

I've chosen Kalea.

We'll try this out and see where it goes. If we break up, at least we tried. What's the worst that could happen?

10

KALEA'S ARIA

It's pretty bad when neither coffee nor breakfast can keep my eyes open at work. I've caught myself starting to nod off three times already, and I haven't even made it to ten o'clock yet. I stand up and pace near my desk while I can talk to customers. But when I have to pull up their information in the computer system, I have to sit down again.

"Just give me a second to pull up your account, ma'am," I tell the customer. "Okay, yes. We did receive your online payment. Your services should be restored within fifteen minutes. Yes, ma'am. Thank you."

With that call over, I log myself out. Then I lean back in my chair and close my burning eyes for just a moment before checking the time—9:57. Close enough. I finally made it to break.

I smell cinnamon. Is that perfume? I turn toward the aroma, and Kalea is standing less than a foot away, holding a large, plastic mug. She looks sympathetically toward me.

"Trouble sleeping last night?" she asks.

"Yeah, you could say that."

"I noticed how tired you looked and got this for you," she continues. "Believe it or not, cold water will help wake you up better than coffee."

"Really?"

She smiles. "Coffee has caffeine. But it dehydrates you, which can actually make you sleepier."

I gladly take the deep blue mug and drink some of the icy water. I can't tell any difference yet. But if I am dehydrated, it may take a while.

"Thank you," I tell her.

"Come with me to lunch today," she suggests. "We can get some food that'll energize you for the afternoon."

"I'd like that," I reply with a smile. "I just clocked out for break. How about you?"

"I'm heading back from break," she says with a shrug. "Let's aim for a noon lunch, okay? I'll text you when I clock out."

"Sounds good."

. . .

When lunchtime comes, Kalea drives us a couple of miles away to her favorite sushi restaurant, Grand Sushi #3. It's a small place with a big window in front that brightens the dining area. The line isn't long.

"Welcome to Grand Sushi!" the bright-eyed young cashier says. Her uniform looks like a dark gray chef's outfit sans hat, but it's her neon pink bob hairstyle that's attention-grabbing.

"I've never had sushi before," I whisper to Kalea.

She grins. "Get the fatty salmon roll. It rocks!" she whispers back.

"Um, one fatty salmon roll for me," I tell the cashier, whose nametag reads Aimee. "And you, Kalea?"

"I'll have the spicy tuna roll."

"Solid," Aimee says. "Can I get you anything else? Drinks?"

"Could we get two large ice waters?" I ask.

"Of course, sir," Aimee answers, tapping a few keys on the tablet in front of her. "That'll be $24.36."

She turns around the tablet, and I put my credit card in its reader. A few seconds later, Aimee hands me a receipt.

"You're order A-fourteen," she says with a smile. "Come pick it up when you hear your number. Thanks for choosing Grand Sushi!"

I take the receipt and smile back. "Thanks!"

We get a table near the window. A few minutes later, an older man with a loud voice calls out "A-fourteen!" I walk up there to get it. As I return, Kalea gestures for me to hurry up.

"I don't know about you, Sean, but I'm starving!" she says. "And this place makes the best sushi in town!"

The salmon in my sushi roll is a bright orange, marbled with white, accompanied by soft green avocado. Combined with the seaweed and rice and dipped in soy sauce, it's amazing.

Her roll looks good, too, but it must be pretty spicy. Her cheeks are flushed, and she just drank half her water after a handful of bites.

"Are you all right?" I ask.

"Sorry," she replied with an embarrassed smile. "It's the price I pay for loving spicy food."

She finishes off her water, and I slide mine over to her.

"I haven't had any yet, I'll go get more water."

"You don't have to do that, Sean."

"It's not a problem," I say, smiling to reassure her.

"Thanks. Really, I mean it."

I nod and go get the ice water. When I get back, Kalea puts her hand over mine on the table and looks at me with concern.

"So, are you feeling any better now, Sean?"

"Yeah, thanks. I usually get enough sleep, but not last night."

She nods, but her worry is still evident.

"Was there a particular reason you had trouble sleeping? I mean, is it okay for me to ask that?"

"It's okay to ask.." I nod. "I needed to make a decision . . . regarding Jennie."

She looks briefly surprised but doesn't say anything.

"I want to be with you, Kalea."

She slightly tilts her head. Is that caution or confusion?

"Are you not in love with Jennie Lou anymore?"

I shake my head. "I took a hard look at myself and . . . my feelings for her. We act different, have different beliefs. That kind of relationship won't work between us now. We're friends, and that's all we'll ever be."

"Uh-huh." She doesn't look convinced yet.

I take my hand out from under hers and place it on her cheek. I look into her eyes.

"I can't deny what you and I have—and I don't want to," I tell her. "You're the one for me, Kalea."

She blushes at that.

"I was *already* yours, Sean. I guess now it's official."

That sends a rush through me. We don't talk anymore about it. I get To-Go boxes for our leftovers. We're both noticeably more relaxed, even happy, as she drives us back to work.

. . .

I complete my last call at 5:23 p.m. and log out for the day. Between the healthy food and drinking water throughout the day, I'm doing a lot better. I think it also helps that I made my feelings clear to Kalea, and she accepted them. I'm not worrying about that anymore.

I walk over to her desk, where she's working on her last ticket. I wave at her, and she waves back. After logging off her computer, she grabs her purse from her desk drawer before locking it. She swings her rolling chair around to face me and flashes a grin.

"I have an idea," she beams. "Now that we're done at work, why don't I just drive us straight to my house? I'll make us a light dinner, and we can hang out."

That's an amazing idea. I like it a lot.

"Sure! That sounds great," I reply.

. . .

After we get to her place, she goes upstairs to her bedroom to change from her work clothes. When she's done, we sit together on the couch.

"I want to know more about you, Kalea. Tell me what you like, don't like, and what you believe in."

"Believe in?" she repeats. "I believe in you . . . and us."

She kisses me, then stands up, walking through the living room. She faces away from me and extends her hands. Then she stretches out her fingers and points toward the framed movie posters on either wall.

"As far as 'likes'—I like the color blue and retro sci-fi—but you knew those things," she begins. Then she turns around and sinks her hands in her pockets, looking up and to the right contemplatively. "I like having enough money to pay my bills, keep food in the fridge, and gas in my car. I like cats, but I'm allergic to them. I like having fun and dancing in my bedroom." Now she looks at me. "I like knowing who my friends are. And I totally like you!"

Still pondering, she takes on a more serious expression and lightly grips her arms as though somewhat uncomfortable.

"For dislikes, I'd have to say romance novels, most politics, Nutella, and rude drivers," she says. "Oh, and people being fake. That's about it."

Pretty simple and straightforward. And that fits what I've seen of her personality so far. I sit down on the couch.

"What about spiritual beliefs?" I ask. "Do you have any?"

She thinks about it a moment. "I believe in karma and not really much else. I wasn't raised with any religion. My aunt and uncle weren't into that. They were all about fending for yourself. What about you, Sean?"

"I'm an atheist."

She smiles. "Then we shouldn't have any problems."

I can't argue with that.

"Now, tell me about you. What are your likes and dislikes?" she asks.

I shrug. "You already know I like *Star Wars*. For music, I like Pure Indigo and Why Shark Why."

"They're pretty cool," she says softly.

"I also like fast food, especially good tacos—"

Her eyes perk up. "I will make you the best tacos you've ever had!" she interjects.

"Really?"

She puts her hand on her hip and smiles.

"I'm an awesome cook," she boasts. "You'll see! I can make Italian food, Hawaiian food, a few Asian dishes—and my Mexican food is out of this world!"

I grin. "I'll look forward to it."

"Just don't be surprised if you gain a few pounds from my meals," she jokes.

That would probably be an improvement for me. And while Kalea's not thin, I think she's got just the right curves.

She sits down next to me on the couch. Being this close, I am drawn to her. I pull her close, and we kiss passionately. Words become unimportant. What matters is only this connection. The time, where we are, what we may have been planning . . . it all becomes irrelevant.

. . .

"Everything okay, Sean?"

"Yeah."

We're blissful, sitting together in the living room. The lamplight is relaxing, and the ceiling fan keeps the temperature reasonable on this warm night.

"I think I already love you, Sean."

I run the words through my head a few times. I can't believe she said it.

"You *think* you love me?" I tease with a wry smile.

"No. I'm sure," she clarifies.

Neither of us know what to say after that.

It's only eleven o'clock. I can still go home and get a decent amount of sleep.

"I'm going upstairs for a quick shower," Kalea tells me.

I follow and decide to explore her room. The walls are cerulean, and she has a small, pecan-colored wood bookcase against one wall. It's filled with classic works of fiction, such as *Alice's Adventures in Wonderland*, *Adventures of Huckleberry Finn*, *Anne of Green Gables*, and *Emma*.

On top of the bookcase is a small stack of papers with drawings. Some look a few years old, corners folded, or even beginning to yellow. Others are much more recent. Some of the drawings are in pencil, others in ink, and the rest in crayon. Kalea's a pretty good artist. There are sketches of men and women, movie titles, and skies with clouds. One thing appears on every page, though, and it's a word: *Aria*. Does she like opera?

I hear the bathroom door open, and Kalea emerges. She's already put on shorts and a halter top. Then I see something unusual. I noticed it earlier but didn't give it any thought.

"What are those?" I ask, pointing at the vertical, rippling, pale lines on either side of her exposed abdomen.

She looks down briefly, then returns my gaze sheepishly. "They're stretch marks."

"From what?"

She looks at me hesitantly. Then she looks away, like she's thinking hard. After a moment, she tilts her head back slightly and sighs.

"They're from when I was pregnant with my daughter," she admits.

"You have a daughter?"

Kalea shakes her head sadly.

"No. I placed her for adoption right after birth. It was four years ago. I was only eighteen."

She had a baby and gave her up? I—whoa.

"Letting Aria go was the hardest thing I've ever done. But I had no way to support her," she continues, speaking slowly. I can hear such heartache in her voice. "I didn't know how bad I would feel later, how I'd regret this . . . and it was too late to stop it."

I step forward and hold her close. I can't even comprehend the magnitude of what she's been through. All I can try and do is comfort her in the ways I know how.

She begins to hold me tighter, saying, "I'm okay, I'm okay." A few seconds later, she looks up at me. "I'm sorry. I probably should have told you, but I didn't know how. And I didn't want to scare you away."

I can appreciate that. It would be difficult to explain under any circumstances.

"It's all right. I know now," I tell her. "It doesn't change how I feel about you."

She smiles at that. "You're a good guy, Sean. Thank you for loving me."

That catches me off-guard.

She winks. "You didn't have to say it. Your actions make it clear."

She makes a quick mini-meal for us to share before I have to go: zesty ham and cheese sandwiches with sides of baby carrots, celery sticks, and ranch dressing. We eat together on the couch.

"I could get used to this," I tell her.

"Me making all your food?" She chuckles.

I laugh. "No, sharing meals with you."

"Oh," she reflects. "We'll just have to spend more time together then."

I take a bite of my sandwich and wash it down with some water. "I'm good with that." The carrots are just sweet enough. They don't even need the dressing. "Next time is at my place, okay?"

She brightens at that. "Sure! When?"

I look at her with a sly smile. "Tomorrow?"

She returns the look. "You could just stay the night?"

"Tempting, but I can't. Work tomorrow."

"All right," she says with a faux pout. Then she smiles. "At least, we'll have something to look forward to."

A few minutes later, we share one last kiss before I go.

II

JUST ADD CINNAMON

INFINITY BOTANICAL GARDENS
OKLAHOMA CITY, OKLAHOMA

Kalea smiles brightly as I take pictures of her next to the delicate bloom of luscious blue windflowers. We've been dating for two weeks now, and we decided to head to Infinity Botanical Gardens in Oklahoma City. The afternoon sun is shining overhead, but it isn't too hot yet. The breeze is soft and pleasant. She wanted us to visit this place on a Saturday.

An unexpected gust nearly blows off her white, wide-brimmed hat, but she catches and holds it in place. The quick action causes her sunglasses to dip down on her nose. Her long hair is not as easy to re-tame, but she makes an admirable effort.

"I hope you got some good shots before the wind turned me into Chewbacca," she frets.

"I sure did," I reply. "About a dozen. And you do not look like Chewbacca."

She does her best Wookie impression, and I bust out laughing. Then she puts her arms around me, and we kiss.

"I'm so happy with you," I say. "I think you could insist we watch every eighties movie, ride roller coasters—which you know I don't like—or ask just about anything of me. And I'd be content as long as I'm with you."

She blushes. "Well, wow! Where did that come from?"

"I just felt like saying it," is my reply. "I want you to know what you mean to me."

She kisses me again. "I love you, too." Then her gaze narrows. "You want me to play more *Droid Wars* with you when we get back, don't you?"

I raise my arms and speak with mock surprise. "What? Why, I would never do that!" Then I grin. "That is, unless you'd be interested in that?"

She cocks her head to the left. "No, I wouldn't," she says flatly. "But I wouldn't mind listening to some more Why Shark Why. I like them!"

"That works for me."

"You're staying over at my place tonight, right?"

I nod. "Yeah. I still don't understand why we can't just share a place, though."

She rolls her eyes. "Not that again? Sean, you know my reasons."

"You don't want me to give up my apartment, and you think it improves our individual credit score to have a solid rent history."

"Exactly right," she answers, looking impressed. "Do you have a photographic memory or something?"

"Something like that," I reply. "I get what you're saying, but I don't mind giving up my apartment. I can build my credit in other ways. I just want to be with you all the time."

She leans so close to me that our noses almost touch, and she smiles. "You practically are, you greedy man."

Kalea and I begin to walk down the path again, surrounded on either side by nature's wonders. We see a clearing up ahead and stop as a dark-skinned man in light-colored clothes goes down on one knee. He's clearly proposing to the almond-hued woman with short, black hair next to him. She grins widely and nods her acceptance. That elicits cheers and clapping from nearby bystanders. He places a ring on her left hand, and they walk off happily, arm-in-arm.

"That was really sweet," Kalea says, leaning against me. She clasps her fingers in mine and turns her head to look me in the eyes.

"You like the idea, hm?" I ask flirtatiously.

She winks at me. "I dare you to try."

I wink back, and we keep walking.

She nudges my shoulder jokingly. "Kalea Winter does sound pretty cool."

I nudge back. "I dare you to go through with it."

She just smiles at that, and we stop to explore some more of the botanical gardens. I gaze at her as much as I do the flowers and greenery.

I remember a week ago, when Kalea showed me pictures of her family from her childhood years. Her parents were a handsome couple, and she's an amazing blend of them both. I think she looks more like her dad. She has his playful smile and kind eyes. She was a cute little girl. I sometimes wonder if she was born with long hair. She has it in every picture, no matter how far back.

I don't have pictures of my grandparents anymore. I only have three old pictures of my mother, Elaine Winter: one when she was a teenager—one of her holding me when I was less than a year old—and the two of us together at a beach when I was seven. The last picture was taken by one of her friends, ten days before Mom died in a car accident. Mom looked happy in each of the pictures. She was slender and carefree with shoulder-length, black hair and green eyes. The pictures prove she was proud to be my mom. That's why I keep them. They're my good memories.

I believe Mom would have liked Kalea. She'd be happy that my girlfriend loves me.

"What are you thinking about so intently?" Kalea asks me.

To Kalea, I must have seemed extremely focused on one particular patch of Desert Willow.

"You," I tease.

"Oh! Well, as long as it's me, that's okay," she says, equally amused.

"Where do you want to go next?"

She considers that. "I'm thinking we should get ice cream!"

We leave Infinity Botanical Gardens, and we take a ten-minute drive to our next stop. Kalea tells me I haven't lived until I experience the Roll Out Ice Creamery. When we arrive, the line is almost out the door.

"Do you already know what you want?" I ask her.

She grins. "Oh yeah! The Fource."

"A *Star Wars* ice cream?"

"Yeah," she replies. "It has four parts to it—dark and white chocolate ice cream with cookie bits and marshmallow cream drizzled on top. It's incredible!"

"Cool," I say. Then I look at the big menu mounted on the wall. "I think I'm gonna get the Mint Dream."

"Mint green ice cream with peppermint pieces and chocolate syrup," she quotes from the menu. "You must really like mint, huh?"

I shrug. "I just wanted to try something different."

She shrugs back. "Okay. Well, thanks for indulging my whims, Sean."

"My pleasure, Cinnamon."

She smiles at that, signaling her acceptance of my new nickname for her.

. . .

It's been two weeks since our visit to the botanical gardens. I'm woken up by Kalea getting out of bed. I groggily check my phone and see that it's five in the morning.

"Kalea, what?"

"I took Miranda's early Sunday shift," she tells me. "I almost forgot last night, so I set my alarm. I need to run by my place on the way there. Sorry I didn't tell you."

The words take too long to process in my brain, but I get there.

"When are you off?" I ask her.

"Three-thirty."

"Okay."

She leans over the bed and kisses me on the lips. "I'll see you this afternoon," she purrs.

"This is the third extra shift you've taken in the last week," I ponder. "Is there a reason?"

"I'm padding my savings account for a rainy day, babe. In a few weeks, I'll reach my goal and won't need to do this anymore, okay?"

I make a mental note to bring this up again. I didn't know she needed to save up for anything. It sounds like there might be more to this.

She kisses me again, more passionately this time. Then I close my eyes and drift back to sleep.

. . .

An hour later, I'm fully awake, showered, and dressed. I decide to go through my phone and delete things I don't need, which includes, apps, emails, and old voicemails. That's when I run across Jennie Lou's voicemails. It reminds me of the huge gap that still remains between us—a gulf I created by my actions.

I may have decided I want Kalea to be my girlfriend, but Jennie Lou and I are still friends, right? But I feel like I abandoned her. I haven't been a friend.

What do I do about this? I can't just call her with no plan, that would be a disaster.

I imagine Sparky gnawing on his fake dog bone in the kitchen, and that inspires an idea. I can believe in a dog that doesn't exist. I can act like I care for him. That is pretty silly, but it means something to me. Jennie Lou believes in God, and I may not share that belief, but it's important to her. I look up toward the ceiling and decide to try something.

"This feels kinda weird to me, but if by some chance you really do exist, God, can You help me and Jennie Lou be friends again? I'd like to believe it's possible. This once, I'd like to believe in You. Thanks."

Did I really just do that? I think I did.

I wait until eight a.m. to call Jennie Lou's number.

"Hello?" she answers.

"Jennie Lou, this is Sean Winter. I'm sorry to call early."

"It's all right. I was up. Is everything okay?"

"I know it's Sunday, but I was hoping we could meet," I tell her. "I feel terrible about the way we . . . parted. And I don't want to leave things like that any longer."

She hesitates a moment.

"Okay," she replies. "We can meet at the Greenback's by your place. I can be there by nine."

I'm very relieved to hear that. "That sounds great. Thank you, Jennie."

. . .

Jennie Lou arrives at Greenback's a few minutes after nine. She's wearing a white blouse with a denim skirt, and her hair is tied back into a ponytail. Her flat expression makes it hard to read her mood. She seems guarded as she sits down across from me at the table.

"I'm sorry I'm late," she says briskly.

"It's all right. I only walked in a few minutes ago myself. What would you like? I'll go order it. It's on me."

"Before we do anything else, I need to say something," she interjects.

"Go ahead."

"I can't keep meeting you in person, alone, like this, Sean. We are friends, but I don't want to give you or anyone else the wrong idea about us."

That's a little surprising, but it's her choice.

"Okay," I reply. "That's fine."

She dips her head slightly and smiles. "Thank you. I'll have a large Americano with an extra shot of espresso."

I see I'm not the only one still needing to wake up some. I nod and go order the coffee. Soon, I return to our table with the caffeinated beverages.

"Thanks for the coffee," Jennie Lou says. She takes a whiff of the air. "Is that cinnamon?"

"Yes. I had them add some cinnamon syrup to my Catapultcino."

She nods. "Interesting choice."

We each take sips of our coffee.

"I want to apologize again for my actions," I begin. "I honestly don't know how to make things right between us, but I want to."

"You don't have to do anything to 'make things right,' Sean. And dwelling on our mistakes won't help either of us. I've already forgiven you."

I find that I can't maintain eye contact with her. I know she's right, that continuing to berate myself for my mistake is counterproductive. But I can't help feeling guilty.

"Thank you," I tell her. "That's more than I deserve."

"Sean, look at me."

That's not easy, either.

"Please, Sean. Look at me."

I take in a slow breath as I lift my head to face her.

"We'll still make the effort to be there for each other . . . right?"

"Yes," I reply.

"I want to learn who you are now," she insists.

"Even if you don't like it?" I ask.

She nods. "Even if I don't like it."

She seems a little stronger, more confident since the last time I saw her.

"Okay," I reply.

"And I want to share who I am with you, even if you don't like it," she tells me.

I nod. "That's only fair."

I can see her relaxing her shoulders. She takes another drink of her coffee. I do the same.

"I wasn't in a very good place emotionally when we found each other again," she confesses. "It took me completely by surprise."

"Me, too," I admit.

"I've had some time to think about all I said to you," she added. "And while every bit of it was true, it . . . probably wasn't the right time. I wish I'd focused more on being a friend." She then straightens up, looking more resolute. "That's what I want to do now."

I take another sip of my coffee and nod.

"Can I ask you something?" she says.

"Sure. Anything," I reply.

"I would like to know how you felt when things ended between us three years ago," she continues. "I didn't ask, and I should have."

Am I up for this? I guess I'll have to be. I asked for this meeting.

I give her a weak smile. "I kinda wish you hadn't asked that."

Her eyes flash with concern, then realization before she blushes in embarrassment.

"It was that bad?" she asks.

I sigh. "Yeah."

"I'm sorry."

I grip my cup a little tighter. "You were my first love . . . and . . . never mind."

"Go on?" she urges.

"You broke my heart . . . and I felt like it was my fault," I explain. "So, I'm having sort of a reverse deja vu."

"Reverse deja vu?"

"I broke your heart this time. And I'm still at fault."

She looks like she's becoming emotional. An awkward silence hovers between us.

"Can I ask what you decided about Kalea?" she says.

I knew she was going to ask about her at some point.

"We're a couple now," I reply gently. "We have been for a while."

She doesn't look happy at that, but at least she doesn't frown.

"Do you think she'll be okay with us being friends?" Jennie Lou asks.

I shrug. "I don't know. She's pretty mellow about most things. I'll let you know."

"Okay."

"For all I know, she might want to meet you."

She shakes her head. "I'm not sure I'm ready for that yet."

"Fair enough," I reply.

Jennie Lou stands up, now finished with her coffee.

"Going forward, let's keep our conversations to phone or text," she says. "That is, unless we're meeting with friends. Is that all right?"

"If that's what you want, sure."

We wave, and she thanks me again for the coffee.

With that, she exits the coffee shop.

12

PERFECT EVENING

I spend a few hours tidying up my place while listening to music. Currently, the *Ouch* album by Why Shark Why is playing. I enjoy the upbeat melodies and nonsensical lyrics. The title track "Ouch (I Need My Leg)" is about dealing with life's challenges, but from a silly point of view. Basically, its message is, "Don't create unnecessary drama in your own life; just deal with it like a normal person."

It's perfect background music as I sweep and mop the kitchen, then sanitize the counters. It gives me a focus that few other activities do. It's repetitive, goal-oriented, and low stress. I don't have to solve other problems if I'm dusting counters or vacuuming the carpet.

I hear the front door unlock while I'm wiping down the bathroom mirror. I know it's Kalea because she's the only other person who has a key.

"Hey, babe, I'm back!" she calls out. She sounds pleasant but kind of tired.

I finish one last stroke across the mirror and briskly walk to the living room. Upon seeing me, her eyes soften. She smiles, rushing to embrace me. We kiss, and she holds onto me tightly. I can feel her pounding heart. When she pulls back, I can see she's misty-eyed.

"Everything okay?" I wonder aloud.

"It is now. I really missed you," she replies. She looks so tender and sincere. "I'm sorry for the way I rushed off this morning."

She's cute when she's like this. I don't know what brings out this side of her so much recently, but I like it. It's endearing. It brings out my tender side, too.

"It's okay. You're back now," I assure her.

She rests her head against my shoulder. I slowly stroke her hair.

"Can I get you anything?" I ask. She turns around to look at me. "Water? Coffee? A snack?"

She blanches at the mention of coffee.

"Want to make a smoothie run instead?" she suggests.

"You like smoothies?" I reply. "I thought you were more of an ice cream person."

"It's true that I love ice cream, but I'm more in the mood for a smoothie today."

I nod. "Sounds good to me."

She kisses me once more. Then she heads into the bedroom.

"I'm gonna change clothes," she says. "I'll just be a minute." It takes more than a minute, but I don't mind. When she returns to the living room, I admire her deep blue sleeveless blouse, white skirt, and white sandals. After we go outside, she pulls indigo cat-eye sunglasses from her purse to complete the look.

There's a Smoothie Universe less than two blocks away. We're the only ones there.

"Welcome to Smoothie Universe!" says the squeaky-voiced teen behind the counter. She's tall, slender, and green-haired. "I'm Sandy. What can I get for you?"

There's a full-color menu under the glass counter. Kalea and I glance over it.

"Ladies first," I tell her.

"Okay," she replies with a grateful smile. Then she looks at Sandy. "Can I have a medium Cyclone?"

Sandy perks up. "Oh, those are great!" she raves.

I look at the menu. Three kinds of fruits and vegetables and a protein mix? Interesting choice.

"Uh, I'll go with a medium Dark Chocolate Banana," I tell Sandy.

"Another nice choice," Sandy says, tapping in my order. "You'll love it!"

"Thanks," I reply.

A few minutes pass before Sandy hands us our smoothies. Kalea and I sit at a corner table. We each sip our smoothies through blue straws. Kalea closes her eyes and smiles, clearly satisfied. I'm pretty happy with mine, too.

"So, what did you do while I was at work today?" Kalea says as she opens her eyes and focuses on me. "Besides cleaning, that is."

I take in a breath before answering. "I worked up the nerve to call Jennie this morning. We met briefly at Greenback's."

Kalea raises her eyebrows at that and leans back in her chair.

"Really? How did that go?" she asks.

"Pretty well, all things considered," I continue. "We both had things to apologize for."

Kalea leans forward again and takes another sip of her smoothie. She gestures for me to continue.

"We're still friends," I say. "I think we've settled things. About our past feelings, that is."

Now, Kalea ponders my words for a few moments. Then she gives me a worried look. "Do you think that's possible, Sean? You can accept her as just a friend? You told me you loved her."

"I did love her . . . but that's the past. I let her know you and I are together now."

She nods. "That's good. So, you believe she's let go?"

"I do."

Out of respect, Kalea tries to minimize her reaction by looking down quickly. But I still see the disbelief in her eyes. She probably thinks I'm being naive.

"Jennie wondered if you might have a problem with us remaining friends," I add.

Kalea smiles at that but says nothing.

"I told her you might actually want to meet her."

That elicits a facepalm from Kalea. "Why would you tell her that, Sean?"

"Well, I also told her I could be wrong," I add, shrugging.

Kalea laughs. "I suppose if you're going to be friends with her, I'll have to meet her sometime!"

"True."

She covers my hand with her own and looks me in the eyes with a bit of sternness.

"Let's make that later rather than sooner, okay, babe?"

"That's fine, Cinnamon."

. . .

The days and weeks continue to pass. Kalea keeps taking extra shifts. That leaves me with more free time than I'm used to. The weeknights I can handle; it's the weekends that are tough. I begin spending Saturday afternoons with Keith. I've learned that he's a baseball fan and also an amateur wood carver.

Today, we're at the Outta Here Dugout taking turns practicing at a batting cage. We've been here a couple of times already. It gives us a chance to talk while honing eye-hand coordination. And even though I'm terrible at batting—I'm lucky to hit the ball one out of four times—I have to admit it's pretty fun. And I'm getting better; at first, I couldn't hit it at all. What's helped is using my video game skills. Just like using blasters in *Knights of Kashyyyk*, I have to anticipate the target and aim in time.

I hear the clack of the automatic pitch. I tighten my grip on the bat, spot the ball, and swing. I miss.

"That's all right, Sean," Keith assures. "You were ready. You'll get it next time."

"Thanks."

He ends up being right. I do hit the next one, though it's technically a foul ball.

"What's the latest with you and Julia?" I ask.

"We've made progress, but there's been some challenges, too."

I swing and miss. "What kind of challenges?" I wonder.

"Through counseling, we've agreed on a few things: we love each other and our daughter. And we want to re-marry," Keith begins. "But Julia doesn't know if she wants to become a Christian. She has no opposition to my beliefs. She just doesn't see the importance of us having the same spirituality."

Another swing and miss. I hold up my hand, signaling I want to rest a minute. Keith walks over, and I hand him the bat.

"Isn't that something you can work out later?" I ask sincerely.

He grips the bat with his gloved hands, adjusts his stance, and plants his feet firmly.

"You would think so, but no. At least I don't think so," he replies. He swings. The ball bounces off in the wrong direction. Foul ball. "A marriage needs to start out with a solid foundation," Keith continues. "I believe that, for me and Julia, that foundation should be Jesus Christ. If He's at the center of our lives and we keep the focus on Him, our marriage will succeed. If we don't, then we'll have more problems."

He swings and gets a solid hit. It's not a home run, but if this were a real baseball game, he would have made it to second or third base.

"Keith, you know I respect you," I counter. "But I don't understand something. What does Jesus have to do with marriage?"

He smiles. "Would you believe me if I said 'everything'?"

"I'd ask you to elaborate. I know that Jesus claimed to be the Son of God, and He was crucified by the Romans. Believers like you think He was resurrected and is in Heaven now."

"All true, yes."

He swings and misses this time. He seems to be concentrating more on our discussion now.

"If Jesus is in Heaven, as you say, how can He help a marriage?" I ask.

"You used to be a believer," Keith replies as he swings and misses again. "So you know that to receive salvation, people pray to repent of their sins and ask Jesus to send His Holy Spirit into their hearts." He taps the ball with the bat. A bunt.

I nod. "I have seen people say they did that, yes. I never experienced it myself."

"Fair enough," he replies. "Well, I have experienced it. When I gave my life to Christ, the person I used to be died, and the Holy Spirit changed me. He cleaned my conscience from within and made me a new person. I face challenges and have temptations like anyone else, but I lean on the Lord now, and His Holy Spirit helps me get through them."

A stronger hit. He definitely could have made it to second base if he was fast enough.

"For the sake of discussion, I'll accept that," I offer. "I still don't see how that affects marriage?"

He swings and misses. "If two married Christians are letting themselves be led by the Holy Spirit, I believe Jesus will give them the grace and answers to whatever challenges they face. And that will help their love mature and grow."

That sounds really nice. But it also sounds like fantasy. I don't know how to respond. I don't want to sound like a jerk.

He swings, and I hear the loud crack as the bat connects. That would have been a home run.

"You want to give it another go?" Keith asks, offering me the bat.

"No, I'm good. Thanks."

. . .

Kalea calls me around five that afternoon. Her timing is good. I've been back at the apartment for a while and had time to shower and change. As a result, I'm in a good mood.

"I wanna do something special tonight," she suggests.

"Okay. What's the occasion?"

"Do we need an occasion to celebrate?" she asks playfully. "Actually, we've been going out for one hundred days. I thought that was a good enough reason."

Has it really been a hundred days already? I guess I can believe it. The time has been zooming by. And I've spent a lot of it with her.

"Sure!" I reply enthusiastically. "What did you want to do?"

"Let's chow down on Greek food first and . . . "

"And?"

"And I . . . *may* have scored tickets to Why Shark Why," she says mischievously.

My jaw drops. "They're in town? Tonight?"

"Yep," she replies confidently. "They're doing a special acoustic set at Aldo's, just for their Oklahoma area OwnMeNow supporters."

"You joined their OwnMeNow to do this? Is that why you've been working so much lately?"

"You could say that," she answers.

I suddenly realize that I haven't been paying attention to the Why Shark Why website and fan club emails for the last three months.

"We have front row seats," she adds. "But we can't be late. I'll be there soon, so dress up."

"I'll be ready," I reply, my excitement barely held in check.

. . .

I haven't been able to take my eyes off of Kalea since she arrived at my apartment. She styled her hair into a high ponytail and is sporting a curve-hugging, off-the-shoulder cobalt blue cocktail dress with soft white, low heel shoes. Completing the look is her deep rose-pink lipstick, sapphire earrings, and silver necklace with a few pearls woven into it. It's a positively stunning look.

She did her best to coordinate my clothing, but I still feel inadequate next to her. I'm wearing a black, long-sleeved shirt with a navy blue blazer, white slacks, and black dress shoes. I've slicked my hair back. She told me it looks cool, but I'm not sure I believe it.

"You really have no idea how handsome you are, do you?" she tells me. I shrug, and she gives me a reassuring kiss. "Believe me, I'm the lucky one tonight."

That's when I notice how tired she appears. Even though her makeup is flawless and almost covers the dark circles under her eyes, I can see past all that and discern what's going on. She's not feeling well. There are no signs of fever, but it could easily be exhaustion.

"Are you okay?" I ask.

"I'm a little tired. I worked from six till four today and didn't get much sleep last night."

Considering she worked late on Thursday and Friday, that's not good.

"You shouldn't push yourself," I tell her. "Do you work tomorrow?"

She shakes her head. "No. In fact, today was the very last extra shift. I'm done with all that."

That's a huge relief to me. I've been concerned about her doing so much overtime. The stress has clearly been getting to her.

I step forward and kiss her.

"That's great news," I say with a grin. She smiles back.

"I know you've been worried about me," she replies. "I'm sorry."

"It's just because—"

She kisses me this time. "I know."

Her kisses intoxicate me. I figure she's trying to distract me, so we can get out the door. But her health is important; I can't just ignore it.

"You know, we can just have a quiet evening at home, and I'd be just as happy. You wouldn't have to lift a finger."

She gives me an appreciative glance and a bright smile, despite her weariness. "That's very kind of you. But don't concern yourself with me anymore. We'll both have a wonderful time tonight. I've been looking forward to this for days."

She fixes my shirt collar. "I want you to know what you mean to me," she tells me. "How much I love you."

I do know how much she loves me. I see it in her smiles, the soft gazes, the way she talks to me—especially when we're alone. She has become so much of my world.

This is different from the way I felt about Jennie Lou. I crave Kalea when she's away, and I feel at peace when she's close like this. I want to be with her. I really care about her and want to be there for her. She gives me a stability I haven't had since my mother died. I don't know if that's what being in love is like, but I'd like to think it is.

. . .

We figured out that we didn't have time for the Greek restaurant. It had an hour-long wait just to get in, and the concert was only two hours away. We settled on the drive-thru at Burger Empire. We usually get a couple of single patty burgers. But today, Kalea gets a junior cheeseburger and barely eats half of it.

"I guess I'm not even hungry enough for this," she says with some surprise.

When we make it to Aldo's about forty-five minutes later, Kalea seems to have rebounded some. Her color is better, and she seems stronger. She pulls out her phone and shows the attendant the QR code for our tickets. The blond-haired gentleman scans the code and allows us to enter the building, a small but posh club with a floor-level wooden stage. It seats up to one hundred people. The ceiling is tall, and the walls are made of gray limestone. There's elaborate, colored lighting above the stage and HDTV screens mounted on the walls showing ads for upcoming shows.

The band's equipment is already set up. I see Lydia Kinn, the lead singer of Why Shark Why, at the back of the stage talking with the guitarist. I can't hear what they're saying, but they're looking over some papers together.

Other fans begin to enter the club, people of different ethnicities and, more surprisingly, different age groups. I guess all kinds of people listen to upbeat indie rock. Then the club's manager, a middle-aged tall and heavyset man with dark brown hair, walks up to the main microphone.

"Good evening, everyone," he says warmly in a deep voice with a British accent. "I'm Aldo Smith, the owner of this establishment. Aldo's is delighted—as we know you are—to have Why Shark Why with us tonight. And we are grateful for you, their fans, for your support of this great band and our business. You fifty are some truly special fans. The band wants to express their gratitude through a meet-and-greet before the actual show."

How much did Kalea pay for this privilege? This must have been too rich for the majority of local fans. I'm another level of impressed.

The full band walks into the room, led by Lydia. She's taller than I thought, and she's cut her raven hair to shoulder-length. Her forest green blouse is long, and with her black leggings and boots, it complements her pear-shaped figure. The barrel-chested drummer with long, blond hair—I think his name is Lars Pinklow—stumbles forward to shake my hand and say, "Thanks for coming." His alcohol-infused breath is noxious, but he seems otherwise pleasant.

Karl Steffanic is the guitarist. Short and trim, his flawless, long, red hair is slicked back and tied into a flowing ponytail. It accents the black, long-sleeved shirt he's wearing, along with his matching slacks and boots. He approaches Kalea instead of me and smiles salaciously at her.

"Glad you could make it, Miss," he says to her, taking her hand in his as if to kiss it. "Wanna lose the dweeb and meet me—"

Kalea's eyes narrow, and I hear her inhale sharply. But before she can tell him off, Lydia grabs Karl by the neck and yanks him away.

"Sorry, you two. I can't take this guy anywhere," Lydia says with an embarrassed smile as the two walk off. She speaks to him in a harsh whisper, but I overhear it. "Do you want another sexual harassment lawsuit? Now, either shut up and be nice, or wait backstage till the show gets started, got it?"

"Fine. I'll shut up and be nice," he replies in a matching tone.

I turn to check on Kalea.

"Are you okay, babe?" I ask.

"Yeah," she replies. "I've been hit on by worse. I just didn't expect that."

"Cool of Lydia to handle it for us."

"Yeah. She's really take-charge. I like that."

The bass player approaches me, smiles, and extends a hand.

"Hi, I'm Igor Allonsy," he says. "Sorry about Karl. He's kind of a work-in-progress as a human being."

The three of us share a laugh at that.

"Anyway, I'm glad you're here," he continues. "It's always great to meet the fans. I hope you both enjoy the show."

"Thanks," we both say.

Before long, the meet-and-greet settles down, and the band offers autographs. I brought my CD of the *Ouch* album, and the band signs the inside sleeve. Kalea and I also get to take selfies with Lydia, Igor, and the whole band. True to his word, Karl behaves around Kalea this time.

. . .

The acoustic set is dazzling. They open with the show with "Danger Kaleidoscope," a hyper tune that gets us all clapping along with the rhythm. The band follows up with two more fast numbers before slowing down with my favorite song of theirs, simply called "Why." Its lyrics are deep and sorrowful, a tragic love song whose end is a mystery. I find myself singing along softly, as do many others. I relate to this one emotionally; it resonates within me in a way I don't fully understand. I see Kalea looking at me with a wistful expression. When our eyes meet, she flashes an embarrassed smile and turns away. What was that about? I'll have to ask her later. When they move on to the next song, I almost want to ask them to play "Why" again.

Another ninety minutes blazes by, even with Lydia taking time between songs to tell us the history of the music or the band itself. This is such a rare experience for me. I've been to concerts before in stadiums and other large venues, but nothing as personal as this. Kalea has been recording a lot of this on her phone. I've been too excited, too nervous. She probably knows I'd record the ceiling or the top of someone's head instead of the band. I'm having a great time. And when I turn to catch glances of Kalea, she's usually looking at me with a smile on her face.

The show lasts forty more minutes, including two encore songs. Then Kalea and I return to my apartment.

. . .

I wake up in bed at about four in the morning and Kalea is next to me. She's on her side, leaning on her elbow, gazing at me lovingly. She freed her hair from the high ponytail when we returned, so it's flowing over her shoulders.

"You sleep yet?" I ask groggily.

She nods. "I got some sleep earlier, yes. Did I wake you?"

"No."

"Good."

She strokes my hair. It's very soothing, and I can tell sleep is reclaiming me.

"I love you, Sean," she whispers, kissing my lips softly.

I hear her get out of bed and walk to the bathroom to shower. Then things go black. My dreams are strange, passionate—and all have Kalea in them.

When I wake up again, hours later, she's gone.

13

FREEFALL

I don't hear from Kalea on Sunday. That's unusual. But given how tired she was on Saturday, I figure she could use a day to catch up on rest.

When Monday comes, I get to work a little early and don't see Kalea then, either. That's surprising, since her shift starts an hour before mine. I find Jessica, who looks distracted today. I ask if Kalea called in sick or something. She looks at me sadly, as though she knows something I don't.

"She didn't call in sick," Jessica says. "She quit. No notice, no real reason. All she said was that it's something she had to do."

I don't know what to think of that.

"She didn't say anything over the weekend about quitting work or changing jobs," I tell her.

I can see that Jessica is frustrated and hurt by Kalea's actions.

"I don't know what else to tell you," she replies. "She called in an hour and half ago."

"Thanks for letting me know, Jessica."

Next, I go find Ben. He's in the breakroom getting a cup of coffee. He glances my direction, and I can already tell he knows something, too.

"Do you know why Kalea quit?" I ask him, concerned.

"Dude, she didn't just quit. She's moving away," he replies, clearly uncomfortable.

"Moving away?" I repeat, not bothering to hide my shock. "Do you know where? Or why?"

He fidgets in place, putting his hands in his pockets as he looks away.

"Kalea called me and Jimbo over the weekend," Ben tells me. "She said she was moving real soon and that she was getting a moving truck. She asked for our help in loading it with her stuff. So, we went over yesterday and packed it all up for her."

He scratches behind his neck and looks at me with embarrassment.

"When you weren't there to help out, I kinda figured she hadn't told you yet," he admits. "But I was sure she'd say something to you before leaving."

"Do you know where she's going—or why?" I ask again.

"She didn't tell us," he explains. "I wish I knew, too. This was all very sudden."

"Do you know when she was leaving?" I wonder aloud.

"Soon, man. She may have left already."

I don't have time to reply. I just start briskly walking and before I know it, I'm jogging.

"I hope you catch her in time!" Ben shouts from behind me.

It takes me a minute to find Jessica again. The way I'm running around, I startle her as I catch her near her office.

"Sean, what's wrong?" she says.

"Kalea," I pant. "She's leaving town . . . right now. I don't know why . . . I have to stop her!"

"Go," she tells me, pointing toward the stairway. "Hurry!"

"I'll make up the time!"

"Don't worry about that. Just go!"

The thirty minutes it takes to reach Kalea's house are anxiety-filled. I definitely can't explain my trepidation to the PayMeRide driver. He just cruises along listening to USPR's ultra-passionless news reports playing on his radio.

I feel a chill in my heart as we approach Kalea's townhouse. There's an unfamiliar car in the driveway, and the door to her home is open. Even from the street, I can see that there's no furniture inside, confirming what Ben said.

I walk across the lawn to the open doorway and knock on the doorframe a few times.

"Who is it?" a gruff man's voice answers from across the living room.

"I'm Sean Winter, Kalea's boyfriend."

I hear his steps echo hauntingly as he walks through the kitchen; then they muffle into soft footfalls once he enters the living room. When he approaches the doorway, he appears to be in his early-to-mid sixties. He's wearing a white dress shirt, blue jeans, and tennis shoes. He's slender, almost six feet tall, and his silver hair is going white on the sides. He initially has a stern expression. But as he continues to look at me, I detect a hint of compassion in his small eyes.

"You missed her, son," he tells me. "She left about two hours ago with the moving truck. She told me she sold her car online to help pay for the move. I've never seen someone in such a hurry to leave a good home. Then again, I suppose that's none of my business."

I stare at him in disbelief. He waits a few seconds and extends his hand.

"I'm Dan Miller, the landlord."

I accept his handshake, but I can barely feel it. I'm having a hard time feeling anything at the moment.

"Wherever she went, she had this well-planned," Dan says, leaning against the doorframe. He turns his head, looks inside the empty space for a second, and returns his gaze to me. "She contacted me a month ago to let me know she was terminating her lease. She paid the fees this morning and cleaned the place out real good. She was a good tenant. Honestly, I didn't want her to go. She always paid on time or early."

A month ago? She's been planning this for at least thirty days and didn't say a word to me? What's going on?

"Thanks, Dan," I say as I shake his hand again.

I book a ride back home. I'm in complete shock. I can only focus on one thing at a time, and even that's a challenge at the moment. Sitting in the back seat, I try to call Kalea. It rings long enough to go to voicemail. Can she not answer because she's driving? I try a couple more times and finally decide to leave a voicemail.

"Kalea, it's Sean. I know you're moving," I say. I'm trying to sound confident and in control. But I'm not. My voice wavers as I speak. "Kalea . . . call me. Let me know what's going on. Please."

Surely, she has to stop and take a break sometime. Won't she check her messages then?

The PayMeRide drops me off in front of the Prosaic building. Jessica sees me and hurries over.

"Did you find her?" she asks.

"She's gone," I tell her, feeling defeated. "She's taken all of her belongings and is . . . gone. Ben, Jimbo—nobody knows where or why."

"Take the rest of the day off, Sean," Jessica tells me.

"I . . . I said I'd make up the time . . . " That sounds so hollow when I say it.

Why is it such an effort to hold my head up? Even focusing my eyes on Jessica is hard. I'm squinting for no reason. I got some bad news, but I shouldn't let it affect me like this. I notice that Jessica is looking at me even more sympathetically now.

"I appreciate that, but you're no good to me—or our customers—like this," she says. "I'll comp you the time. Don't worry about it. Just go home and work through this. If you need to take tomorrow, too, let me know."

"Why are you, um—"

"Being so nice? Look, Sean, I just lost one good employee. I don't want you getting yourself fired over a breakup."

I don't quite understand what she means, but I accept it.

"Thanks," I tell her.

I slowly trudge home. My mind floods with memories of all the wonderful times I spent with Kalea: laughing together, holding one another, savoring each other's presence. All of the passion and joy.

Was it just a lie?

Then I think about Saturday night. Kalea insisted on taking me to see my favorite band, even though she was so exhausted. Was that her version of a goodbye—to do something really wonderful for me, spend most of the night with me, and then leave town the next day with no explanation?

Each time I take a step in the direction of my apartment, my feet feel heavier and heavier. I bump into a woman on the sidewalk and can barely mumble "sorry" as I continue on. Sheer force of will is the only thing that keeps from dropping to my knees or passing out. I don't know if it's day or night. I just have to make it home.

By the time I enter my apartment and collapse on the couch, the numbness starts to wear off. I have time to think. And that's when my emotions swell within me, threatening to burst through.

I miss her so much already! Am I really never going to see her again? Is this some kind of test for me, to see if I'll stay true to her? I don't know. And I really need to know.

So much has happened on this couch. It was so dull and lifeless when I first moved in. It was functional. A thing I used to watch TV, listen to music, or sit on and eat my meals. That all changed when Kalea and I started going out. How many movies did we watch here together? How many times did we make out?

I learned so much just talking and laughing with her. I came alive as a person. I forgot my loneliness, forgot the pain of the past. The present became everything. Kalea became everything to me. And now she's gone. With no explanation. Why? Was it me? If it was, what did I do to drive her away?

Somewhere along the way, I forgot about Sparky. I guess I didn't need him anymore. I had Kalea. I . . . had a life.

The warmth of my retrospection is replaced by the leeching coldness of Kalea's absence. It stabs at my insides and feeds my insecurities. I start to feel like less than nothing.

"I didn't even merit a goodbye from the woman I love."

Great. I finally said I love her. To myself. After she's gone.

Could it really have been love if I had never said those words to her? And why didn't I? She said it to me plenty of times.

And yet, she's off to who-knows-where with some big plan I know nothing about.

I sigh.

You know, thinking about this situation now, it wouldn't have taken much to satisfy me.

"I made a mistake, Sean," I imagine her saying. "It was fun; but I realized I don't actually love you, and I need to move on."

"I've got a great opportunity to start up my own business in France. I won't ask you to come with me, but I have to do this. I'm sorry. Let's still be friends, okay?"

"This isn't working. You're a jerk, and I hate you. Bye."

Any of those would have ripped me to shreds, but they would have given me some understanding of what was going through her head. I might not have agreed with it, but it would have brought more closure than this. It's hard to have closure when you're given nothing to work with.

The sad bleakness and misery slowly transform into anger. Still sitting on the couch and staring at the skyline through my glass balcony door, the twilight sky darkens the room like my mood.

How could Kalea do this to me? Doesn't she know how selfish and cruel this is? How could she abandon me if she loved me? And I know she really loved me! I felt it! So why? What could be so important that she had to leave like this? How dare she! She said she'd always protect me! How can she do that if she's not here?

I lay back on the couch, overwhelmed by my emotions. Tears stream down my face, and I don't care. A cold hole within me is threatening to drain away all that I have left. It gnaws at me and taunts me with her name. *Kalea! Where is Kalea?*

I want to reach out to her with both arms and feel her warm embrace, but it's not possible. The void laughs at me. *She's not there. Guess she didn't love you after all.* In my thoughts, I curse at it and fight to drive it away. One moment I win, but it always comes back. As my tears start to dry, hot, new ones coat my cheeks.

Without even thinking, I pound the couch's back cushion several times and abruptly stop. *What good did that do?*

For some time after that, I drift in and out of sleep.

. . .

My phone rings, waking me up. I see that it's Keith.

"Yeah?" I answer groggily.

"Sean, I heard about Kalea and that you went home," he says. "Are you okay?"

"Not . . . even . . . close."

I tell him the small amount of information that I know.

"Sean, I don't even know where to begin. I'm so sorry this has happened," he says.

"Me, too," I reply.

"I just finished here at work. I can come over if you want."

Part of me still wants to be alone, but my intelligence wins out. It would be a terrible idea to spend this whole day alone with my thoughts and feelings.

"I'd like that. Come on over."

"Cool. I can be there in about fifteen minutes."

I already know I'm going to make awful company. But he knows that, too, and he still wants to come over. That's why he's my friend.

. . .

"I tried to tell her we weren't the Internal Revenue Service, but she wouldn't let me get a word in," Keith says, shrugging. Then he switches to a mock-stern expression. "She says, 'Sir, I'll have you know I've paid my taxes in full every year since 1982. But I keep getting calls from some people who insist they're with the IRS and that if I don't pay what I owe, I could be arrested. I want to speak to someone in charge about this!' And finally, she paused. So, I told her, 'Ma'am, it sounds like a scam call. Those people weren't with the IRS. They just want to trick you into giving out your credit card or bank information.'"

It was a pretty amusing story. And Keith was doing what I imagine was a good impression of the caller.

"So how did she respond to that?" I ask.

"She said, 'Well, it's a good thing I hang up on them every time!' And I said, 'Yes, ma'am.' She wrapped up with, 'So I'm not in trouble with the IRS then?' And I said, 'It doesn't sound like it to me. You have a good day, ma'am.'"

"You handled that one like a real pro, Keith."

"Thanks," he replies. "I'm just glad she didn't get scammed."

"Sounds like a feisty, old lady," I add with a slight smile.

I appreciate Keith's efforts. He's trying really hard to cheer me up. But given my mood, I think he'd be more effective at cheering up the couch pillows. It's not his fault or a lack of effort. I'm kind of a lost cause today.

Wisely, he doesn't say a word about his relationship with Julia or his religion. I'm glad that he cares enough about me to be sensitive to what I'm going through and who I am. I really am grateful. I hope I can convey that properly someday.

"Hey, I was gonna go for a drive," Keith tells me. "Wanna come along?"

"Where to?" I ask.

"I dunno," he answers. "Sometimes, I just go drive to get some fresh air and clear my head."

That sounds good right now. "Okay."

We head outside to his new Chevy truck, and he unlocks the doors. A minute later, he drives out Interstate 40 and then takes 44 over the Oklahoma River. Somehow, my thoughts find their way back to Kalea's car, a used 2010 Toyota Tercel. It was blue, of course.

"Why haven't you learned to drive yet, Sean?" she asked me once.

"It hasn't been important," I had answered. "I don't mind taking the bus or getting a PayMeRide. And most places I need are within walking distance."

She would usually give me a side-glance and smirk. "A car's too expensive for you right now, huh?"

"That, too," I had admitted.

"I understand. It was a long time before I could afford a car. But it was worth it. I saved up for the down-payment. With that and working full-time, I was approved."

I could spend whole car rides looking at her. She knew I'd do that, but I guess it flattered her. She acted like she didn't mind. I memorized every line and curve of her face and body. Sometimes I wished I had her artistic ability. I'd paint immortal portraits that would take the world by storm. It would help people perceive what I saw in Kalea Nadeaux.

Eventually, I have to force myself to stop thinking about her. I don't want to fall apart again, especially in front of a friend.

"Got any music?" I ask him. "I'm not choosy, just something for the ride, y'know?"

Keith smiles. "Sure! Give me a second."

He turns on the radio and presses the CD button. Some instrumental guitar music starts to play. It's probably some Christian tune, but I don't care about that right now. The music is nice. Soothing, really. I close my eyes and get lost in it.

I feel so empty right now, like more than half of me is missing.

I guess it is.

. . .

I ignore Jessica's advice and go to work the next day. I need to restore some semblance of normalcy, some kind of schedule. If I spend another day trying to work out my feelings without any additional information about Kalea, I'll just drive myself nuts like yesterday. I spend an hour before my shift psyching myself up for the day. Then I get a double-shot Catapultcino from Greenback's Coffee on the way in.

My idea mostly works. The calls keep my mind on business and procedure. But every now and then, I find myself looking at where Kalea used to sit. I know she won't be there. I know it's pointless. But I do it anyway because I can't help it. Aside from that, I keep taking calls straight through break.

Jessica clears her throat behind me as I finish a call. She puts up a hand, indicating I need to stop. I put my system in "stand-by" mode and take off my headset.

"What is it, Jessica?"

"It's almost one," she says. "Take a lunch."

"Can I take one or two more calls first?"

She shakes her head. "No. I will remind you now that we are legally obligated to give you a lunch break. And you are legally obligated to take one. So *take* it, okay?"

I sigh. "Okay, okay."

She stands and watches as I log out of my computer, lock my desk, and walk to the breakroom.

I barely have an appetite. And all of the eateries around here remind me of times I went there with Kalea. A soda and granola bar from the vending machines will do just fine today.

I make it through the rest of the day and try to focus on calling Jennie Lou when I get home.

"Gone? What do you mean 'Kalea's gone?'" she asks.

"I missed her by two hours," I tell her over the phone. "Kalea had two friends pack up her belongings in a moving truck Sunday, and she left yesterday morning."

There's a moment of silence.

"You had no idea she was going to do this. Sean, I'm so sorry. I can listen. Tell me what you're feeling."

"Remember that tornado I told you about when we met again?"

"Of course."

"This is much worse. As scary and damaging as it was, it had an end. I knew what caused it. This? I have no answers, and I know it's just beginning."

She listens to me as I ramble on. "I feel like it's happening again," I say through my sobs.

"What's happening again?" she asks sincerely in her Peppermint Patty voice.

I try to find the right words. It takes a moment. "Everyone leaves me, Jennie Lou. You're the only one who ever came back."

"Everyone? I don't understand."

"My mom left me when she died in a car accident," I explain. "Then you left me. My grandparents left me when they died. And now . . . "

"Now Kalea, the woman you gave your heart to, does the same thing," she sympathizes.

"I didn't just give her my heart, Jennie," I say through my sobbing. "I gave her everything! All of myself—my free time, my body, my hopes and dreams! Literally everything!"

Jennie Lou pauses at that.

"And now she's gone," she finally says.

"I don't know why this happened, so I don't know what to do!" I shout loudly. Then I calm myself down a little. "I don't know how to feel."

I can almost feel her compassion through the phone. I hear hints of her own soft, tearful sighs.

"You shouldn't be alone. Do you want me to call Keith or . . . someone?" she asks.

"No," I urge, resisting the urge to chuckle. "I was poor enough company with Keith yesterday. I can't do that to him again."

"The only other thing I can think of is . . . maybe Hopes and Prayers? I could call a few volunteers, and we could meet?"

I laugh. I don't mean anything by it. She's making a real effort to help but being prayed over by her and strangers is the last thing I want or need. I just can't take anymore. If what she's offering is all that's left to me, it feels as pathetic as I am. I force back the absurdity of it all and calm myself as best I can.

"I don't think so, Jennie," I tell her, sounding somewhat hoarse. "Sorry for the way I—anyway, I'll get through this somehow."

"Sean, don't—"

"Good night. I'll . . . call you soon."

. . .

A month passes. During that time, I've texted Kalea every single day and gotten no responses. I'm not blocked; she just won't answer. I've probably left fifty voicemails. Nothing.

I've managed to get through the days, but the nights have been slowly stripping me of my pride and resolve. It's like being constricted tighter and tighter by an emotional python.

I stopped letting Jennie Lou and Keith spend so much time with me. It really helped the first couple of weeks, but I could see the toll it was taking on them. I decided it wasn't fair to them.

I've also had to admit to myself that I'm addicted to Kalea, physically and emotionally. And I've been experiencing serious withdrawal. Every hour of every day is living in continual heartache. The depression is bad enough, but my longing for her is torturous. It's slowly beaten me down into a shell of who I was. I can't keep going like this. I can't endure it.

I know she will never return my calls or texts. I accept I'll never know her reasons for leaving. I have no idea where she is or how to find out.

The normal world seems so far away now. I look at the wall clock and see that it's eight in the evening. It must be Saturday. I don't work Saturdays. It's always the single longest day of the week.

I want it all to stop—all the pain, languishing, the endless circle it's become to me.

I still don't own a car, so I can't use that. And I don't own a gun. I consider hanging myself or dropping off a building. But I don't want to suffer the horror of slow asphyxiation or the terror of jumping from a high altitude.

I decide there's only one solution. Ironically, I owe the idea to my grandparents and a three-year-old memory. *That* memory. The one that haunts me every day of my life.

. . .

I was back home from college for a visit, and Grandma was in another one of her foul moods. Grandpa went into action quickly and brought her some of her favorite whiskey. She was grateful for it and soon calmed down, becoming playful with Grandpa and ignoring me. A little later, she even took the bottle with her to her evening bath while Grandpa and I watched television in the living room. After some time, it registered with him that something was wrong.

"Sean, how long you figure we've been watching the show?" he had asked me.

I looked at the wall clock. "Almost an hour."

He stood up, alarmed. "The longest your grandma's ever taken in the bath is maybe thirty minutes. I better go check on her."

I stayed where I was. But after Grandpa didn't come back in five minutes, I went to check on him. As I approached the bathroom, the door was half-open, and I saw Grandpa on his knees by the bathtub, sobbing like a baby.

"Grandpa, what's wrong?"

When he couldn't answer due to his crying, I stepped forward and saw Grandma. Her whole head was still underwater—her eyes closed—and she wasn't moving. It took a few seconds for me to comprehend that she was actually dead.

"Debra, I'm so sorry!" Grandpa had cried. "I just wanted to help you; I didn't mean for this—"

He choked on the last word and started crying again. I didn't know what to do, so I went back to the living room. I heard Grandpa half-stumble back to their bedroom and yank open a drawer, where I knew he kept a revolver for self-defense.

Then I heard a shot, followed by a crash when Grandpa hit the ground. I ran to him, but it was too late. One bullet to his right temple had accomplished its deadly purpose.

I didn't know how long I hopelessly cradled his bloodied body in my arms before the police arrived. But it was the last day I stayed in that house. After I explained what I knew to the authorities, I avoided anything family-related. I couldn't even bring myself to attend the funerals. All I was able to do was focus on finishing college at OU.

. . .

IN THE PRESENT

Trapped in my misery, I'm too much of a coward to risk drowning like Grandma. But I can buy whiskey. I still have a pathetic tolerance, and that will help.

It only takes ten minutes to walk to the liquor store around the corner and buy the alcohol. I chose a fifth of eighty-proof whiskey. That should be strong enough. It takes less than ten minutes to return home.

A few weeks ago, Keith let me borrow the instrumental music CD from his car, since I liked it so much. I want to be as comfortable as possible. I haven't had anything to eat since breakfast.

I take a sip and lean back against the couch. The liquid burns on the way down. After a few more drinks, I start to feel warm all over. I'm determined to take my time and be consistent.

It isn't long before I start to feel buzzed. Then I'm in a really pleasant stupor. I continue on, feeling sleepy now. I fight that feeling; I don't want to pass out yet. I push myself further and further, past what I know is my limit.

I can tell I'm in trouble when I can't tell up from down, whether I'm conscious or not. I'm beginning to have trouble catching my breath. And that scares me.

What am I doing? Do I really want to die because of this? Do I really want my existence to be over?

If I'm truly an atheist, this is the end. No afterlife. No do-overs.

If I die, I'll never get any answers from Kalea. And if she finds out I committed suicide, she'll probably blame herself.

Good.

No. I don't mean that.

Whatever her reasons, I still love her. At least, I think I love her. We were so close just a month ago, closer than any friends. As close as two people can get. There's so much I'm unsure about. No matter her reasons for leaving, she did say she loved me. And if she loved me, isn't that enough reason to keep living even if it hurts?

I can redouble my efforts. I can find her! I just have to try hard enough!

But I can't do anything if I'm dead.

That thought swirls through my head over and over as I drift through this dark haze.

That's when the truth hits me. *I don't want to die anymore!*

I try to make myself sit up. If I can get some food and water in me, maybe I can clear this out of my system. I'll be crazy hungover tomorrow, but at least I'll be alive.

No! I can't make my body work like I want it to. I put all my strength into my arms, and I'm so sluggish, all I've managed to do is land my hands in my lap. I can't move to the left or right. It's hard enough to keep my eyes open. I can sort of see my phone on the coffee table, but I can't make myself lean forward to reach it. I have a terrible dread wash over me. *I'm going to die, anyway!*

"*You don't have to die.*"

Who said that?

I'm so drunk, I can't even tell if someone is in the room with me or not.

"*You have a lot to live for,*" the soft voice tells me, whoever it is. "*Grab your phone. Call Jennie Lou.*"

Somehow, the sound of this voice calms me down. I feel weightless. I know the danger is still here, but I'm not afraid anymore.

Who are you? I ask in my thoughts, since I'm unable to speak.

The comforting feeling permeates the entire room. It's amazing.

"*You know Who I am. I have always been here, Sean. Go ahead; pick up the phone and call Jennie Lou. Don't be afraid; you can do it.*"

I try to move forward again. This time, I feel Someone gently push me forward until I can grab my phone and pull it toward me. Then I don't feel the presence anymore.

But it was enough. In my hazy state, I don't question it. I'm just grateful.

I manage to unlock the phone and stab at the call feature. Jennie Lou is number three on my autodial, and I hit it hard with my finger. I put the phone to my ear and hear it dialing her number. I'm so glad when she answers.

"Sean? I'm glad to hear from you—"

"He'p!" I manage to blurt out.

"What was that?"

"Jen . . . neeeed . . . he'p! Pleez!"

The room spins. I feel my cheek strike the coffee table, and I crumple to the ground, along with the phone. I can't open my eyes. I have no strength anymore. And though I can't understand what Jennie Lou is saying, she sounds frantic.

Then I lose consciousness.

14

COMING TO TERMS

The next thing I'm aware of is how cold I am. Slowly, I gain enough strength to open my eyes. Everything is blurry at first, but after a moment, I can see more clearly. There are blue curtains surrounding the bed I'm in, which has its side-railings raised. When I look down toward my chest, I see I'm in a light blue hospital gown. This looks like an emergency room.

My cheek is really sore. I touch it with my right hand and feel the bandage over it. I move my left arm and realize there's an intravenous line attached to it. I feel so groggy and weak.

A middle-aged, red-haired nurse enters through the curtain to check my vitals.

"Feeling better?" she asks me. Her name tag reads "Celeste."

"Y-yeah," I manage to say.

"You had a blood alcohol level of .23," the older woman says sternly. "Were you trying to kill yourself?"

I'm still confused, and my memory is hazy. I got that drunk? Why?

Then a memory of Kalea flashes in my mind. She's gone; she left. I must have . . .

"No," I lie. "My girlfriend left me. I . . . wanted to get really drunk."

She raises an eyebrow at that but doesn't immediately comment. She checks my temperature, blood pressure, and heart rate instead.

"You succeeded," she finally replies. "If your friends hadn't brought you in when they did, you probably would have died."

"Friends?"

"A man and woman about your age," Celeste tells me. "They're still in the waiting room. I'll tell them you're awake, but you can't see them just yet. Dr. Elvey needs to talk with you first."

That fills me with some dread until he comes in a few minutes later. The doctor is short, African American, and has a deeply receding hairline. Perhaps in his forties and slim, he stands close to my bed and looks at me with concern for a few seconds.

"Mr. Winter, you are very fortunate," the doctor begins. "You took in an acute amount of alcohol, but you don't appear to have any long-term poisoning effects."

"It was my first time drinking so much," I admit. "I . . . made a big mistake."

He nods. "Yes, you did, sir. But thankfully, you're still here. That could have been fatal. Now, I have to ask you a few questions to determine our next steps."

We spend the next fifteen minutes discussing my evening and state of mind.

"Yes, I was depressed over Kalea—that's my girlfriend—leaving me," I admit to the doctor. "And that's why I started drinking. I just didn't think it would . . . go south like it did."

I quickly determine that it isn't in my best interest to volunteer that I was attempting to commit suicide. "Like I told the nurse, I made a mistake."

Dr. Elvey nods, but he looks like he's still assessing me.

"I, um . . . I actually have a lot going for me," I add. "I graduated college not long ago and landed a job at Prosaic Industries."

"Do you like your job there?" he asks.

"I do. I've got an apartment right down the street from it. It's a solid."

I can tell he still doesn't buy my whole story, even though it's laced with the truth. But he must be accepting some of it.

"Can your friends in the waiting area take you home?" he asks. "And maybe stay with you a while?"

"Sure." I nod. "You can ask them, Doctor. They should agree."

He nods back. "I'll have a nurse do that. I want to keep you another hour or so, just long enough for that I.V. to finish replenishing your fluids."

"All right."

"I also recommend you consider counseling for your depression, Mr. Winter," he says. "We all need help sometimes. There's no shame in that."

"Okay," I say without meaning it.

We shake hands, and he leaves.

A few minutes after that, Celeste opens the curtain to let Jennie Lou and Keith in. They both rush to my side. Jennie Lou's face is a mixture of devastation and pure relief. Keith looks worried.

"Sean, are you okay?" Jennie Lou peers deeply into my eyes. Standing over me as she is, it's kind of intense. I'm just glad she's here.

"I think I will be," I tell her. "Thanks for getting me here."

"I called Keith, and he met me outside your apartment," she replies. "We knocked on the door, but you wouldn't answer."

"That's when I forced the door open," Keith interjects. "I'll probably need to replace your lock."

I think I manage some kind of smile at that. "No worries, man."

Jennie Lou takes my right hand in both of hers. She's close to tears.

"What happened, Sean?" she asks.

"I can't tell you the whole story here," I confess, switching to a whisper. "Or they won't let me leave. But I'll tell you this: it's never going to happen again."

Jennie Lou embraces me and whispers, "I'm so glad to hear that!"

It takes almost ninety minutes to get me discharged from the hospital. I make the co-pay with money from my savings, and Keith drives me home. Jennie Lou follows us in her car.

As it turns out, Keith didn't break the lock on my front door. After I secure it behind us, we go to sit down on the couch in the living room. Keith goes to turn on more lights than what I'd left on. I don't mind, since the previous atmosphere was toxic and depressing, anyway.

I still feel awful—a lousy combination of nausea and wooziness. The lights feel too bright, and my head feels like I just pried it out of a vise. And it's still sore.

Jennie Lou goes into the kitchen and gets us some bottled water from the refrigerator. Then she grabs a pillow from my bedroom and slides it behind my back where I'm sitting. She still looks so worried. Keith sits next to me, and Jennie Lou sits down in a nearby chair.

I look at each of them warmly. It's good to have them both here right now.

"I really am grateful for both of you," I tell them. "You're the only ones I still have, the ones I can depend on."

Keith smiles at that, and Jennie Lou nods in relief.

"You know I've been going crazy since Kalea left," I say. "Today, I'd finally had enough. I was going to die, and I had my grandparents' example to inspire my plan."

"What does that mean?" Keith asks.

I take a breath. "My grandfather always soothed my grandmother's foul moods by getting her drunk. The last time he did, she passed out in the bathtub and drowned."

"I didn't know she died like that," Jennie Lou says, looking downward.

"When Grandpa realized he'd accidentally killed her, he went downstairs and shot himself."

"You . . . you were there?" Keith asked, looking sad.

I nod. "I saw the whole thing. I still have nightmares about it sometimes."

"That's . . . awful," Jennie Lou says, looking at me sympathetically. "But—"

"I didn't want to drown or shoot myself," I say, answering her unspoken question. "But I knew alcohol would do instead."

Both Keith and Jennie Lou look at a loss for words.

"Remember, my mother died when I was young," I continue. "And even though my grandparents provided shelter and the essentials, they didn't give me any emotional stability. They called themselves Christians, but they drank and cursed. They lied to me and others. They were . . . abusive."

Not wanting to hide anymore, I unbutton my shirt suddenly and pull it halfway off. It exposes the burn scars from cigarettes that dot my lower neck, chest, and upper arms. Keith squints and looks down. Jennie Lou's eyes are wide, and she puts her hand to her mouth as she gasps.

"My grandmother did this to me as punishment," I add. "In the end, they ended up killing each other. Getting away from them to finish college was the best thing that ever happened to me."

Tears are streaming down Jennie Lou's face. "Sean, I had no idea. I'm so sorry!"

Keith looks at me with a hardened expression. "I suspected something like this, but . . . not this bad."

"Kalea saw this the night we met," I tell them. "She told me she understood and asked me to trust her. She told me she wanted to protect me, that she would keep my secrets. And she did. She never told anyone."

There's silence for another several seconds. Jennie Lou nods knowingly.

"But then she left you, too," she says.

"She had secrets of her own," I declare. "I just didn't know how many."

"I still don't understand why she left without telling you," Keith says.

Welcome to the club, my friend.

"That's why I've been torturing myself all this time, trying to figure that out," I resume. "But she cut off all ways of finding out. That's why I had no choice but to give up on Kalea. And when I did that, I gave up on myself. I saw no future."

Jennie Lou looks like she's going to say something, but I shake my head.

"I really did think I wanted to end my life, but something incredible happened," I tell them, thinking back to those fateful moments.

"What do you mean?" Jennie Lou asks. Keith looks equally curious.

"After I had drunk all that liquor and it was taking effect, I got scared," I reply. "I decided I didn't want to die, but it was almost too late. I was too sluggish; I could barely move at all. Then I heard a Man's voice. It told me comforting things. It told me I didn't have to die; I had a lot to live for. And it told me to call you, Jennie."

Jennie Lou's eyebrows raise. "A Voice told you to call *me*?"

I nod. "But I was too intoxicated to do it. I felt Someone push me forward. That's how I grabbed the phone to call you."

I can feel my emotions swelling within me. But for the first time, it's not anxiety, fear, or self-loathing. It's gratitude and relief.

"I couldn't see anyone, but I knew He was there. I asked Who He was," I explain. "He said I already knew; that He'd always been here and not to be afraid. Then He kept encouraging me to call you, Jennie Lou. He told me I could do it, and I did."

I close my eyes and lower my head. I put my hand to my face and feel my own tears. I remember the feeling of comfort and bliss in those moments and begin to chuckle. I put my hand down and look at my friends.

"I guess I can't call myself an atheist anymore if God saved my life," I share with them.

Jennie Lou hugs me, and I can feel her shaking. I don't know if that's shock, relief, or happiness, but I won't question it. Keith puts his hand on my shoulder.

"That's an amazing testimony, Sean!" he says.

I take a few moments to calm down. Jennie Lou does, too.

"I know there's a God now, and I'm grateful He kept me from dying. But there's something I still don't understand."

"What's that?" Keith asks.

"I'm glad for Christians like you two, believe me. So, how come there are Christians like my grandparents?"

Keith considers my question a moment. Jennie Lou remains quiet.

"That's a good question," Keith replies. "I think Jesus gave us the best answer. It's found in the book of Matthew in the Bible in chapter seven and verse thirteen. He said, 'Enter ye in at the strait gate: for wide is the gate, and broad is the way, that leadeth to destruction, and many there be which go in thereat: Because strait is the gate, and narrow is the way, which leadeth unto life, and few there be that find it.'

"Jesus also said in Matthew 7:21-23, 'Not every one that saith unto me, Lord, Lord, shall enter into the kingdom of heaven; but he that doeth the will of my Father which is in heaven. Many will say to me in that day, Lord, Lord, have we not prophesied in thy name? and in thy name have cast out devils? and in thy name done many wonderful works? And then will I profess unto them, I never knew you: depart from me, ye that work iniquity.'"

I don't think I've ever heard those passages before. Jesus said those things? Then again, now that I recall, Jesus didn't like hypocrisy in the church. He threw the money changers out of the temple. He spoke against the Pharisees and Sadducees of His time because He said they weren't doing God's will. They wanted to kill Him for that and because Jesus said He was equal with God.

"So, are you saying my grandparents . . . weren't Christians?" I ask.

"That's not for me to say," Keith answers quickly. "God will judge them, not me. But I can tell you this much: someone who is living for God would never do what they did to you."

That's strangely comforting. I accept that. Let God judge them, not me. I need to let go of all those years of hurt. Somehow, I know I need to forgive them and move on with my life. Kalea, too. It's not worth holding onto my pain anymore. That's what nearly killed me.

"I'm just glad to be alive," I share. "My problems are still here, and I'm a mess. I don't want to miss Kalea anymore, but I do. I don't want to be depressed, but I am. I need help."

Jennie Lou smiles. "Sean, we're going to be here for you."

They certainly have been. I couldn't have asked for more steadfast, loyal friends.

We talk well into the night.

"I have to insist you two go home and get some sleep," I tell them. "Maybe we three could meet tomorrow and have lunch or dinner and talk some more?"

"I'm up for that," Jennie Lou replies.

"Me, too," Keith adds. "You pick the place, and we'll meet there, okay?"

"All right. It's settled then."

"If you need to, you can call me, Sean. Anytime," Keith tells me.

"I feel the same way," Jennie Lou concurs.

We share a group hug, and then they go.

. . .

Keith left me his King James Bible and suggested I read through the book of John. I've been sitting on the couch with all the lights on pondering whether to pick up the Bible lying beside me. After a few minutes, I flip through the pages until I get to John.

John 1:1-5 caught my attention. "In the beginning was the Word, and the Word was with God, and the Word was God. The same was in the beginning with God. All things were made by him; and without him was not any thing made that was made. In him was life; and the life was the light of men. And the light shineth in darkness; and the darkness comprehended it not."

Then I remember what the Voice said to me: "You know Who I am. I have always been here, Sean."

He is *always* with me.

I continue reading and come across this in John 1:29-33: "'The next day John seeth Jesus coming unto him, and saith, Behold the Lamb of God, which taketh away the sin of the world. This is he of whom I said, After me cometh a man which is preferred before me: for he was before me. And I knew him not: but that he should be made manifest to Israel, therefore am I come baptizing with water.'

"'And John bare record, saying, I saw the Spirit descending from heaven like a dove, and it abode upon him. And I knew him not: but he that sent me to baptize with water, the same said unto me, Upon whom thou shalt see the Spirit descending, and remaining on him, the same is he which baptizeth with the Holy Ghost.'"

Was that what happened to me? Did I encounter the Holy Ghost? Is that Who gave me the strength to move and call Jennie Lou for help?

I'm so fascinated, I have to read more. I read the third chapter several times to truly comprehend what Jesus was saying to Nicodemus:

Verses eleven and twelve really stick out to me. "'Verily, verily, I say unto thee, We speak that we do know, and testify that we have seen; and ye receive not our witness. If I have told you earthly things, and ye believe not, how shall ye believe, if I tell you of heavenly things?'"

This sums up my cynicism of Keith and every Christian over the years. Some of them, like Keith and Jennie Lou, were trying to tell me their experience, and I just couldn't understand.

"'And no man hath ascended up to heaven, but he that came down from heaven, even the Son of man which is in heaven. And as Moses lifted up the serpent in the wilderness, even so must the Son of man be lifted up: That whosoever believeth in him should not perish, but have eternal life.'"

These verses from John 3:13-15 seem very familiar.

"'For God so loved the world, that he gave his only begotten Son, that whosoever believeth in him should not perish, but have everlasting life.'"

This! This sixteenth verse of John 3 was the Scripture I thought I knew, the one Derek Simmons tricked me with in college. I had never read and memorized the verses that came before or after this one. I really didn't know what it meant back then. I was foolish to think I did.

"'For God sent not his Son into the world to condemn the world; but that the world through him might be saved. He that believeth on him is not condemned: but he that believeth not is condemned already, because he hath not believed in the name of the only begotten Son of God.'"

I think verses seventeen and eighteen are talking about the difference between being a sinner and a Christian.

"'And this is the condemnation, that light is come into the world, and men loved darkness rather than light, because their deeds were evil. For every one that doeth evil hateth the light, neither cometh to the light, lest his deeds should be reproved. But he that doeth truth cometh to the light, that his deeds may be made manifest, that they are wrought in God.'"

I see myself in the passage of John 3:19-21. I have lived my whole life hating the light. I didn't understand it. I thought my grandparents represented the light, but they didn't. They were misguided sinners themselves.

But I'm being given a real chance right now. I can feel it. I feel like I'm being called toward His light, toward Jesus.

I get down on my knees in front of the couch. I rest my elbows on the cushions and close my eyes. I'm so serious. I know this is the most important decision of my life.

"God, I'm calling out to You," I say aloud. "I don't know if I'm doing this right or not, but I pray in the name of Jesus Christ, Your Son. I . . . I thank You that I'm still alive. And I thank You for Keith and Jennie Lou."

I press my face into the couch cushion, feeling the weight of my mistakes and regrets. I start to cry. It just seems right. I need to let this out.

I lift up my face up, just enough to speak again. "God, I've messed up! I know I'm a sinner. And I'm sorry for everything I've done wrong. I know now that You have the answers and I don't. I know You love me, or You wouldn't have done what You did tonight. You have a strength that I don't, that no one else does."

When the words come to me this time, they feel natural, not awkward like before. I know they're my true feelings, and I want to express them.

"I don't want to feel far from You anymore. I've stopped running away."

I remember some of the things I learned about Jesus from when had I attended church as a child. Jesus left Heaven and was born into the world to be a sacrifice for everyone's sins. My sins. He died and was resurrected. Jesus sent the Holy Spirit into the world as the Comforter.

All of it was true. The Holy Spirit reached out and helped me today. It's not myth. It's not stories made up by flawed people, like I used to tell myself. It's real!

Comprehending that, it makes me all the more ashamed of my behavior.

"Jesus, I need You! I don't deserve what You're offering, but I need You! Please—please send Your Holy Spirit into my heart and heal me. Make me who You want me to be. I'm tired of being who I am. I can't do this on my own anymore!"

The couch is wet with my tears, and that's okay. I'm tired of the way I've been living; I want things to change. And I know this is my only chance, so I keep calling out.

"Jesus, please—I need You! I'm begging You, please help me! Save me!"

After some time, I feel the same warmth and peace I sensed when I was dying. I feel a Love I've never known before embracing me, showing me that everything is all right. In that moment, I feel both joy and hope. The huge weight of my guilt lifts away—it's gone! *I feel forgiven!* I cry and laugh and praise God. Why had I run away from this for so many years?

. . .

Once I'm coherent enough to complete a sentence, I call Keith.

"Sean?" he answers groggily. "Is everything okay?"

"Yes. Actually, everything is great! It's amazing!" I say with more cheer in my voice than I've had since . . . well, since my mom was alive.

"Um, what happened?" he asks.

"I did what you suggested," I answer. "I read in John, and it really made me think about the Lord and what He did for me tonight— what He's been doing for me my whole life. I started praying. I asked Jesus to save me—and He did, Keith! He's with me now! I feel His Spirit in me!"

"Thank you, Jesus!" Keith exclaims loudly. "I'm so happy for you, Sean! This is incredible!"

"It is," I reply. "I've never felt like this. So happy, so . . . free."

"That's the Lord for you," Keith replies. "It's His grace and mercy. His love."

"Thanks for not giving up on me, Keith."

"It's all good, man."

"Go ahead and get some more sleep," I tell him. "I just wanted to share my happiness and what the Lord did for me."

"I'm so glad you did, Sean. Good night."

"Good night."

This changes everything.

15

SUDDEN SHIFT

A surprise greets me as I wake up the next morning, which is a Sunday. I hear music, an acoustic guitar strumming outside in the neighborhood. I get out of bed and step over to the window, raising it slightly to hear it better. Down on the street is a man in dark clothing and a cowboy hat sitting on a fold-out chair with his instrument. He's playing a folksy tune and begins to sing with his raspy tenor voice. I don't recognize the song, but it's catchy. Next to him is a dark-skinned woman with shoulder-length, black hair. She's wearing a light yellow blouse and blue jeans, swaying to the rhythm. She offers a soprano harmony that complements the man's efforts.

It looks like they're playing for tips. I've never seen anyone perform in front of this building before, but maybe they've come on hard times because of the tornado or something else. There's a fair amount of people out walking right now, and some drop dollar bills or change in the man's open guitar case. He smiles, and the woman thanks them individually as they pass by. I close the window and head over to the bathroom.

I get washed up and then call Jennie Lou.

"Good morning," I begin.

"Good morning. How are you doing?"

"A lot better, thanks. I was wondering if we could meet for breakfast. I know you don't like meeting me alone, but something amazing happened, and I'd like to tell you about it. Maybe you can bring someone with you?"

She hesitates briefly before responding.

"Where do you want to meet?" she asks.

"How about the Greenback's Coffee by my apartment building?"

"All right. I can be there in about thirty minutes. I'll see if my friend, Lynn, can join us, okay?"

"Sure. Thank you. I'll see you then."

When I leave the building several minutes later, the singers are still performing. The man and woman both look to be in their forties or maybe a little older. He's heavyset, has a graying mustache and deep blue eyes. She's slimmer, has deep brown eyes, and is wearing round glasses. Their melodies are infectious and make me want to dance, even though I'm not a fan of the genre. Since I'm in a good mood and feeling generous, I drop a couple of ten-dollar bills in the guitar case.

"Thank you, sir," the woman tells me. "You have a blessed day!"

I tell her thanks and walk on.

· · ·

Jennie Lou and Lynn are waiting outside the coffee shop when I arrive around eleven o'clock that morning. Lynn is very polite, but I can tell she's still cautious around me.

"I almost can't believe how much better you seem than last night," Jennie Lou tells me, looking intrigued as we sit down together at a booth. "You said something happened?"

"Yes. And I do feel different," I reply. "I'm not even hungover at all."

Jennie Lou leans back into her chair and studies me a moment. Then her eyes widen briefly.

"You accepted the Lord," she says in a kind of quiet awe. It's not a question.

I quiet down, just giving a quick nod. She looks happy. Lynn seems intrigued now.

"That's so wonderful!" Jennie Lou says.

"You prayed for me, didn't you?" I ask.

"You have no idea," she replies.

Considering what a mess I was last night, I can only imagine.

"Can you tell me what happened?" she asks. "I'd really like to know."

"I'd like to know, too," Lynn says nervously in her soft voice.

"Okay, sure," I answer.

I spend the next fifteen minutes sharing what happened to me, how the Lord heard and responded to my crying out to Him.

When I think about it, the man I was before would be appalled at me now. Sean Winter, a Christian? The old Sean would have laughed at me and called me names. But that's okay. He didn't want to live anymore, anyway. And since I've been spiritually reborn, that means old Sean died after all.

By the time I finish, Jennie Lou's eyes are brimming with tears.

"What the Lord did for you, it's so beautiful," she tells me. "I'm truly happy for you. You have an incredible testimony. I think people need to hear it."

"I don't know if I'm ready to do anything like that yet, Jennie. So far, you two and Keith are the only ones who know."

She holds out her hand before me. "That's all right. What's important is that you have Jesus."

Lynn nods in agreement, finally smiling a little.

A thought occurs to me then.

"You both volunteer at Hopes and Prayers. Do you think I could do that, too?" I ask.

Jennie Lou's face brightens. "Of course! They always need volunteers. There's a lot of work to be done."

I feel my face flush with nervousness. "I—I wouldn't be doing it to be near you or to bug you. I just thought it would be a good way to spend my free time."

She nods thoughtfully. "I understand. That was my thinking when I first started with them."

. . .

I begin attending Keith's church on Sundays. I like the humble, respectful atmosphere. I'm also pleased that Keith's ex-wife and daughter join him fairly often. I'm hopeful they will successfully reconcile.

Between church and Hopes and Prayers, I slowly start making new acquaintances. I find that I like helping with the soup kitchen. I'm not a very good cook, but I can serve meals to people. By watching my fellow volunteers, I learn how to be friendlier toward strangers without seeming weird or awkward. I now sense when people are hurting the way I used to. I want to help others. I don't fear or distrust them like before.

Even more important than things like my volunteer work, I've seen changes within myself. I have a calm that wasn't there before. I don't see only problems anymore. I don't see myself as causing everything that's wrong with my life. And though I can't fully put it into words, I know the Lord's love is what's changing me for the better.

. . .

It's almost nine o'clock on a Thursday night when I get a text notification. For the moment, I ignore it. Walking back after distributing flyers for an upcoming event, my friends Caleb, Regina, Kathy, and Vic accompany me.

"We should probably hurry up and get back to the center," Regina says, looking up briefly. "I think we're in for icy roads and snow tonight."

"Sean, you don't have a car, right?" Caleb says. "I can give you a ride home."

"Thanks, Caleb," I reply.

"Yes, thank you, Caleb," Regina echoes.

"I think we've got a couple of hours before it gets serious," Kathy notes.

We pick up our pace and make it back to Hopes and Prayers less than ten minutes later. Vic secures the remaining flyers inside just before Caleb locks the building and we all say our goodbyes. It only takes a few minutes for Caleb to drive me home. I could have walked, but his offer was right on time; it's been a long day. I thank him for his kindness and tell him to be careful. We all come from completely different backgrounds, but we already function together like a well-oiled machine. Even though we have such different personalities, it helps to think of us as family. We can lean and depend on one another if we need to, just like I have with Keith and Jennie Lou.

I enter my apartment and have a light salad dinner. I just want to relax. After a hot shower and a change of clothes, I sit on the couch, reading the Bible while I listen to some instrumental guitar music.

I marvel at how much my life has changed in the last six months. I'm so much more at ease since letting go of my past burdens and forgiving myself. I've really been learning how to live again. In the midst of these thoughts, I find myself nodding off. Realizing how tired I am, I get ready for bed. I reach over to my nightstand and grab my phone. I need to make sure my morning alarm is on. That's when I see the text notification.

And I freeze. Literally everything in my world stops when I see my phone screen.

It's Kalea.

16

A MESSAGE FROM KALEA

She sent a video. I take a deep breath and pray without words.

There she is on my phone screen: Kalea Nadeaux. The woman I thought I loved, who shared my life for a few months. She's holding her phone up high to get as much of her in the camera as possible. The shape of her eyes, her deep tan skin, that flirtatious smile, and the super-long frizzy hair are all unmistakably Kalea. Yet I'm astonished at how different she looks, too. There are dark circles under her half-open brown eyes, which, combined with her slightly furrowed brow and lack of makeup, make her look quite tired. She's also added red highlights throughout her ever-lengthening hair.

However, what's most striking is how much weight she's gained in the last six months—at least fifty pounds. She stands there in a deep orange, loose-hanging t-shirt, confident and pleasant in the pre-recorded frozen frame. I wish she had made a video call, so I could directly ask questions. But this is what I got. And the only way I'll get answers is to press the Play button.

"Sean, I hope you're well," Kalea tells me. "I know it's been too long, but I finally felt ready to share everything with you. I'm living in Canada now with relatives of my father's. I'm sorry I didn't say goodbye or return your calls and texts. I didn't want to risk you coming after me . . . or losing my resolve."

Well, at least she's honest about that. The old Sean would be furious and cursing at the phone screen by now. I'm sad and a little frustrated, but that's all.

"You have every right to hate me, but please keep listening," she continues in a cautious-sounding tone. "It's very important that you hear—and see—this part."

That sparks my curiosity. Then she takes her phone and swings it around, facing away from her. It's almost dizzying, but the camera quickly refocuses. What I see next almost makes me drop my phone. I can't believe my eyes. She shows me two very young infants in a baby bed. There's a cloth divider between them, allowing each child room to move unencumbered. The newborns, whose skin bear lighter shades of tan than Kalea's, are both wearing white onesies and matching beanies. One looks asleep, and the other is staring up at Kalea in amazement, making cooing noises.

"You're a father, Sean!" she declares proudly, brightening up.

My attention is now totally glued to the phone screen.

"I knew I was pregnant before I left," Kalea tells me as she turns the camera back around. "In fact, that's what pushed everything else into motion. I had been waiting for confirmation before I gave notice to my landlord or did anything else. But once I verified the pregnancy with my doctor, I knew exactly what to do."

She changes expressions, looking concerned.

"Sean, I can only imagine what's going through your mind now. But you're one of the few people who can understand my reason for doing this."

She's right. It makes sense. And I fell for it like an idiot.

"Aria," I say aloud.

She nods, as if she knew I'd say that. Then she becomes pensive, sadder. "I placed my daughter, Aria, for adoption when I was eighteen," Kalea confirms. "That decision nearly destroyed me. It tore at my heart every day for four years. I could barely keep going."

I grip my bed with one hand. I'm starting to get angry now that the initial shock is fading. "Until you met me," I say, unable to hide the bitterness in my tone.

"And then you came into my life, Sean," Kalea says happily. "You gave me new hope!"

She seems to realize how that sounded and becomes more serious.

"Please, don't get me wrong. I did mean *everything* that I told you when we were together," she says. "Every moment that I shared with you was precious to me. However, as soon as our attraction evolved into a sexual relationship, I believed you could give me a child to replace Aria."

Simply put, you'd used me.

"What I didn't know until after I left was that I was carrying twins, a boy and a girl," Kalea shares, the pride shining through her voice. "You doubled my joy! And I will honor you through them."

I let go of the bed and start massaging my temples with the fingertips of that hand.

"Honor me?" What does that even mean?

"I named them both after you," she clarifies. "Sean and Shawna."

Even across the miles, that pleasantly tugs at my heart. She still knows how to manipulate me. Yet it seems too little, too late.

She zooms back in on the infants.

"I will always let them know who you are, Sean Winter," she continues. "And if they want to reach out to you when they're old enough, I won't get in their way. I will always assure them that they were conceived in love."

Sure they were. I did love her at the time. At least, as much as I knew how to. But would Sean and Shawna be fine with knowing their mother left their father the way she did? I don't like where this is going. It's already one-sided, and she's trying to control all the information.

Then she turns the camera back to herself.

"I will never ask you for financial support or to help raise them," she tells me. "This was my decision. These are our children, but I consider them my responsibility. I've gotten a job I can do from home, and I will care for them on my own. That's what I want."

A tear falls from her left eye. I can't tell whether she's acting or if it's genuine. I suppose it doesn't matter now.

"I do love you, Sean. I live that love every day through these babies. I won't ever forget you. But our time together has come and gone."

She looks down and briefly laughs before looking at the camera again. She's still crying a little.

"I hope you've moved on and gotten together with your Jennie Lou," Kalea says. "I'm glad for what we had, but I feel she's the one who can make you happy, not me. All I want to be is a mother. I'm content with that. And based on what you told me, she loves you in a way that I can't."

Jennie Lou and I are just friends. Neither of us is looking to take that relationship anywhere else.

"I want you to be happy and fulfilled, Sean, the same way that I am," she continues. Then she takes on a pained expression. "I know I hurt you. I am so deeply sorry for that. I won't ask you to forgive me.

204 THE FORMER THINGS

But I do hope this video brings you some relief . . . in the answers and the promise it contains. I will also send you regular pictures and videos like today."

Is that really supposed to console me? According to what she just said, I'll probably never see my children in person. Instead, I'll get some pictures and videos?

I have to remind myself that she could have chosen not to do this at all. In that case, I would have never known. I'm not sure which is worse.

"I have no right to ask this, but I will, anyway. Please do not call me or try to visit me in person," she adds. "You can send texts and I will read them, but I won't reply. I really can't."

Sure you could. You just don't want to.

"I don't want to move again, but I can do it at a moment's notice if I need to. Don't force that," Kalea admonishes. "We have a great start here. I can provide them with a good life. Please let me do that, and I'll share as much as I can."

She looks away briefly and nods, as if reluctantly agreeing with herself before she speaks again.

"When they're older, I'll let them record videos to you. You are their father, after all," she adds. "And . . . you can record videos for them, too. Just know that I will review everything before I show them anything."

I chuckle at that. Does she think I'm going to send them subtle messages to rebel against their mother and run away to the U.S.? Or is she anticipating that possibility because that's the kind of thing she might do if our circumstances were reversed? That's a troubling thought. But so was the warning.

"I truly wish you well, Sean. I hope we can make this new chapter in our lives work. I am so proud to be the mother of your twins. Thank you for everything. I'll be in touch."

With that, she blows a kiss at the camera and ends the video.

While I was watching the video, she sent three pictures: one of each child on their own and one of them together. They're so young; but both seem to have her nose, lips, and forehead. The boy has her eyes, and the girl has my eyes.

I lay the phone on the bed and fall to my knees. Now that I've seen everything, I'm too stunned to sort out my feelings. My mind is still combing through the facts.

The signs were right in front of me. I was just too blinded by how enjoyable our relationship was to see them. She was becoming moodier and more withdrawn. She had stopped drinking alcohol and started making healthier meals for us. The last day I saw her, she must have been dealing with morning sickness.

This is unbelievable. Why reveal this information to me and then ask me not to contact her directly? Why tell me I have children and then block access to them, except through pictures and video? She must not have any idea how cruel that is. Like before, she must think she's doing me a favor.

One thought keeps replaying in my mind: I'm a father.

How do I feel about that? How *can* I feel about that? This is the very last thing I could have imagined happening. I never even considered having children. I thought I was doing good to have a girlfriend.

Despite my newfound confidence and peace, my head is swimming right now. This doesn't seem real. I have a son and a daughter! Twins? I went from single guy to dad in just a few minutes.

What am I supposed to do?

Part of me is glad. I stare at their pictures. The children are beautiful. They look content, and I know on some level that Kalea will never harm them. She wanted them enough to go to all this trouble. All this . . . scheming. She said it: she wanted to replace the daughter she gave up. And she has. She can probably raise them just fine without me.

Except I know now. If she wanted to do this without me, why tell me? *Our* children. Kalea and I have children together.

This is surreal.

Still on my knees, I begin to pray. I know I can't fully deal with this right now. I don't know how to. I share my rawest emotions with the Lord, the ones that can't even spring tears or drive a yell of frustration through my lungs. What consoles me is that I already know He understands me. I can feel that. It keeps me sane and focused.

Even so, I know I'm not going to be able to sleep. Not yet. I call Jennie Lou and hope she's still awake.

"Hi Sean! Is everything okay?" she says.

"No, not really," I reply.

This might be as hard for her as it is for me. Then again, I've already called her.

"What's wrong?" Jennie Lou asks.

"I need to talk to a friend," I answer.

"Sure. Tell me what's going on."

She'll find out, anyway. I might as well be the one to tell her.

"I finally heard from Kalea," I continue.

"Oh! What? Um . . . what did she say?"

"She sent me a video; we didn't talk. She's somewhere in Canada now, staying with relatives."

"I see. Is she all right? Did she tell you why she left the way she did?"

I'm dreading what's going to happen next.

"Yes, she did. She moved away . . . once she confirmed she was pregnant."

I hear Jennie Lou gasp. "That was months ago! Has she had the baby already?"

I take a moment to softly inhale and exhale.

"Yes. It was twins."

"Twins," Jennie Lou repeats numbly.

She didn't want to hear that any more than I wanted to say it. I know her well enough to know that. She understands the implications of what I've just told her. Kalea's and my choices during our relationship are going to shock a lot of people.

"She wants to raise them where she is," I continue. "She doesn't want contact with me."

"What? But that's so wrong!" she blurts, clearly upset. "She just told you about these children. How can she keep them away from you *now*?" Her voice rises an octave on the last word.

I'm still too overwhelmed to explain things properly. She's extremely sympathetic. Yet she has no more answers than I do. She just lets me talk for a while until I'm tired enough to go to sleep.

. . .

I wake up at five-thirty so I can go into work early. I want to see Jessica in private before my shift starts. We go into her office, and she shuts the door behind us. She's understandably curious as she sits down at the desk. I sit down as well. I'm not ready to give another explanation. I hand her the phone.

"The video is from Kalea. Just . . . just watch it," I tell her.

"All right," she says with a dubious look.

In nearly a year's time, I don't think I've heard her curse so much as she does while watching it. Once it's done, she puts the phone on the desk, then leans back in her chair. She clenches her fists, clearly frustrated.

"Sean, this . . . this is crazy!" she says, finally sitting up straight. "Is she really that crazy?"

I shrug. "I think this all makes sense to her."

Jessica turns her chair on its wheels and looks away while shaking her head.

"I knew I should have said something!" she mutters.

"What are you talking about?" I ask her.

"Office romances are usually a bad idea, Sean. I could have warned you, but . . . Well, I thought you two were a nice couple. I was rooting for you. It really hurt to see the breakup tear you apart."

That's very kind of her to say. Jessica has a very maternal side to her management.

"What are you going to do now?" she asks, turning to face me.

"I'm not sure. I'm still trying to process this," I answer.

"Do you need some time? You've earned some PTO."

It's true I have accumulated paid time off, but I don't think this is the time to use it. Not yet.

"I'm going to keep working," I tell her. "I need to stay focused. Besides, I still don't know where she is. Canada is a big country."

Jessica nods. "I can respect that. But if things start getting to you and you need time off, let me know, okay?"

"Sure thing, boss."

. . .

The lunch hour comes soon enough. I ask Keith, Ben, and Jimbo to join me at Loggie's Pizza, where I bring them up to speed on Kalea as we wait for our food.

"Are you serious?" Ben exclaims, outraged.

"I'm afraid so," I confirm. "The video and pictures prove it."

"Can we see the video?" Ben asks.

"That's kind of personal. Sorry," I tell him. "But you can see the pictures in a minute."

Jimbo looks shocked; Ben is angry; and Keith looks apprehensive.

"I understand, man," Ben adds. "I just never thought Kalea would pull something like this. She always had our backs. She's been solid since I met her here at Prosaic two years ago."

"Did she tell you her reasons, Sean?" Jimbo interjects. "There had to be, well, something, right?"

"There was," I confirm. "She had a baby girl when she was eighteen and had to place her for adoption. She never got over that decision and wanted another child."

Ben and Jimbo look down at the table. I think they're in mild shock at their former friend's actions. Keith is looking at me. I feel his brotherly care and concern.

"What are you going to do?" Keith asks me.

"I've thought a lot about it between last night and this morning," I tell the group. "To keep peace and maintain a relationship with her and the kids . . ."

Her and the kids. Wow. It just keeps smacking me in the face.

" . . . I'm going to accept Kalea's terms."

"Are you sure that's a good idea?" Ben objects. "You have paternal rights, Sean. And she might not keep her word . . . "

Thanks for that cheery thought, Ben. While his support is heartening, suggestions like that don't help.

"So far, I have no reason to believe Kalea will break her word," I insist. I've run this whole scenario through my head a dozen times. "Right now, she has things the way she wants it. She's in control of the communication. She has the children and won't do anything to harm them. Consider this: even if I had the financial means to take off from work, fly to Canada, and somehow locate them—what would that accomplish? Kalea would just take the twins and go into hiding again. I'd lose what little contact I have and put her in a worse position than she is. And that could endanger our children."

Our children. It sounds so strange to say.

"He's right, Ben," Jimbo says. He leans back in his chair and puts his hands in his lap. "The way things are right now, Sean can work with it and maybe turn it to his advantage. If he goes after her . . . "

Ben slaps the table and shoves himself back in his chair. "I know. I just wanted to be able to do something! You have no idea how much I regret getting Sean involved with Kalea. I thought I was doing right by you, Sean." Ben shakes his head and looks off. "Now, I see I've gotta change some things. I got a lot to think about."

I reach over, put a hand on Ben's shoulder, and give him a reassuring smile as he turns to look at me.

"Neither of us could have known how this would play out, Ben," I tell him.

"Sean, we're here for you, man," Keith says. "No matter what."

"Definitely," Jimbo agrees.

"No matter what," Ben adds.

. . .

Kalea must be happy with our arrangement. Over the next few weeks, she texts me dozens of photos and more than a few videos of Sean, Jr. and Shawna. From what I can see, they're well-nourished and seem to be happy. The more I see of them, the more connected I feel. They're in my heart now. They're my children, and I'm growing to love them more by the day.

It's a mixed blessing. I know my feelings are normal. Yet the fact that I can't be there with them and they can't come here makes me ache inside. I have to pray about it daily, asking the Lord to build me up to bear this.

I don't have an answer to this, but in my soul, I know this arrangement is not right. It's not about whether it's "fair" or not. Life isn't fair. It's about whether or not I'm doing the right thing just accepting this and suffering the grief of being denied access to my children.

I continue praying and even go on a three-day fast about this the following weekend. I want to get closer to Jesus. I'm seeking a resolution by faith. I feel like the Lord can help me. I know that prayer changes things.

During the fast, I can really begin to feel the Lord's presence. As I pray and study the Bible, I ignore television, the internet, and only take vital calls. By the first evening, I'm encouraged to push further ahead. I can feel in my heart that I'm being heard, so I cry out in my thoughts.

"Lord, I praise Your Holy Name! I know there is nothing beyond Your ability! I need Your help, Lord. You know I want to see my children,

Little Sean and Shawna. I want to be a part of their lives, to see and hold them, to show them how much I love them to be their father.

"Help me to forgive Kalea and lose my resentment toward her. Lord, I do want her to be all right. Actually, I want her to find salvation like You gave to me. But that's not up to me. Let Your will be done, Lord."

I continue my fast throughout the weekend. By the end of the third day, I feel a joy within my spirit. It's a bliss more powerful than anything I've felt before. And in that moment, I know the Lord has already answered my prayer.

The sun is setting outside, and there's no wind—just a beautiful stillness surrounding me. So here, alone in my apartment, I praise Him with my lips and everything I have within me.

Even though I'm no singer, I begin singing a hymn—"It Is Well With My Soul." It's just what I feel within me. I learned the words as a child, though I didn't know what they meant until this year.

When peace, like a river, attendeth my way,
When sorrows like sea billows roll;
Whatever my lot, Thou hast taught me to say,
It is well, it is well with my soul.

It is well with my soul,
It is well, it is well with my soul.

Though Satan should buffet, though trials should come,
Let this blest assurance control,
That Christ hath regarded my helpless estate,
And hath shed His own blood for my soul.

It is well with my soul,
It is well, it is well with my soul.

My sin—oh, the bliss of this glorious thought!—
My sin, not in part but the whole,
Is nailed to the cross, and I bear it no more,
Praise the Lord, praise the Lord, O my soul!

It is well with my soul,
It is well, it is well with my soul.
And Lord, haste the day when the faith shall be sight,
The clouds be rolled back as a scroll;
The trump shall resound, and the Lord shall descend,
Even so, it is well with my soul.

. . .

During the next month, Kalea continues to send me pictures and videos of the twins. It eventually becomes a daily occurrence I look forward to. She dresses the babies in such cute matching outfits in soft colors.

The following month, however, the quantity of pictures and videos begins to slow down. And then they stop altogether. I receive no texts explaining this change, nothing to let me know when they might resume. It feels disturbingly familiar. And Ben's words haunt me: "She might not keep her word."

I dismiss the thought. There's a better explanation; I just don't know what it is yet. The Lord has already assured me there is an answer to all of this. It will happen. I just have to be patient and wait on Him.

It's Saturday afternoon, so I've been doing laundry and some cleaning with some light music playing. I find that I'm not comfortable with Why Shark Why anymore. I think I should stop listening to most of the music old Sean liked. I've bought a few CDs of Christian music and various instrumentals. I stream similar online selections.

Suddenly, there's a gentle knocking on the door. That's a surprise. No one had mentioned coming over, and I didn't order any food.

The knocking almost sounds hesitant. But whoever it is, they keep doing it.

I walk toward the front door. "Hold on, please."

I feel a strange sensation inside as I release both locks and start to open the door.

That's when I find myself face to face with Kalea Nadeaux, who's standing there with a twin baby stroller.

17

THE RUNAWAY

"Kalea?" I say, completely stunned. "What are you doing here?"

She's wearing a white trench coat over her cobalt blue blouse and a black skirt that matches her boots. Her hair is so full, framing her soft face and flowing behind her. Her makeup is flawless and attractive. But her demeanor is what strikes me as different. Her usual confidence is nowhere to be found. There's a sadness in her eyes, coupled with something else—maybe regret?

"May we come in, please?" Kalea asks quietly, looking down to the children, then back at me.

I take a breath before I speak. "Yes."

Kalea rolls the stroller to the couch. As she passes by, my eyes are glued on Little Sean and Shawna, who seem to be sleeping. I can't move. My breathing is quick and shallow. I'm looking at . . . our children. I can barely believe this is real.

Kalea sits down and looks at me glumly. Then she peers down at the twins, and her mood lifts some.

"Hi, Sean," she says, sounding a little nervous as she looks up again. "Thanks for inviting us in."

"You're here . . . with our children," I reply, more stiffly than I intended. "Of course, I invited you in. We need to talk."

She gazes at me for several seconds. Is she trying to figure out my mood?

"Yes. We do," she finally says. She looks so tired. "That's one of the reasons I'm here."

"You look like you're not feeling well," I state, unable to mask all of my bitterness. My eyes don't move, locked onto hers.

"Physically, I'm fine," she says. "Emotionally, I don't know."

Where is she going with this? I don't want to think ill of her, but I keep expecting some self-serving ball to drop.

"Having the twins has changed me. It's changed the way I look at the world around me," she continues, turning her gaze back to the infants. "Taking care of these two all the time, putting them first . . . I've never done that for anyone before. It's taken so much. Some days, I don't know how I pulled it off, but I did. And it felt right."

Is she really praising her own her parenting, right in front of me? That's just . . . wow. I feel my whole body tensing up. If she didn't have the babies with her, I'd tell her to get out right now.

She raises her head and makes eye contact with me once more, seeming sorrowful. "I didn't put you first at all, Sean. I only took from you."

Now she says this? I rest my forehead in my hand. "What do you want, Kalea?"

"I'm here to talk. The first day we met, I said I would protect you . . . but I didn't," she admits. "I meant to. I really wanted to at the time . . . but I'm a coward. I ran away to have the twins in secret. And when I finally worked up the nerve to tell you about them, I still kept you at a distance. I'm always protecting myself." She looks down again. "And I end up hurting you."

I peer at her in amazement. In all her self-reflection, she truly doesn't understand what she did to me. My temper flares. I can feel my pulse starting to race.

"This is bigger than that," I tell her. "You basically held our kids hostage in front of me! Do you have any idea how that affected me?"

She narrows her gaze at me. "What do you mean, I held them hostage? I didn't do that."

"You threatened to move if I tried to find the three of you," I say angrily. "Isn't that blackmail?"

I need Your help right now, Jesus! I'm getting too angry. I know this isn't good. Please show me how to handle this.

I feel a new calmness soothing me from within. Thank you, Lord!

"*Just listen,*" a soft Voice says within me.

I take a deep breath and let it out slowly. Kalea looks like she doesn't know what to say to me.

"I'm sorry," I say as humbly as I can. "I guess I'm getting too upset."

"Should I take the twins and go?"

"No. Please don't. I . . . want to hear what you have to say."

She appears surprised to hear that and sits back down.

"Thank you," she tells me. "Sean, I didn't just come for a visit."

"What do you mean?"

"We've moved back to Oklahoma City," she adds. "I can do my job from home. I'm renting a place about two miles from here."

What? What about her grand plans? I don't get it.

"I'm not running anymore," she says. "I *had* to come back."

She pauses and looks directly into my eyes. I see a shadow of what we shared.

"I'm connected to you," she says with a sincerity that chills me.

It makes me immediately defensive again. I will my mouth to stay shut. I don't know what I'd say if I let myself talk. I mentally count to ten before responding.

"Through the children?" I ask flatly.

She shakes her head, looking flush. "That's not what I mean. Even before I got pregnant, we had a special tie."

"We?" I repeat, stung by her choice of words. "That implies there was an 'us.' You said we could never have been 'just friends,' so I trusted you. I committed myself to our relationship. But you made it abundantly clear in your video that there's no 'us.' It was all about you."

Ease it down, Sean. Take deep, calming breaths. This is tough.

Kalea puts her hands in her lap. She nods once silently.

"You're right. It was all about me then," she admits. "I've handled everything wrong. I'm sorry . . . for everything."

I want to believe her. I want this to be the answer to my prayers. But even if it is, I still need to be very careful. She might be trying to manipulate me.

In nervousness, I begin to pace. As I swiftly pivot, my foot jars the coffee table and causes one of the babies to stir. Kalea and I both turn to observe Shawna's tiny, troubled face. I suddenly feet guilty for causing her distress. And that feeling becomes a catalyst for all of my own confusion and inner pain. It starts pouring out.

"You don't know . . . what you're apologizing for," I say, trying to keep my voice as quiet as I can. I wanted to say, "You don't know the half of it!" but I stop myself. I want to say what I feel, but it would make me sound angry or cold. So I ask the obvious instead. "What. Do. You. Want?"

Our eyes meet once more. She takes a moment, sniffles, and looks back down at her lap.

"I've messed it all up, haven't I?" she asks sadly. "You don't trust me anymore." She sighs. "I can't blame you. I'd be furious if our positions were reversed."

"Why did you really come back, Kalea?"

It's a simple question. I'm asking sincerely. There's a pocket of silence before she answers.

"As much work as I put into my original plan and carrying it out, I still feel—incomplete," she says carefully.

I want to slap those words out of the air. *It was a bad plan! What did you expect?*

"I mean, I succeeded. More than succeeded!" she continues. "I tried for one baby to replace Aria—and had twins!"

More self-praise. She's unbelievable! I want to scream, but I won't let myself. It wouldn't help, anyway.

"But I feel haunted. It's been hanging over me ever since I left. It affects how I sleep and eat."

Am I supposed to feel sorry for you? You set this all up. What does this have to do with "I'm connected to you"? More deep breaths, Sean.

She sinks back into the couch and lets her arms hang at her sides. She leans her head back, closes her eyes, and sighs.

"Our children are fine, but . . . I'm not. I went through the pregnancy and these last few months trying so hard to figure out what was missing in my life," she continues. "And the only answer I could come up with . . . was you."

Ah, there it is. She finally got to the point . . . kind of.

"What do you want to happen?" I ask with my hands held out. "Do you honestly think things can be like they were before?"

"No," she shakes her head, eyes still closed. "I've messed things up too much for that to happen."

At least, she understands that. Then she sits up straighter and looks at me.

"But Sean, one thing is very clear to me now, even if you don't believe me," she says humbly. "I *do* love you. And I will always love you."

I don't say anything. I stare hard at her. I feel tears welling up, and my jaw is clenched tight. I ball up my fists and release them a few times. Her being here, seeing the twins, the things she's saying—it's all building into one big, growing wall of anxiety inside me.

Suddenly, there's a glint of alarm in Kalea's eyes.

"Sean? What is it?" she asks, concerned.

I feel cut off. I'm frozen in place, and all I can feel is the devastating hurt she put me through. So much loss and betrayal. The tears fall.

Warm hands grip mine and shake me. "Sean!"

Kalea is wide-eyed with fear now. I can't speak yet, but I look at her.

"What's going on?" she asks urgently. "I've never seen you like this!"

I take in a shaky breath. "There's . . . things you don't know about."

She lets go but continues to stare at me.

As I walk over to a chair, my legs feel like there are weights attached to them. I slump into the chair louder than I intended, and Shawna is startled awake. She starts to fuss. Kalea rises to check on her.

"She's hungry," she tells me a moment later. "Are you going to be all right?"

I nod. "I will be."

"Do you mind if I feed her? It shouldn't take long."

I wipe the tears from my face. "Sure. Would you mind using my bedroom? I'll stay out here . . . with Little Sean."

"All right."

She picks up Shawna and walks out of the living room.

The mood slowly diffuses, and I feel a little better.

I look over at Little Sean and see that he's looking at me. I don't know if he's studying me or just trying to focus his eyes on my shape, but I'm glad he's calm. I step over toward him and gently pick him up. It's very awkward at first, and I'm terrified I'll hold him too tightly or drop him. After a few moments, I find a balance that's comfortable for both of us.

Now that he's aware of me, this tiny, little boy and I look at each other in amazement and curiosity. My son. He's a blend of me and Kalea. Was it like this for my mom when she held me when I was this young? Did she think about my father, or did she just focus on me? I imagine she did both. But it's comforting to think that maybe she only thought of me.

I put my fingers near his hand, and he grasps my index finger tightly. For only being a few months old, he has a strong grip. I think he's as intrigued by me as I am of him. I find myself smiling and grinning without thinking about it. I'm holding my son in my arms! I tell him who I am, knowing he won't understand my words. But hopefully, he'll sense that I like him and care about him. I want to get to know him. I know this is just the beginning of that, but it feels so right.

I smile at him and say his name. I tell him we have the same name. I must have sounded funny when I said that because he makes a sound that's half-laugh and half-gurgle.

Kalea takes a little over twenty minutes before returning to the living room with Shawna. She sets her back in the stroller and sits back down with her diaper bag on the couch.

"Your daughter is going to get jealous," Kalea teases, cooing at Shawna.

I bring Little Sean to her, and we swap.

While he's a handsome, little guy, Shawna has inherited her mother's beauty. She's delicate and quieter. I feel like she's definitely studying me, as if asking specific questions: "Who are you? Is it safe to be with you? Why did Mommy give me to you? I thought there was only Mommy?" I feel like I have to earn her trust, so I try.

I talk more gently with her, using soothing tones. I assure her that I'm her father. I tell her how pretty she is.

"You must have been around kids a lot," Kalea interjects. "You're a natural at this."

"Not really," I answer. "I was around other kids in church when I was growing up, but that's it."

She gives me a satisfied smile. Then she turns her head back toward my bedroom.

"I didn't mean to be nosy," she states. "But I was surprised to see a Bible by your bedside."

I nod. "I became a Christian a few months ago."

She raises her eyebrows briefly at that. "Interesting. What changed your mind?"

"Something significant. I'm not sure if now's the right time."

"I'd really like to know. Can I ask what happened?" she inquires.

I put Shawna back in the stroller, then return to my chair. I can tell Kalea my testimony, but there's no way to avoid inflicting guilt for her part in it. Maybe she needs to know.

"I didn't take your leaving well," I begin. "I tried to move on, but I couldn't. I missed you so much. Honestly, I . . . was addicted to you. But I had no way to contact you, didn't know where you were. And I got to where I . . . couldn't live without you."

She knows what I'm alluding to, but she can't say the words. She just slowly shakes her head in denial, her eyes wide with fear.

"I tried to commit suicide," I admit.

Her mouth drops open, and she looks crushed.

"I thought I had run out of options, out of reasons to go on," I continue. "So I was going to drink myself out in one go, one night. And I almost succeeded."

Since she knows how my grandparents died, her wide eyes relay her understanding of the significance and the tragedy of my decision.

"I got scared and changed my mind at the last minute, but I was already in a bad way," I tell her. "I had been trying to sit up and reach my phone on the coffee table, but I was too blitzed to move. And right then, God intervened."

Kalea is silent, but her quizzical expression says, "What do you mean?"

"God spoke to me and pushed me forward enough to grab my phone," I add. "I called Jennie before I passed out. She and Keith got me to the emergency room and stayed with me, even after I was released."

She's been listening quietly, patiently. And she's crying again. When she speaks, I can hear the weight of regret in her strained voice.

"Sean, if you'd . . . died . . . because of the way I treated you . . . I never would have forgiven myself," she says, still choked up. "I truly didn't see . . . anything, I guess. I was only thinking about my needs. I'm so sorry!"

She looks pale and haunted.

"This is terrible. I feel terrible about all of this," she continues. "Maybe . . . maybe I should just go."

She starts to get up, still holding Sean.

"Wait, Kalea," I suggest. "Please don't go."

Something else needs to be said. I don't know what specifically, but this conversation can't stop here. What is it You want me to do, Lord?

"What?" she replies, startled.

She sits back down.

Tell her what you're feeling, I hear the Holy Spirit say.

What *am* I feeling? I'm still reeling from her sudden visit and seeing our children in person for the first time. But what else is there? When I look at her, I'm hurt by what she did. I'm hurt because . . . because . . . ah, that's it. Okay, Lord, I'll trust You.

"I don't want you to go," I tell her.

She looks at me with knit brows, like I've said something impossible.

"Why? I treated you so badly," she says. "Why would you want me to stay now?"

"Because it's the right thing to do."

I get us both some bottled water from the refrigerator and sit back down across from her in the chair. She smiles nervously as I hand her the water. I can tell she's still uncomfortable.

"I'm happy that you moved back," I begin. "Of course, I'm glad to see the children. But . . . part of me is glad to see you, too."

"I find that hard to believe, with all that's been said," she tells me.

I take a sip of my water. *Lord, please give me the right words to say to Kalea.*

"I've been through a lot, yes, and your actions did hurt me," I continue. "But I do care about you. And . . . you are the mother of our children."

She just looks at me for a moment, at first confused. Then her features soften into a hopeful expression.

"Does that mean . . . do we still have a chance?" she wonders aloud.

It's way too soon to know that for sure. I don't want to discourage her, but we both need to be realistic.

"I don't know, honestly," I reply. "I think we need to take this slowly. Let's get to know who we are now . . . and be good parents to these kids."

She drinks some of her water, contemplating my words.

"Would it help if I converted to your religion?" she asks.

I suppose I should have expected that. She's very driven right now. But I need to address this directly.

"It's an individual and very personal choice," I respond. "I would love for you to discover your own need for Christ. But you can't do it for me or to make me happy. You have to make that decision for yourself. It has to be because you want it."

I can tell by her narrowing gaze that I've further confused her. I notice my right foot is tapping nervously. I try to ignore it and keep going. I recall Keith's words to me not long after we met.

"For us to have a real chance, we need to build a solid foundation for our relationship," I tell her. Keith was referring to his relationship with his ex-wife, but it applies here, too. "I'm still a new Christian, but I didn't just convert. I saw that I was a sinner. I was ashamed of how I'd handled my life and wanted to change. I had to realize that I couldn't make that change on my own. I needed Jesus."

She inhales slowly while looking at me. Then she stands up, so I stand also.

"I can't say I fully understand everything you just said," she tells me. "But I want to. And if there's a way for us to have a second chance, I'll do anything to achieve that."

"Kalea—"

She cuddles our son, Sean, close to her for a moment. He squeals in delight, then calms down when she places him in the stroller and offers him a white pacifier.

"You're the only one for me, Sean. I know that now," she says while sitting back down, still looking at our son. "Maybe it's too late, and maybe I don't deserve you. I wish I knew then what I know now. I wish I had stayed with you."

I look at her for a few seconds before speaking. "We all make mistakes."

She looks up at me then, taken aback.

"You're more forgiving than I would be," she says, shaking her head.

"That's the Lord, not me," I explain. "He's been teaching me how to forgive."

We spend a few more minutes talking and paying attention to the kids. Then she tells me she needs to return home, giving me her new address. She secures both children in the stroller, and I walk her to her vehicle.

As I stand in the parking lot and watch her drive off, I feel the cool breeze waft over me. Once the car is out of view, I look up to the afternoon sky. It's a rich blue with very few clouds. A few months ago, I went from single guy to being a father. In the last hour, I was reunited with my new family, which has to include Kalea.

This family was just a concept, an idea, to me before—an abstract reinforced by videos and pictures. But after holding these two little humans in my arms and looking in their eyes, they are now a very firm reality to me. I feel responsible for them.

I start to walk back toward my apartment. But I stop and lean against one of the walls. I close my eyes, squinting in frustration as I try to wrap my thoughts around all of this. My fingers bounce off the wall again and again, forming an unintended rhythm. I'm confronted with another firm reality: how am I going to do this? I really don't know how to provide for this new family. I mean, I have a job that covers my needs and allows for a little savings. But my—no, *our*—son and daughter have needs, too, a lot more than financial ones. They'll need my time and commitment. And . . . so does Kalea. This family has become such a high priority in my life.

I never had a father, but now I am one. I want to be who they need me to be. And in order to do that, I'll have to see Kalea. We'll have to work together as parents.

This . . . I've never faced anything like this. I don't know what to do. Lord, please help me.

18

PRODIGAL DAUGHTER

As I'm getting ready to go to sleep, I get a call from Kalea.

"Sean?"

She's breathing hard and sounds afraid.

"What wrong?" I ask.

"I need your help! I—I think I'm having an anxiety attack!"

I've never heard her sound unsettled like this.

"Easy, Kalea," I reply as I sit on the side of my bed. "Breathe in, nice and slow. I want to help, but I need to know what happened, okay?"

I hear her take a couple of deep breaths.

"I'm not sure exactly," she answers. "We got back to our apartment, and I had a little something to eat. After putting the babies to bed, I was taking time to clear my phone of the first video that I sent you . . . 'cause we don't need it anymore."

My heart feels relieved to hear her say that.

"But I saw the videos before that one, the night of the concert we went to . . . our last night together . . . "

I forgot! She did record parts of the concert.

"I saw that, and then I thought about our times together—the days, the nights. It all started to loop in my mind, over and over."

I've been there. I know how torturous that can be.

"I thought about what I did, leaving you like I did . . . and how I sent the video, the one I wanted to delete," she continues. "I watched it again, and I realized something, something awful!"

Her breathing has sped up again, and it sounds like she's crying. I want to say something reassuring, but she starts talking again first.

"What I went through with Aria, I did the same thing to you!" she exclaims. "I didn't mean to . . . I thought I was doing the right thing, but I wasn't! I was only thinking of healing my hurt . . . and I nearly *killed* you! I pushed you to the brink of suicide! How could I *do* that to you?!"

"Kalea, calm down, please!" I suggest. "I'm here; I'm all right. The worst didn't happen."

She's silent for a moment, but I can still hear her ragged breathing.

"You're right," she responds eventually. "But no thanks to me. I'm an awful person."

"You weren't trying to hurt me. Like you said, you thought you were doing the right thing. We all make mistakes. I definitely have."

"I don't know how I got things so wrong in the first place. I've messed it up so bad," she laments. "I'm so scared! Even if we can . . . fix these mistakes . . . I'm afraid I'll do something else just as bad. I don't want to ruin things again!"

As hard as it is to hear her sound so miserable, I think it's good she has a more realistic view of herself.

"I love you, Sean! I need you so much. I'm filled with these regrets, and I want to fix everything—but I don't know how!" she blurts out. She sounds so frantic. "Honestly, Canada wasn't worth it. And it wasn't hard to come back here. It—it was a relief! Because I need to be with you. But now, I feel like I'm coming apart inside! Please, Sean—help me!"

"Kalea, I'll help you. I'll stay on the phone with you, and we'll get through this."

For a few seconds, all I hear is her sobs and breathing.

"Thank you!" she finally says.

I keep praying for the right things to say.

"I . . . experienced what you're going through. It happened months ago," I begin. I shift my position on the bed to get more comfortable, since I may be here a while. "I missed you terribly and wanted to be with you . . . but I couldn't. I thought I could deal with it on my own. I tried to make it go away with extra work shifts or spending time with friends. I managed for a short time; then it would all come back . . . to you."

"That's not encouraging," she says, despair lacing her words.

"Sorry. What did help was the Lord. Even after He spared me from dying, I realized I still needed something. I didn't want to die, and I was tired of always hurting inside. Keith let me borrow his Bible. And when I read it, I saw that Jesus was offering me the very things I needed. So I called out to the Lord. I was so desperate, I said everything I could think of, asking for His help. He showed me I just needed to trust and accept Him. So I did. That was my starting point. After that, everything started getting better."

"That sounds good for you," she says, sounding dejected. "How does that help me?"

"You can have the same thing," I reply.

"But you said I couldn't convert to your religion," she counters. "You're not making sense again."

I can understand her frustration. I pray harder in my thoughts. I don't want to discourage her.

"Let's just get through tonight," I say confidently. "And sometime in the next couple of days, would you be willing to talk to my pastor?"

"About what?" I hear the frustration in her voice.

"I trust Pastor Anderson. And you know, I don't easily trust people," I begin. "I think he can help. He can talk with you about how to find your peace in God."

"Like you did?" she asks.

"Yes."

She pauses a moment.

"Will you be there?"

"Yes," I reply. "I'll be there."

"Okay . . . then I'll do it. I mean, I've got nothing to lose, right?" she says. "Set it up, and I'll meet with you and your pastor."

"That's awesome!"

Thank You, Lord!

For the next hour and a half, I talk to Kalea about my work with Hopes and Prayers and the new friends I've made. She tells me about traveling to Canada and back, her pregnancy, and some little tidbits about our children.

"Thank you, Sean," she says, sounding much calmer than before. Tired, too. "I feel much better. I'll be okay now."

"I'm glad."

There's a brief silence.

"Hey," she says.

"Hm?"

"I'm happy it was you. Of all the men in the world that I could have had a relationship and these children with, I'm so relieved it was you."

How am I supposed to respond to that? I'm stumped for a moment.

"Are you sure you're going to be okay?" I ask her.

"Yes. Thanks for listening to my craziness. Good night, Sean."

"Good night, Kalea."

Not long after we hang up, I send a text to my pastor, Charles Anderson. I ask him if we can talk on the phone tomorrow to discuss an important matter.

. . .

I find myself in the mountains with Kalea. I think it's a dream, but I'm not sure. It's morning; the sun is low in the red and orange sky. The air is cool, though not uncomfortable. We're ascending a dirt path that's surrounded by trees, grass, and flowering plants. I know where we're going, and she's following close behind me.

There's a foggy mist near the ground. It's kind of pretty and doesn't get in our way. The dirt trail becomes rockier. It doesn't slow us down, though.

I cross a suspension bridge—the final hurtle in our short journey. Once I get midway, I no longer hear Kalea's footsteps. I turn to check on her and see that she hasn't stepped onto the bridge. She's just looking at me fearfully.

I don't understand why she's so worried. I smile reassuringly and motion for her to follow me. I know she'll be fine. She shakes her head and takes a step back. That confuses me; but we're so close to where we're going, I point at her and then motion for her to join me once again. Still frightened, she points at me urgently. No, not at me. She points at the bridge beneath me, so I look down.

There are no deck planks beneath my feet. There's the sky above and a
chasm below. Yet I'm safe and feel no fear.

. . .

I startle awake, surprised. I open my eyes but don't move my
body for a moment. I turn my head to look around the dark bedroom,
replaying the dream while it's fresh in my mind. Kalea only saw
danger. I knew there was a bridge there, whether I saw it or not. She
only saw the gaping chasm and me floating in mid-air. That's when
I realize something: even though I became disillusioned with my
religious upbringing, it did introduce me to the idea of God, Jesus,
and the Bible. And when God rescued me, I recognized Him. He had
already given me some faith.

I don't think Kalea has any of that. Her parents died when she was
young, and the relatives who took her in had no Christian background.
Her whole life, she's been the only one she could believe in. I want to
help her see that she doesn't have to do this alone anymore.

. . .

By mid-morning, I get a text response from Pastor Anderson
while I'm at work. I decide to call him during my lunch and share
Kalea's unexpected return and her anxiety. I also tell him she's open
to talking with him if I'm present.

"Okay, then let's meet this evening at my house at seven," he tells me.

"Sure. I'll call and invite her," I reply. "I'll let you know if there are
any problems."

He tells me it's all right to give his address and phone number to
Kalea.

. . .

Evening comes quickly. I get a ride to the pastor's residence, a one-story home in the Forest Park neighborhood. As I step out of the vehicle, I see Kalea drive up and park at the curb in front of the house. She exits, and I go to help her get the twins into the stroller. She looks a bit stressed until we make eye contact; then she relaxes some.

"Hey," I say.

"Hey yourself," she replies.

I release Little Sean from his car seat and gently put him in the stroller.

"I'm glad you're here, Kalea."

"I'm glad *you're* here," she tells me as she gets Shawna.

"Everything will be fine," I reassure her.

Kalea did a nice job styling her hair. It's kind of slicked back on top and pulled into a long, braided ponytail. I'm used to seeing it sprawl over her shoulders, so this is positively restrained for Kalea. Her long-sleeved, white blouse and navy blue skirt also look nice. She has Sean and Shawna in pastel outfits with matching beanies. I'm still wearing my work clothes.

We follow the short sidewalk path from the driveway through the grass to the dark brown front door. I press the doorbell, and a moment later, Pastor Anderson opens the door. He's in his mid-forties, tall and broad-shouldered with an average build. He has a simple, kind face; compassionate, brown eyes; and short, receding brown hair.

"Good evening," he says. "I'm Charles Anderson, the pastor at Finding Hope Church."

"I'm Kalea Nadeaux," she tells him.

"Thank you for coming," he tells her, extending a hand.

She shakes his hand briefly and lets go. I can see she's nervous. He shakes my hand, too.

Mrs. Anderson walks from the living room to the doorway. She's almost the same height and build as her husband. She has strong cheeks; a button nose; wavy, blonde hair; and deep green eyes. She's wearing a light yellow dress and matching low heel shoes. Lightly touching Pastor Anderson's shoulder, she passes him to greet Kalea with a wide smile.

"Good evening, Kalea, I'm Carrie Anderson," she says, shaking Kalea's hand. "It's a pleasure to meet you."

Then she sees the twins in the stroller and brightens even more.

"Oh, look at these beautiful babies!" she chirps. "They're adorable!"

Kalea blushes with pride. "Thank you."

"What are their names?"

"Sean and Shawna."

Mrs. Anderson looks to me and smiles. "Good evening, Brother Winter," she says, shaking my hand. Her eyes convey an unspoken question about the twins' parentage. I nod my answer, smiling back.

"Kalea, I know you're here to speak with my husband. Do you mind if I care for your children while you do that?"

"That's very kind of you, but I'm used to caring for them."

We all walk inside to the living room. I push the stroller, while Kalea continues speaking with Mrs. Anderson.

"We had three children, and our last two were twins," the pastor's wife says.

"Really?" Kalea replies.

Mrs. Anderson nods. "You have to be a super mom to take care of twins. But even super moms need help sometimes. Our kids are grown now, and we have a couple of grandkids already. They're not much older than your kids, and they stay with us sometimes. So, we set up a room in the back for them."

"So . . . it won't be any trouble?" Kalea asks.

"No trouble at all," Mrs. Anderson says. "And I'm happy to do it."

"All right," Kalea relents. "Thank you very much, Mrs. Anderson."

"You're very welcome," the older woman beams.

I step back from the stroller, and the pastor's wife wheels them past the living room to a hallway.

I've only been over to the pastor's house a couple of times. We enter the living room, which has a brown-tiled floor; a long, tan couch; and several pieces of framed art and family pictures on the walls. A fireplace and a large bookcase span the back wall. Pastor Anderson leads us into the dining room, and we sit down in tall-back chairs surrounding a rectangular table with a clear glass surface. It's set with four ceramic plates and silverware.

"We prepared some refreshments to enjoy during our conversation," the pastor says. "Would either of you like some coffee, tea, or bottled water to drink? Miss Nadeaux, do you have any food allergies?"

"No, sir," Kalea replies. "And please, just call me Kalea."

She then opts for bottled water while I ask for some tea. A minute later, Pastor Anderson brings our drinks. There are already small bowls of fresh fruit on the table as well as crackers and some asparagus dip.

"Pastor Anderson, Sean trusts you," Kalea says. "And he said you could help me with . . . the way I've been feeling since I moved back to Oklahoma City recently."

The pastor nods. "Well, the best way to start is with prayer. Do you mind if we do that before we begin?"

She thinks about that a moment. "All right."

Pastor Anderson asks us to close our eyes and bow our heads.

"Father, it's in the name of your beloved Son Jesus that we come humbly before you now," he begins. "We ask that You visit us here tonight. We seek Your will and Your favor at this time. Please bless Miss Kalea Nadeaux and her children this evening. We ask that You guide our words and our hearts. Please bring healing and reconciliation. We thank You and ask these blessings in Jesus' name. Amen."

Kalea takes a drink from her water and then tries some of the asparagus dip with a cracker. I try a strawberry and have some tea.

"Kalea, would you tell me about what you've been going through?" the pastor asks.

Kalea takes a long breath. "I'll try." It's a minute before she speaks again. "It's . . . like I lose control of my emotions sometimes."

"In what way?" Pastor Anderson asks. "What triggers it?"

"Thinking about Sean," she says softly. "And . . . all we have been to each other. But—" She suddenly chokes up. "When I got back, Sean told me what he . . . that he went through a lot . . . because of me. He almost died because of me." Now she's crying. "And the thought of losing him forever . . . because of what I did . . . it did something to me. It tears at me, and I feel so guilty! I never wanted to hurt him—I love him!"

She breaks down into sobs. I rest my hand on hers to try and comfort her. The pastor is respectfully silent. After a couple of minutes, she calms down.

"I've made a big mess of things," she continues, trying to wipe the tears from her eyes. "I can barely keep up with my kids, and they deserve more. I want to be with Sean, but I don't know what to do."

In that moment, I think about my dream from last night.

"Kalea, you've done a good job with Sean and Shawna," I tell her.

She looks confused and a little embarrassed as she turns her head to look at me.

"Thank you, but why say that now?" she asks.

"You've only had yourself up 'til now, right? You were the only one you could count on?"

She slowly nods. "That's right."

"I was the same way for a long time. I couldn't count on my grandparents, so I had to do everything myself. But I was always scared, afraid I would mess up."

She doesn't say anything, but I can tell she relates to what I'm saying. I make brief eye contact with Pastor Anderson. His warm expression and slight smile encourage me to continue.

"That approach got me through college and into my first job," I continue. "But I was falling apart inside. The more I fought to gain control, the more out of control things got, including our relationship and . . . what happened after."

Her face pales at the mention of it.

"Kalea, my point is when I was at my lowest, God was there for me. All I had to do was trust . . . in Him—that He wanted to help me, that He loved me. It was just a little bit of faith, but it changed everything."

She relaxes her shoulders some and allows herself a nervous smile.

"Just a little bit of faith, huh?" she repeats.

I don't hear any sarcasm in her voice. And I feel like she's lowered a wall.

. . .

Forty minutes later, I watch Pastor Anderson humbly work with Kalea. She has questions about a lot of things: the natures of God and Jesus, what purpose the Bible serves, and what sin really is. The pastor uses Scriptures to answer each point.

"I have to make a decision, don't I?" she asked him. "Either I want this Jesus in my life, or I don't . . . right?"

"We all have to make that decision at some point," the pastor replied. "But it's entirely up to you."

"Hmmm, I get it."

She looked down for a moment, contemplating something.

"I've decided," she says calmly, pausing briefly. "I want . . . I *need* the Lord to save me, Pastor." Then she looks at him, tears forming. "I don't want to live another minute like this."

As the pastor prays with her, she doesn't speak out loud. I close my eyes and pray, too. Several minutes later, I hear her stand up, so I open my eyes again.

"Do you feel the Lord answered your prayer?" Pastor Anderson asks.

"Yes, sir."

"Can you tell me what happened?" he adds.

She nods, smiling but teary-eyed. "I came here feeling weighed down by . . . everything in my life. All the wrongs I ever did pulling me down . . . and then, I felt love all around me. That's the only way I can describe it. I felt that Jesus was there." Then she puts a hand on her chest near her heart. "And now, He's here."

We both look at each other.

I can feel myself grinning. I'm feeling euphoric at seeing Kalea receive Christ. I don't hear all of their following conversation. I'm so happy for her . . . and I think I'm happy for me, too.

Then I notice Pastor Anderson looking at me.

"What is it, sir?" I ask him.

"I believe there's . . . something you didn't bring to the altar, Sean."

I freeze. "What do you mean?"

"I think there's something from your past that you haven't let go of."

I wonder what it could be? I'm pretty sure I confessed everything.

Kalea is looking at us, not saying a word. She seems like she doesn't want to interfere. She sits back down.

"I'm not sure what it could be?" I say nervously.

"Take some time and ask the Lord to show you your heart. When He reveals it to you, there'll be no doubt, and we'll be able to talk about it together."

"All right."

Soon, Mrs. Anderson gingerly brings out the children in their stroller. Shawna is asleep, and Little Sean is grumpy. At the news of Kalea's salvation, Mrs. Anderson gives her a hearty hug. After we thank them for everything and say goodbye, we head outside.

"You took PayMeRide to get here?" Kalea asks.

"Yep, like always," I reply.

"You really need to get a car," she says. "Mind if I drive you home?"

"Thanks."

19

GIVING BEAUTY
FOR ASHES

As we leave the pastor's neighborhood, I know we're in uncharted territory. Who will Kalea and I be to each other now? I feel a little awkward and don't know what to say. Despite those concerns, I feel like I'm supposed to be here.

"Sean, thank you again for . . . putting up with all of my craziness," she tells me. "This is new, but I . . . I have hope now."

"It will get better from here," I assure her.

She nods. "I've never felt like this," she continues. "I know everything is okay. I . . . I feel free!"

"You are."

She sighs.

"Part of me worries that something will go wrong, or this is a dream or something," she says.

"I know the feeling," I reply. "But Christ is always with me. And He's with you now, too. We're not going to face these things alone."

She smiles at that. We drive for a minute in silence.

"How's the job?" Kalea wonders. "Still at Prosaic?"

"Yeah, I'm still there. Everything's fine."

She keeps her focus on the road ahead.

"The same crew there?" she asks.

"There's been some turnover; but Jessica, Ben, Keith, and Jimbo still work there," I answer. "Jimbo even got a promotion. He's the chief network admin now."

"Good for him!" she says sincerely. "I always liked Jimbo."

"Miranda got another job," I mention. "She left a few months ago."

Kalea smirks but says nothing. I can't say I blame her. Miranda didn't really get along with anyone.

"I should talk to Ben," Kalea says. "I asked a lot of him before I left with no explanation. I should apologize."

I remember. That really did upset Ben.

"Would you like me to go with you?" I ask.

"No, but thanks," she answers. "I'll handle it."

There's a brief silence.

"So, you said you have a job that lets you work remotely?" I ask.

She nods. "I do customer service and booking for the Beryl International hotel chain."

"Very cool."

"Yeah. They let me set my own hours, as long as I work a total of eight hours a day or more."

"That's great!" I tell her. "Is the pay good?"

"It's about the same as I made at Prosaic," she replies. "But I do get benefits now like medical insurance, and that's important with the twins."

"That's good. Um, listen Kalea, I want to help . . . with the twins . . . and you, too. If I can, that is."

Still looking ahead, she grins this time.

"That's really sweet," she says. "That's the Sean I remember."

I smile at the compliment. We enter the parking lot of my apartment complex. She pulls into one of the spaces and eases to a stop before putting the car in park.

She turns her head to face me. "For the first time in my life, I have no idea what to do next. But . . . somehow, that's okay."

I chuckle a little. "Yeah. Just take things one day at a time."

She nods. "Good night, Sean."

"Good night, Kalea."

. . .

Over the next week, I start spending a couple of hours each day with Kalea and the twins after work. At first, I had some reservations about making this a daily routine. I thought it might be awkward—and Kalea seemed as nervous as me at first. She wouldn't say much unless I asked her questions about the infants' care.

Now, it's Thursday. When she opens her door, the sound of simmering meat and the delightful scents of spices let me know she's been cooking. That and the light blue apron Kalea's wearing over her white blouse.

"Come on in, Sean. I'm just making a taco supper for us. I hope you don't mind."

"No, I don't mind," I say with a grin. "I'm starving!"

She smiles. "It'll be ready in about fifteen to twenty minutes."

"Thanks."

Once we're inside, she heads back into the kitchen. I enter the living room. Then I get on my knees to greet our children, who are laying on a soft mat on the floor. I see recognition in their eyes.

"Hey there, Little Sean, Shawna! It's Daddy! I missed you. I'm happy to see you!"

I notice I've started exaggerating my expressions a little bit when I talk to them. I feel the tugging at the corners of my mouth as I watch their wriggles and kicks.

"They look forward to your visits now," Kalea says from behind me in a warm voice.

Curious, I turn my head to look at her. "How can you tell?"

"They get excited when they see you," she replies. "I think they know it's their daddy."

I guess I'll attribute that to maternal intuition. And I'd like to think it's true.

Kalea walks back into the kitchen and turns off the oven burner. Then she brings two plates to the dinner table, where two glasses of water are already set.

"Have a bite and let me know if it needs anything, okay?" she asks.

"Do you mind if we say the blessing first?"

"What do you mean 'the blessing'?" She's never done that, I guess.

"The blessing is saying a short prayer to thank God for the food. It's also asking Him to literally bless the food," I add.

She looks surprised. "I didn't know that was needed. And it's important?"

"It is. The Lord does so much for us. So, we should thank Him whenever we can."

"I get the idea," she replies. "Go ahead and say the prayer."

I have to mentally swat away bad memories of Grandma and all the times she forced me to recite her specific idea of a "good and proper blessing." As long as what I say honors the Lord and is from my heart, it will be fine.

I close my eyes and lower my head.

"Heavenly Father, we thank you for providing for our needs. Please bless this food to our good health. We ask this in Jesus' name. Amen."

"Amen," Kalea repeats. "That was a nice prayer. Are we supposed to do that with every meal?"

"You're not required to do it. But it's good to do. And you can word it your own way."

She considers it briefly then smiles. "Okay. That's one more thing to get used to, I guess. But I don't mind."

"You don't?"

She shakes her head. "No. I'm still trying to understand everything. But I know the Lord changed me. I want to show Him I'm thankful."

I nod in response and then take a bite from one of the tacos. It's delicious and spicy, just like I remember. She's still a good cook.

"This is the first meal we've had together since I left," she tells me.

"Yeah," was all I could think to say.

We eat in silence for a minute.

"Thank you," she says.

"For what?"

"For wanting to be in our children's lives."

She barely looks up as she talks. She's clearly uncomfortable with the subject.

"They're our children," I reply. "I—it's not just a want. I *need* to be in their lives."

"And that's why you'll be a good father."

I feel my cheeks warm up as I blush.

"You're a good mother to them."

Now she's the one who blushes.

Little Sean, as I've come to call him, cries for her attention. I can finally tell the difference between the twins' voices now. Kalea checks him.

"He needs changing," she says. "Can you do it?"

"Okay."

This is another thing I've learned this week. But I don't mind. It's a way that I can help with them. I have just finished changing Sean's diaper when Shawna begins to wail.

"She's hungry," Kalea says. "You'll have to excuse us ladies for a bit."

. . .

What I notice over the next month is how natural it feels to be around Kalea and the children. It becomes more than a routine. I look forward to my time with them, sharing meals with Kalea, and even going to church together. In my daily prayers, I ask the Lord to guide my steps. I ask Him to show me what my relationship with Kalea is supposed to be.

One evening, as I'm preparing to leave her apartment, my feet don't want to move. I'm five feet from the door. It should be easy, but not tonight.

"What is it, Sean? Did you forget something?" She's right behind me. This moment feels right.

C'mon Sean, of all the times to be spontaneous, this is it!

"I love you, Kalea."

I turn around easily, and she locks eyes with me, stunned. "What?"

"I love you. If it's the Lord's will, I want to be a real family—with you and the kids."

She studies my face for a long moment. I see her worry begin to melt away, and it turns into joy.

"I—I—yes!" she stammers, putting her warm hand on top of mine. "Yes?"

"You just asked me to marry you, right?"

I did do that, didn't I?

My nervousness is gone. I've decided. And I'm at peace about it. I want Kalea to be my wife.

"Yes," I reply confidently.

She lifts her hand and puts it to my cheek as she peers deeply into my eyes.

"So, my answer is yes, Sean Winter."

I grin in response. Inside, I'm thrilled with her answer.

We hug, and it feels good. When she lets go and moves back, she wipes a tear from her eye.

"How soon?" she asks.

"Well, we have to tell everybody," I answer. "And I'd like it if we could talk to Pastor Anderson and get some marriage advice before the wedding."

"Those are good points," she concedes. Then she raises an eyebrow. "So . . . how soon are we getting married?"

I think about that for a few seconds. Then I put my hand to her soft cheek and smile at her. "How about a month from now?"

She blushes bright pink as she grins at me. "Sean, I'd marry you right now if I could! But, sure, a month from now will work."

. . .

When I enter my apartment thirty minutes later, I go change into a t-shirt and shorts before turning off the bedroom light. Sitting on the edge of my bed, I take in my surroundings as my vision acclimates to the moonlit room. This apartment has been my home for more than a year now. It still isn't decorated very well, especially this room. There's just a few old *Star Wars* posters on these off-white walls and a small, framed graduation picture on my nightstand.

A lot is about to change. When Kalea and I get married, this place won't be big enough for the four of us. We could probably manage at her apartment for a while, at least until we get something better. A house, I suppose. Can we afford that? I probably shouldn't get ahead of myself.

Relaxing, I lay down in bed and pull the covers over me. I can hear a plane flying overhead nearby. Part of me wants to follow the sounds of it into a deep sleep, but my thoughts and memories are too active.

Tonight, I told Kalea I love her. I asked her to become my wife. It certainly wasn't a conventional marriage proposal. Some people might even call what I did lame or foolish—asking her to be my wife without getting on one knee or even having a ring. Then again, we haven't done anything in a "traditional" way, starting with sleeping together the first day we met. We embarked on a whirlwind romance, each of us with different agendas driven by our past hurts. But the Lord saw past all that and saved us. He's leading us down a better path. All we have to do is trust in Him and follow.

20

CATCHING UP

Four days later, I open the door and let Ben Deconde into my apartment.

"Hey, Sean, thanks for meeting me on short notice like this," he says.

"You caught me just in time; I was about to go see Kalea and the kids."

"I won't take too much time," Ben adds. "But it's Kalea I wanted to talk to you about."

"Okay," I reply as we walk toward the couch. "Want something to drink? I've got water, fruit juice, coffee—"

"No, thanks," he says, shaking his head nervously.

We sit down and he shares his experience with me.

"I was still at work, about to head home, when I got a call on my cell phone. When I saw Kalea's name and number show up, I just answered it.

"She said, 'Hi, Ben,' and I said, 'Kalea. Wow.'

"She said, 'I owe you a big apology, Ben. I asked you and Jimbo to help me move without telling you what I was really planning. And that was wrong. I'm sorry.'

"I didn't want to get angry in front of a bunch of people, so I walked to the breakroom real fast.

"I said, 'Why didn't you trust me? You and I go back a little ways. You could have told me.'

"And she said, 'I could give you a bunch of excuses, but the truth is, I was scared you might try to talk me out of leaving. And because of our friendship, I knew if I didn't tell you, then I could count on you and Jimbo.'

"She had a point.

"I said, 'I probably would have tried to talk you out of it, yeah. But either way, I would've respected your wishes.'

"She said, 'I believe you. I guess I didn't trust myself, either. I was already an emotional mess from being pregnant; I could've changed my mind very easily.'

"I told her I wish she had.

"And she said, 'I know I hurt you all—especially Sean. If I could go back in time, I'd change things.'

"So I said, 'Look, Kalea, if you just called to say you're sorry, it's okay. I've been more angry at myself than you.'

"Then she asked, 'Why?'

"And I told her, 'Where do I start? I introduced you two at the party, encouraged Sean to drink when he didn't want to. I even rooted for your and Sean's relationship.'

"But she said she encouraged you to drink, too.

"She said, 'I had a part in that. But what's wrong with rooting for me and Sean?'

"I laughed at that. Then I said, 'Do you really need me to explain that? Your relationship . . . was a disaster.'

"I felt kind of bad about saying that, but I had to.

"She said, 'It almost was. And that was my fault. It was . . . all my fault. But I'm trying to change that now. I've changed.'

"I said, 'That sounds good. But you've always talked a good talk.'

"Then out of nowhere, she said, 'I've moved back to Oklahoma City with the twins.'

"Did you know that, Sean?

"Anyway, I said, 'Really? You moved back?'

"She told me, 'I want to make things right, Ben.'

"I wasn't really convinced, so I said, 'Do you really think you can do that?'

"And she said, 'I know words aren't enough. I'll have to let my actions prove it.'

"I didn't expect her to say something like that. So I said, 'You have changed, haven't you?'

"I heard her chuckle a little. Then she said, 'Yeah.'

"After that, she told me she needed to go, but I felt like I needed to tell her something else.

"'Kalea?' I said.

"She said, 'Yes?'

"I told her, 'I'm sorry, too. And I'm glad you're back.'

"That seemed to make her happy. We said goodbye, and that was that."

. . .

"I just thought you should know," Ben says, looking relieved.

"Thanks. I'm glad you told me," I reply. "I've been wanting to talk with you, too."

We're both still sitting on the couch.

"Yeah? What about?" Ben asks, turning his head to look at me.

"Kalea came to see me first when she moved back to town. We talked, and I told her everything that's happened since she left . . . including my suicide attempt."

His eyes widen briefly at that. "How'd that sit with her?"

"She took it hard," I tell him. "She was very sorry for everything. And she said she came back so I could see the kids regularly. And that's what I've been doing."

Ben nods slowly. "I guess she really is trying to do better by you."

I stand up and go to get a water from the refrigerator. I offer again to get something for Ben, but he waves it off. I walk to the couch but remain standing.

"Kalea's become a Christian, Ben. And . . . after spending the last month or so with her and the kids, I asked her to marry me. She said yes."

Ben looks kind of shocked at first. I did just drop a lot on him. After a few seconds, he stands up, smiles, and offers me his hand.

"Congrats, Sean! If you two have made peace and this is what you want, I'll support you!"

I shake his hand firmly and return the smile. "Thanks, man!"

We talk for a few more minutes, and then Ben has to go.

21

DISTANT THUNDER

I wake up to the sound of rain splashing against my bedroom window. I don't remember showers being in the forecast. I'm glad it's Saturday morning, and this isn't a severe storm.

After I wash up and get dressed, I kneel beside my bed and pray for a few minutes. I'm looking to the Lord for direction, especially with what the pastor told me the other day about the "something from my past that I haven't let go of."

Following my prayer, I start some coffee and lean against the counter while I'm waiting for it to brew. I imagine the future, a few years from now: Little Sean and Shawna are sitting at the dining table, asking what's for breakfast. In this scenario, Kalea and I have been married for a while. She's already up and doing her work-from-home job in an adjoining room. Instead of this one-bedroom apartment, I see us in a medium-sized house. That feels right to me.

I envision walking over to Kalea, after the kids begin eating. She's sitting at a desk with a laptop. I gently put my hands on her shoulders. I massage out some of the tautness that's already built up. Then I give her a kiss.

Suddenly, my phone rings, pulling me back to reality.

"Good morning," Kalea says, almost singing the words cheerfully.

"Morning. How are you?"

"I'm still on Cloud Nine—about being your fiancée," she replies. "And how is my future husband?"

"Not bad," I reply. "Just making some breakfast before I head over."

"I guess it's good to keep up your skills," she teases. "So, how long do you think you'll be?"

"An hour? Maybe less."

"Okay," she says. "See you then!"

As I hang up the phone, I hear some thunder in the distance. That's odd.

. . .

It's pouring rain even before my ride picks me up. The lightning and thunder along the way put my nerves on edge, and the driver is going under the speed limit to compensate for the bad weather. In my mind, I know this storm probably won't produce a tornado. But that doesn't prevent my memories of living through it once before. Is this not a good day to be out?

No. Kalea's counting on me to come over. And I want to keep learning how to care for our children.

Even so, the wind has started picking up quite a bit, making the PayMeRide driver have to slow down even more. I see twigs and leaves flying past in the rain, which is streaming sideways against the car's windows. I'm not so sure about the skies anymore.

Arriving, I walk to the first-floor apartment and knock on the door more loudly than I intended. While I wait for her to answer, I wipe some rain from my forehead. I'm not too nervous, but I'll be glad to go inside.

Several seconds later, Kalea opens the door, holding Shawna against her chest. She looks past me to assess the weather before grabbing my arm.

"Come on, get inside," she says, sounding concerned.

We move through the hallway and into the living room. Little Sean is looking at us from a playmat. At Kalea's prompting, we sit down on the carpet next to him.

"This is turning into tornado weather," Kalea sighs. "A watch is already in effect."

Instinctively, I grab my phone from my pocket and pull up the weather app. I use my fingers to enlarge the live radar map, closing in on the red. I spot a few pockets of dark purple, and my anxiety grows. I fight the feeling, but it's tough. I put the phone away and look at Kalea again.

A memory flashes through my mind. "You were at Prosaic the day the tornado hit, right?"

She nods grimly. "I'll never forget it."

"Me either," I reply. "That was the day I met Keith. I got mad at him because he was praying, but I think those prayers made a difference. The Lord let the tornado pass by our building and leave us unharmed."

"I didn't know that," she considers. "But I believe it. We . . . we should pray now, shouldn't we?"

"Yes."

Right there in the living room, we close our eyes and bow our heads.

"Dear Lord, we praise Your holy name and thank You for our salvation," I begin. "Right now, we ask Your protection through this storm above. Please keep our family safe. We give You all the honor and glory, Heavenly Father, because You deserve it. We pray in Jesus' holy name. Amen."

"Amen," Kalea says.

I pick up Little Sean and pay attention to him while Kalea has Shawna in her lap, soothing her fussiness. For the first time, I know deep within myself that I'd protect this family with my life.

The rain gets more intense. The lightning is almost blinding at times, followed by strong thunder that makes the windows shudder. The babies cry and cling to us throughout the wait. Then the storm gradually lessens until it's just a light rainfall.

Now, I take a deep breath and exhale. I check my app again; the radar shows me the storm has passed south of us.

"Thank you, Lord!" I say softly as I close my eyes and smile.

"It's over?" Kalea asks.

"Yeah, the worst has passed us already."

She lets out a sigh of relief and looks toward Heaven. "Yes! Thank you."

. . .

It continues to lightly rain throughout the day. Kalea had wanted us to take the kids for a stroll, but that's not happening now.

"I might have some board games. They'd be in one of the boxes in the hallway near my bedroom. I never did finish unpacking," she chuckles. "Would you mind checking? You can choose if you like any of them."

"Okay, sure."

I go to see if I can find the games. The first box I open only seems to have clothing. The second box is full of her artwork. The papers near the top look recent. I'm glad she's continued her sketches. I know I shouldn't take too much time with these, but she really is good. She's started drawing the kids and other backgrounds like trees and flowers.

But I freeze when I see the next piece of paper. It looks like she made it in the last year but . . . it's a different baby's face. And she wrote the word "Aria" next to it. The papers below have even more drawings of Aria. It's almost overwhelming. Then I hear Kalea rushing toward the room. I turn and see a guilty expression on her face.

"I didn't want you to see those!" she spits the words.

"I don't understand," I say honestly. I'm disturbed by this discovery and can barely speak. "Why?" I whisper.

"I still miss her," Kalea admits. "I guess I always will."

I suppose that makes a kind of sense, but . . . does this mean she wants her back? Isn't she satisfied with *our* children? I can't help it. My field of vision narrows, and I tense up. Hasn't she changed?

Did she really accept the Lord?

No, I can't think that way! I know this hurts, but I'm not the person I used to be. I need to find out what's really going on. I need to give her a chance to tell her side.

"Let's go back to the living room," she says sadly. "I'll try to explain."

I'm still angry inside, but I make myself get up and follow her. We sit back down on the couch.

"I was ashamed to admit this to you. I should have told you sooner," she confesses. "But it was like saying I failed. My whole point in getting pregnant with the twins was to replace Aria. I honestly thought that would heal me and . . . fix everything."

Obviously, it didn't.

"The twins have been in my heart since the pregnancy," she continues. "They're beautiful and gave me new purpose . . . but they didn't replace Aria. They're her siblings. I don't know what I'm doing wrong. I thought getting saved would fix this, too." She looks down a moment, closing her eyes.

I'm torn inside. Part of me is glad she's finally being honest about all this. And part of me is furious.

"I'm jealous of Aria, jealous for our twins," I snap at her. "Will they always come second to their sister, who they'll never meet? It's so unfair! Reason tells me that you can't help how you feel. But you have to let go!"

She stands there silent and still. She isn't crying, and it doesn't seem like she will.

"Do you truly feel guilty for what you've done, or are you just resentful you can't see your daughter?"

"Sean . . ."

Even though I'm still upset, I do feel some pity for her. She looks miserable.

"I—I don't want to keep feeling like this. I want peace about Aria," she tells me. "But I don't know what to do!"

I sympathize now. I believe her.

"When I don't know what to do, I ask the Lord to help me," I say. "Even if I just think it."

She nods slowly. Her eyes plead with me. "Then will you say a prayer for me . . . for us?"

If anyone can fix this, it's Jesus. I tell her I will pray about this. Then I close my eyes and bow my head.

"Dear Lord, we pray in the name of Your Son, Jesus," I begin. "We thank You for Your grace, mercy, and salvation. And we're asking for Your help again, Lord."

I hear Kalea whisper, "Please."

"We ask you to free Kalea from the pain tied to her daughter, Aria."

"Help me let Aria go," Kalea sobs. "I want to love this family right!"

I can hear the desperation in her voice, and it moves me. I really want the Lord to help her.

"Please bless us, Lord. We need you so much! And we're handing this over to you. We ask these blessings in Your holy name, Lord Jesus. Amen."

"Amen," she whispers.

I open my eyes at the same time as Kalea. She looks tired.

"Now we just need to believe the Lord will help us."

"I do," Kalea says. "Sean, I meant what I said to the Lord. I want to give my everything to our family."

"I believe you, Kalea," I say with a new smile. "And I want to do the same."

When it's time for me to leave and the driver arrives, I give the kids kisses on their foreheads and Kalea a gentle hug. I don't want to leave. I feel even more protective of this family.

22

A JUXTAPOSITION OF FLOWER SEEDS

The ride home is very different from the one to Kalea's. There's a light rain as we cruise through the neighborhood. However, there's no tension or sense of foreboding. The overcast sky has made it seem to get dark earlier than usual, and most of the passing cars have their lights turned on.

The female driver is listening to some classical jazz on her satellite radio. Grandpa loved jazz and usually played it as he worked. Many times, he'd tell me about the different artists and their music. I recognize "Yardbird Suite" by Charlie "Bird" Parker as the current song. It's almost finished when we get to my apartment complex without incident. Once I get to my door, I send a text to let her know I got home safely. She replies a minute later, thanking me for that.

I go over and sit on the couch. I haven't thought about Grandpa much since the night of my suicide attempt. He may have had a lot of problems, but I know he loved me. Even so, I don't know if I feel safe reliving memories of him and Grandma. If I've truly forgiven them, that shouldn't be hard, right?

I take in a deep breath and slowly release it. Then I go to the URVidiot app on my phone and find a classical jazz playlist. I want to reminisce some, keeping the volume low. This is just for me, a way to relax before going to bed.

. . .

Half an hour later, I get a new text. This one's from Jennie Lou. It's then I realize we haven't chatted since Kalea got back. We have a lot to catch up on.

Hey, Sean! How have you been?

I'm okay. It's been quite a week.

Really? What's been going on?

Am I up for this conversation, even through text? Aren't we friends? She'll find out soon enough, anyway. I may as well tell her.

Kalea moved back to OKC with the twins.

There's a pause before she replies. As I wait, I notice the hum of the refrigerator behind me and the icemaker as it rattles out some cubes.

Why?

I lean forward on the couch, a little nervous.

She had a change of heart. It's kind of hard to explain. But she and I met with Pastor Anderson not long after she returned. Kalea gave her life to Christ. I've seen the change in her.

Another pause. I stand up and start to pace around the living room, wondering what to write next. But a lot of that will depend on Jennie Lou's response.

This is a lot to take in. Of course, if she really became a Christian, that's great.

She's skeptical, even after what I wrote?

262   THE FORMER THINGS

Now, I hesitate a moment, not sure if I want to share everything. Then again, I've come this far.

Jennie, I've asked Kalea to marry me. And she said yes.

There's no delay in her response this time.

What? Marriage? So soon?

We love each other, and we have the twins to think about, too.

Love? She just got back!

I know. A lot has happened in the last month.

Sean, it's your life. I'm just your friend. But . . . I'm not okay with this.

I don't know how to respond to that. And she doesn't text anything else.

. . .

It's been two weeks since I talked to Jennie Lou. Kalea's been out running an errand for a while. I came over to her apartment after I got off work at five. We talked while I played with the kids.

"I need to go for a bit," Kalea said. "Can you watch the kids?"

"I don't mind." I replied. "Little Sean and Shawna are used to me being around now."

It's been over an hour since Kalea left, and I'm getting concerned. I send her a text, but there's no reply yet. I try not to worry; she could be driving.

I've laid the babies on their child's mat, which is soft and has small, hanging cloth made to look like different animals for them to reach up to, touch, and shake. I enjoy watching them do that, talking with them as they play.

Forty-five minutes later, I hear the front door lock unlatch and breathe a sigh of relief. When they see her, the kids squeal in delight.

She's carrying two takeout bags and sets them on the dining room table before coming into the living room. Kalea sits down next to me on the couch. I'm not sure how to read her expression. She seems sad and relieved at the same time. She stretches her neck from side to side for a few seconds. Then she turns her head to look at me and takes my hand in hers.

"Sean, I need to apologize to you about something," she says. "The errand I went on . . . it was to see Jennie Lou."

"What? I don't understand. Did she contact you?"

"No," Kalea replies, shaking her head. "She contacted you. When you set your phone down to play with the kids, I heard a notification and saw that she sent you a text. So I read it."

I'm not sure how to feel about that. I grab my phone from the coffee table to see Jennie Lou's text myself. It reads: *Sean, I'd like to meet and talk about your relationship with Kalea. I'll be waiting at the Infinity Botanical Gardens by the zephyr lily exhibit at six o'clock. This is urgent. I really need to see you. Call if you'll be delayed.*

The only thing I can say out loud is "I see." I'm more confused than anything. Why would Jennie Lou want to meet like that?

"I decided to go in your place," Kalea adds. "I'm sorry for not telling you."

"Tell me what happened," I ask her. She nods.

"I arrived a little early, which gave me some time to find her. There was just one problem: I'd never seen her before. I only had your description of her to go off of.

"I also took some time to think about what I might say to her. But I didn't want a fight. I knew that would be wrong. So, I took a few seconds to whisper a short prayer.

"As I got closer to the middle of the gardens, I was surprised the exhibit area was blocked off. It was mostly dirt, and there was a sign that read, 'Please excuse our redecorating. We've recently reseeded this area. Please continue on to the rest of the gardens.' I could see more lush, flowering plants and greenery a few hundred feet away on either side.

"Then I saw a woman walking in my direction slowly, looking down like she was deep in thought. She was about my age and dressed nicely, as if she'd just came from work. I wondered if it was Jennie Lou. She slowed down more as she got closer, looking at all the dirt. And she read one of the signs.

"'Great,' she said in a huff.

"I decided to walk over to her then.

"'It looks like they did this pretty recently,' I said pleasantly, deliberately not introducing myself.

"'Yes, I think you're right,' she said to me. 'This is where the zephyr lilies usually are. They're my favorite.'

"'At least it's a small area,' I continued. 'There's plenty of garden left to enjoy.'

"The blonde woman smiled at me briefly, but I could tell she wasn't satisfied.

"'I asked someone to meet me here,' she added. 'I thought it might—never mind. I don't want to trouble you.'

"'It's no trouble,' I told her.

"She was silent for a few seconds, looking over the area before us.

"'My friend came here once . . . with a date,' she said. I could hear some serious disapproval in the way she said it. 'He said they really enjoyed their time at this exhibit. Anyway, the mood here now isn't exactly what I was hoping for.'

"I knew she had to be talking about our date, when we came here almost a year ago. Now I was sure it was Jennie Lou.

"'I remember it well,' I said softly.

"She turned her head sharply to look at me. 'What did you just say?'

"I extended a hand and smiled. 'I'm Kalea Nadeaux. It's nice to meet you, Jennie Lou. Sean isn't coming.'

"Her eyes went wide, and she stood there stiffly for several seconds. Then she folded her arms across her chest, and her gaze narrowed. Since she didn't accept my handshake, I withdrew it.

"'What do you mean, he's not coming?' she asked.

"'I saw your text, not him,' I replied. 'I thought we should talk instead.'

"There was a hot breeze, and it was already warm out today. Jennie Lou sighed and then sat down on a nearby bench, but I chose to remain standing.

"'I don't understand,' she muttered, leaning her head back and closing her eyes in frustration.

"I asked, 'What don't you understand?'

"'Forgive my bluntness, but why is he with you? You're the one who tricked him and hurt him,' she continued, leaning forward, and turning to look at me. She looked so resentful. 'He tried to kill himself over you!'

"That was low, but it's the truth. She meant to hurt me! I wondered if she wanted to hit me. I prayed silently right there. I still didn't want to fight her. I closed my eyes a moment and just breathed, waiting for the right words.

"'I know that. You're right,' I told her. 'And for reasons only God knows, Sean forgave me.'

"That settled Jennie Lou down some.

"'Yes, he did,' she said. 'He obviously did. He even asked you to *marry* him.'

"'I love Sean with everything I have. I—I'm not the way I used to be.'

"'Prove it.' She looked so cold, kind of intimidating. It surprised me, but I wasn't about to back down.

"'I don't have to prove anything to you,' I told her. 'You don't know me, but Sean does. That's why he chose me.'

"I knew she wouldn't like that, but it was the truth, too. And she was starting to upset me.

"'You're right; I don't know you,' she said. There was an edge in her voice now, and she gripped her arms tighter. 'So, I don't have to believe you, either.'

"I had to take some deep breaths because I was getting mad now.

"'You're his friend . . . and you're trying to protect him—' I started to say.

"But she interrupted me. 'I love Sean!' she erupted. 'I've loved him for years!'

"You did tell me before that she loved you. But I wasn't prepared to see her like this, passionately expressing those feelings for you. She looked angry, sad, and desperate all at once. She believed every word she was saying.

"But I saw the flaw in her approach, and I wasn't angry anymore. I felt sorry for her. This conflict was already over. We both just had to see and acknowledge it.

"'The person I used to be would have fought you over that challenge for Sean's love,' I told her. 'But even if you and I fought each other, it wouldn't matter.'

"She hesitated, thinking about what I'd just said. So I continued.

"'I don't have to fight you, Jennie Lou. It's not up to me or you what God's will for Sean's life is—or *our* lives, either. God has made His choices. We just have to accept them.'

"Jennie Lou stared at me for a few moments. Her expression was hard and judgmental. But slowly, that look faded. I could see she realized something.

"'I . . . had hoped that maybe it was all an act,' Jennie Lou said. 'You were still tricking him, trying to have your twins' father to yourself . . . or something. But now, I see that's not it.'

"I heard her sigh loudly. It was irritating. I didn't know how to take it. But then, she looked at me, and I could see a change. There was still anger there, but it wasn't as strong.

"'I just thought that when the Lord brought Sean back into my life, it was for us to be together at last,' she said.

"Words just came to me, and I had to say them. 'Jennie Lou, you helped Sean when he was at his lowest,' I told her. 'He told me what happened the night he attempted suicide. You were there for him, along with Keith. Your testimony, your friendship, your support, meant the world to him.'

"Jennie Lou looked at the ground for a few seconds, thinking. 'My testimony . . . my friendship . . . my support,' she said. 'Was it the Lord's will for me to just do that much—and no more?'

"She looked up at me a few seconds later and was very sad.

"'Like I said, I've loved Sean a long time. I assumed . . . I just assumed,' she said. 'And I—I made my desire to be with Sean more important than what God wanted.'

"I was shocked she admitted that, so I stayed quiet.

"She looked up at the sky. 'What if God just wanted my testimony to help Sean find Him . . . and that's it?' Then she turned toward me. 'Maybe Sean *is* supposed to be with you and his children.'

"Tears fell from her eyes then as she closed them. I sat down next to her and put my arms around her to comfort her. I was grateful that she let me. We stayed there a while until she was okay again. I offered to walk her to her car and make sure she was all right, but she asked me not to. She told me she needed some time to herself, but she'd be okay."

Sitting on the couch with Kalea, I'm not sure what to say at first. I'm stunned. Thinking it over, I don't think I could have handled things any better with Jennie Lou.

The babies are still playing on their mat. They're blissfully unaware of what their mother's been sharing with me.

"Are you okay, Sean?" Kalea asks, gently putting her hand on mine.

"Yeah, thanks," I reply with a nod. "Are you okay?"

"As confrontations go, that one wasn't too bad."

Despite her reassuring smile, her eyes are still a little red and puffy. She must have cried a lot before she came back. This was tougher on her than she's letting on.

"Thank you, Kalea."

"For reading your text and interfering with your friendship?" she half-jokes.

"No, for trying to make things right for everyone involved," I tell her.

"I'm just glad the Lord helped me so much."

She leans on me, and we're quiet for a while. Later on, I help her get the kids to bed. On my way home, I say a prayer for Jennie Lou in my heart. I hope she can find peace with all of this, so she can move on with her life.

23

LOOSE ENDS

My work shift is pretty typical for a Tuesday. By mid-morning, I'm definitely ready for some more coffee and a snack. As I walk toward the breakroom, I see Keith leaning against one of the hallway walls. He's on his cell phone, and he looks kind of upset.

"I wish I could explain, Julia," he says. Then he squints in frustration and breathes in sharply. "Look, I'm sorry. I shouldn't have called right now. I'm sorry. I'll call you later." He rushes that last sentence and hangs up.

I've never seen him so troubled like this. I close the distance between us and put a hand on his shoulder. It startles him, but he relaxes when he sees it's me.

"Hey, what's wrong, Keith?"

"I—" he starts to say. But he looks like he's about to cry, he's so overwhelmed. It really surprises me.

"Let's go to one of the empty offices. We can talk more privately," I suggest. He nods, and we go.

Soon, we're alone in a conference room. After locking the door, I close the blinds to reduce the sun's glare. Then we sit down.

"Is there a problem with Julia?" I ask. "I thought things were going better with you two."

Keith looks miserable. His fingers are clasped together on the wooden surface of the table, and he won't look up at me.

"Things have been going great," he replies with a shrug. "The problem is with me."

"How?"

"We've had great relationship counseling the last few months, between the one she recommended and, more recently, with Pastor Anderson," he begins. "Julia even gave her life to Christ. On Friday, we set a date to remarry."

I feel myself relax. "That's all great news! So, what's the problem?"

Now Keith looks at me with very haunted eyes.

"Throughout this whole process, I've felt really conflicted about going through with the marriage."

"What? Why?"

"Sean, I hurt her so badly when I cheated on her. The counseling helped me understand that very clearly. Even though we worked through it and Julia has forgiven me, I still have trouble with what I did."

I just look at him for a moment, taking in what he's just said.

"Why would you have a problem with it if she doesn't?" I ask.

"I keep feeling like . . . like I don't deserve her, not after betraying her that way," he says sincerely. "It's tough to hold her hands. And I haven't been able to kiss her since we reconciled."

I don't know what to say to him. Is this the same man who boldly witnessed Christ to me in the middle of a tornado? After all the Lord's done for Keith, how can he act like this? I'm fighting being disappointed in him.

"Pastor Anderson has been working with me one-on-one," Keith continues. "He believes I am wrestling with something spiritually—guilt and the need to forgive myself for what I did to her back then."

I slowly nod. "That makes sense. I'm glad he's talking with you about this."

"Opening up about it helps. You're one of the few people I feel comfortable speaking with about this."

"Sure, man. I'm here for you. I'll pray for you, too."

He stands up, still somewhat unsteadily. But he manages a smile for me. I stand up, too.

"Thanks. This has helped me, just talking with you," he says. "I think I can make it through the workday now."

We walk out of the conference room together. He heads back to his cubicle while I go to get coffee. I really am glad I can help in some way. And as many times as he's listened to me, I want to do the same for him. But it still troubles me that a strong Christian like him could go through something like this. Am I missing something here? Do even strong Christians struggle like this?

. . .

My conversation with Keith hangs over me the rest of the workday like a bad mood. I just can't shake how it made me feel in the end. As I leave work, the gray skies that threaten more rain match my mood pretty well. I manage to get most of the way home before the first drops fall.

Even when I enter my apartment, I don't feel relieved. I make some herbal tea and hope it will relax me. I hear some thunder close by.

Why am I so conflicted about this? It's not even my problem. Keith can handle this, right?

Is this even about Keith, or is this really about how I feel about his situation? What am I missing here?

Then my phone rings.

"Hi, Sean," Kalea says on the other end. She sounds a little down.

"Hey, what's up?"

"The power just went out here."

"Really? How about you three come over here?" I reply. "I could use the company."

"Thanks, that sounds good. We'll be there soon."

She arrives about thirty minutes later. I go out with my umbrella. I help get the babies out of the stroller and into the apartment as quickly as possible. It's raining pretty solidly now.

Once inside, Kalea and I hug and then sit on the couch. She turns her head to look at me and smiles.

"You're a real lifesaver," she says. "The kids were not happy with early lights-out."

"My pleasure. It's always good to see you."

"You, too," she says.

She looks at me a moment longer. Her calm gaze changes to one of concern. "What's wrong, Sean?"

I involuntarily smile at that. I guess it makes me feel good that she's starting to read my moods.

"Something unusual happened at work today," I tell her. "And I guess I'm still trying to figure it out."

"Want to talk about it?"

"I think I do, yeah."

She nods.

There's a flash, outside followed by thunder. The lights flicker but don't go out.

"I have some candles," I remember. "Maybe I should set a few out, in case we lose power, too."

"That's a good idea," she replies.

The candles are packed away in a box in my bedroom closet. I head that way, but as I enter my room and approach the closet, I get a sense of dread. Fighting it, I open my closet door and look down and to the left for the box. It's a medium-sized cardboard box that has the candles and a few keepsakes from my grandparents' house. I haven't opened it since I moved in here. But we may need the candles, so I pick it up and leave the closet.

As I walk across my room, I feel like the box is getting heavier in my arms with each step. Intellectually, I know nothing has changed about the box. It's me. My steps slow until I can't keep going.

I see their faces. Both Grandma and Grandpa. Alive. Dead. Grandma angry. Grandma hurting me, and Grandpa not doing anything about it.

Just then, Pastor Anderson's words come back to me: *"I believe there's . . . something you didn't bring to the altar, Sean."*

Grandma and Grandpa stumbling around drunk. Such pain when Grandma put out another one of her cigarettes on my neck. Watching Grandpa sobbing over Grandma's body in their bathtub. Then Grandpa's lifeless eyes staring at me after he took his own life.

"I think there's something from your past that you haven't let go of."

I don't even feel the box slip out of my hands while I remain standing. I don't hear it smack against the floor. I barely notice my knees hitting the ground. But I do feel my tears.

"Sean? What happened?" Kalea says, rushing into the room. She gets down on her knees and holds my shoulders.

I can't look at her. I'm still seeing all those painful moments. I can't speak at first, even though I try. Kalea holds me and does her best to comfort me. It takes a few minutes to recover.

"I'm . . . I'm sorry about that," I finally say.

"What happened, Sean?"

"The box with the candles—it's from my grandparents' place. It triggered so many memories."

She looks very worried for me. "Good or bad?"

"Mostly bad."

She nods sympathetically.

"Pastor Anderson . . . he was right," I tell her. "I haven't let go of my past . . . just like Keith."

I know I haven't told Kalea about Keith's problems, but I have to get this out.

"I . . . I haven't forgiven my grandparents. I told myself it was God's place to judge them, not me. But I never forgave them for what they put me through—and the Lord's showing me that I need to."

Kalea pulls me into a close hug. Nothing more needs to be said right now. But Jesus forgave me for all I did. And the Lord can help me forgive my grandparents.

EPILOGUE

It's the day of our wedding. Kalea and I stand together inside the sanctuary of Finding Hope Church. We're surrounded by friends, and a couple of Kalea's cousins even traveled from Canada to be here today.

It's not a large church, seating about 150 in its wooden pews. The bright sun outside is illuminating the sanctuary through its six stained glass windows, three on either side of the brown and white veneer walls.

Kalea is wearing a simple, light blue wedding dress. Her hair is pulled back and flowing gently behind her. She doesn't have to try to be beautiful to me, it just comes naturally. Her brown eyes have a sparkle to them, and she hasn't stopped smiling since joining me before the pastor. I feel like I'm in a dream. I'm nervous, but I've been looking forward to this for weeks. Now, it's really happening.

I asked Keith to be my best man. He's become my best friend over this last year. I don't think I would have made it through without the Lord and Keith. He looks really proud for me. I see him sneak a glance at Julia and their daughter Karen in the audience.

With the Lord and Pastor Anderson's help, Keith was able to forgive himself. He and Julia remarried, and I got to be one of his groomsmen.

Kalea has become good friends with one of the Hope and Prayers volunteers, Kathy Harwood, who is standing with Kalea as her maid of honor. We chose not to have additional groomsmen or bridesmaids. We wanted to keep things simple.

There's about seventy-five people present. Some are from the church congregation; others are from Hopes and Prayers; and there's even a few from Prosaic. I'm glad that Ben and Jimbo and his family are here. Even Jessica and her husband came.

I haven't seen Jennie Lou. She called me a couple of days ago to humbly decline our wedding invitation.

"Sean, I truly wish you and Kalea well," she had said. "But I'm still getting used to this, and . . . it would be too much for me right now. I'm sorry."

"I'm sorry, too, but I respect your wishes," I had replied. "We are still friends, right?"

She paused a moment. "Of course. We will always be friends. Just please be patient with me. We'll see what the Lord has planned for my own life."

"Okay, I understand. I . . . hope we'll see you soon."

I know the Lord will bless her. She's an incredible person. In the past, I would have said I didn't "deserve" her as a friend. Now, I know it's not about that; it's about what the Lord's will is for our lives. He sends us who we need, even if that doesn't match what—or who—we imagined.

"Sean Addison Winter," Pastor Anderson begins. "Do you take Kalea Ariel Nadeaux to be your lawfully wedded wife? Will you love her, comfort, honor, and cherish her above all others—in sickness and in health, forsaking all others, as long as you both shall live?"

"I will," I reply.

Then Pastor Anderson looks at Kalea.

"Kalea Ariel Nadeaux, do you take Sean Addison Winter to be your lawfully wedded husband? Will you love him, comfort him, honor and cherish him above all others—in sickness and in health, forsaking all others, as long as you both shall live?"

"I will," she answers proudly, briefly meeting my eyes before returning her attention to the pastor.

Only moments later, Pastor Anderson declares us husband and wife, both legally and in the sight of God. When Kalea and I close our eyes and kiss, it's simple and genuine. And when we pull back and look in each other's eyes, it's almost like we can hear our thoughts:

We did it! We're married!

We're a family. At last.

I love you!

It's a blissful moment. We hear the clapping and cheers of our loved ones, but it's something outside ourselves. We're just happy being together.

Kalea winks at me. "I told you Kalea Winter sounds pretty cool."

"It does," I agree.

. . .

We won't have the luxury of a honeymoon—at least not for a while. We could probably afford a weekend away, but not just anyone could babysit the twins. Also, Kalea doesn't want to be away from them, and honestly, neither do I. So, we decide to start saving up for a family vacation as a late honeymoon.

I've given notice to the apartment management that I won't be renewing. I've been in the process of selling or giving away things, mainly furniture I don't want to bring to Kalea's—and now *our*—apartment. As my old apartment becomes sparser, I realize I'm not going to miss those things . . . or the apartment. It served its purpose, housing me during one of the most difficult stages of my life. But now it's time to move on.

I've also decided that it's time for me to learn to drive. We're using Kalea's car for now, but eventually, I want to get my own vehicle.

I've gone through most of my life feeling uncertain about things—who loved me, who was my friend, my own worth, what I wanted to do, and who I wanted to be. Those ambiguities held me back and kept me from growing as a person. I let fear and anxiety control who I was.

All of that changed when I finally became aware that I didn't have to go through life alone. Jesus was there for me all along. All I had to do was reach out to Him and trust Him. I couldn't change myself. But with God, all things are possible.

Now, I'm a husband and father. I have this family that depends on me. And I'm strong enough now. I can be reliable. I want to do this because I love them. And because I have hope.

Now the God of hope fill you with all joy and peace in believing,
that ye may abound in hope, through the power of the Holy Ghost.
—Romans 15:13

THE END

ACKNOWLEDGMENTS

I want to thank God and His Son, Jesus Christ, for inspiring this novel. I had not planned to write it. But in April 2020, during the lockdown in Texas, the Lord gave me the main concept that turned into *The Former Things* and encouraged me to complete the first draft in thirty-three days.

My wife, Angel, helped me tremendously in further developing the characters and storyline. She is always there for me, and her love for these stories and the Lord shines in this novel.

I thank my two sons and my daughter for their love and support. They get to hear about my books all the time and occasionally give their feedback, which is helpful.

I am grateful for the support of the rest of my family and friends, including those from social media (especially Facebook, Twitter, and Instagram), during this endeavor. Special mentions to Parker J. Cole, Ariel Paiement, Joshua Reid, Larry Walker, Michael Bridges, Jeff VanMeter, and Alexzander Maldonado.

I am grateful to Ambassador International for believing in this novel. My special thanks to the publisher, Dr. Samuel Lowry, for his personal attention in helping me with *The Former Things*, and my editor, Daphne Self, for her tireless efforts. Kudos to everyone who had a hand in bringing this novel to fruition.

ABOUT THE AUTHOR

Allen Steadham created comic books and webcomics before he started writing novels. He has been married to his wife, Angel, since 1995 and they have two sons and a daughter. When not writing stories, Allen and his wife are singers, songwriters, and musicians. They have been in a Christian band together since 1997. They live in Central Texas.

www.allensteadham.com

www.facebook.com/iamallensteadham

Allen Steadham FB Readers Group: www.facebook.com/groups/2756807194616682

www.twitter.com/Mindfirenovel

www.instagram.com/allensteadham

www.bookbub.com/profile/allen-steadham

www.goodreads.com/allensteadham

ALSO BY ALLEN STEADHAM

Leia Hamilton's powers are awakened, and her life is forever changed. Suddenly her birth mother, the infamous supervillain Malevolence, is determined to be in her life. As she comes to terms with her new powers and her parents, former members of a superhero group called The AR-Men, guide her, Leia discovers she is pregnant. Life, death, and the future hang in the balance as each of the characters in *Mindfire* struggle to find the balance needed . . . and as they discover forgiveness in Christ.

Jordan and her mother are abducted. For five years they have lived on a strange planet so far away with a different sun and different night sky. They have lived with the tribe and become one of them, but Jordan longs for home on Earth. In order to secure her place in either her new world or the old one, she must find The Abductors and the way back to Earth.

War has come to Algoran. The Gulstaa nation is determined to expand their territory with merciless resolve. Their end goal is revenge for a past defeat—they want to conquer the Mountain Mokta and anyone else in their way. Loyalties are tested. Decisions are made. And Algoran will never be the same after Jordan's Arrow finds its target.

The Onchei are back, and this spells trouble for the Mokta tribe. Zeetra is kidnapped, and her life is endangered. Only an heirloom—back on Earth—that contains the ultimate Onchei knowledge can save them.

Father Vera Daniel serves as a parish priest in the rural regions of the Kingdom of Parvion, one of the great powers of its day. While Father Vera was raised to be a loyal citizen, he found himself increasingly at odds with the very monarchy he had sworn to obey. As Parvion's chronic warfare, economic woes, and increasing intolerance of dissent feed the calls for Revolution, the charitable clergyman finds himself in the greatest danger of his life.

After his wife dies, Marco finds himself lonely and desperate for companionship. Katie is an abused woman, who is now tied to caring for an invalid husband. When Marco and Katie meet, they form a bond quickly. Realizing they are walking a line outside of God's will, Marco returns to his life in New York with Katie telling him to forget her forever. But she is never far from his mind. Does God bring beauty from ashes? Can God repair what has been broken and "make all things new"?

Dalton Russell is a man broken-hearted by loss. He grapples with his own inner demons and feelings of abandonment. After his best friend also commits suicide, he inherits a boat, but not just any boat. Dalton soon discovers the boat left by his friend has an incredible secret. Soon, the entire Russel family is swept up in a wave of what can only be described as miracles. Inspired by what they've seen and Who they've talked to, the Russell family begins new projects and a mission to share what they've learned.